Praise for Reed Farrel Coleman and *Walking the Perfect Square*

"Reed Farrel Coleman is a terrific writer.... a hard-boiled poet... If life were fair, Coleman would be as celebrated as [George] Pelecanos and [Michael] Connelly."

—Maureen Corrigan, NPR's *Fresh Air*

"Reed Farrel Coleman is one of the more original voices to emerge from the crime fiction field in the last ten years. For the uninitiated, *Walking the Perfect Square* is the place to start."

—George Pelecanos, best-selling author of *The Way Home*

"Among the undying conventions of detective fiction is the one that requires every retired cop to have a case that still haunts him. Reed Farrel Coleman blows the dust off that cliché in *Walking the Perfect Square* . . . with a mystery that would get under anyone's skin."

—Marilyn Stasio, *The New York Times*

"The author makes us care about his characters and what happens to them, conveying a real sense of human absurdity and tragedy . . . a first-rate mystery. Moe is a fine sleuth. Coleman is an excellent writer."

—*Publishers Weekly*

"Whenever our customers are looking for a new series to read, they often leave with a copy of *Walking the Perfect Square*. It has easily been our best-selling backlist title. Thank you, Busted Flush, for bringing this classic 'Moe' back into print!"

—Gary Shulze, Once Upon a Crime (Minneapolis, MN)

"The biggest mysteries in our genre are why Reed Coleman isn't already huge, and why Moe Prager isn't already an icon. Both are to me. Read this book and you'll find you agree."

—Lee Child, best-selling author of *Gone Tomorrow*

"Originally published in 2001 . . . *Walking the Perfect Square* has been reissued by Busted Flush Press, good news for mystery lovers, since Reed Farrel Coleman is quite a writer, and this is only the first of five books about Moe Prager. The story and the characters will hook you, and Coleman's lightly warped take on the world will make you laugh, dark as the tale is. As soon as I finished *Walking the Perfect Square*, I started the next in the series, *Redemption Street*. The only problem with the following three (*The James Deans*, *Soul Patch*, *Empty Ever After*) will be to decide whether to read them immediately or savor them over a period of time."

—Marilyn Dahl, *Shelf Awareness*

"Moe's back—if you haven't already discovered Reed Farrel Coleman's wonderful, award-winning ex-cop-turned-PI, Moe Prager, here's your chance. He's for real, and so is Coleman's handling of cases that stay with you long after the book's end. *Walking the Perfect Square*, *Redemption Street*, and *The James Deans* belong in every mystery fan's personal library, because the writing is fine, the realization is believable, and the character is true to himself. This is the man to measure the rest by, a writer with a passionate belief in giving his best, and an eye for what makes the PI novel work at a level few can match."

—Charles Todd, best-selling author of *A Duty to the Dead*

"One of crime fiction's finest voices, Edgar Award-finalist Reed Coleman combines the hard-fisted detective story with a modern novel's pounding heart and produces pure gold. Moe Prager belongs with Travis McGee and Lew Archer in the private eye pantheon. Coleman's series is a buried treasure—dig in and hit the jackpot!"

—Julia Spencer-Fleming, best-selling author of *Once Was a Soldier*

"Moe Prager is the thinking person's P.I. And what he thinks about—love, loyalty, faith, betrayal—are complex and vital issues, and beautifully handled."

—S. J. Rozan, Edgar Award-winning author of *The Shanghai Moon*

"What a pleasure to have the first two Moe Prager novels back in print. In a field crowded with blowhards and phony tough guys, Reed Farrel Coleman's hero stands out for his plainspoken honesty, his straight-no-chaser humor and his essential humanity. Without a doubt, he has a right to occupy the barstool Matt Scudder left behind years ago. In fact, in his quiet unassuming way, Moe is one of the most engaging private eyes around."

—Peter Blauner, Edgar Award-winning author of *Casino Moon* and *Slow Motion Riot*

"Reed Farrel Coleman makes claim to a unique corner of the private detective genre with *Redemption Street*. With great poignancy and passion he constructs a tale that fittingly underlines how we are all captives of the past."

—Michael Connelly, best-selling author of *9 Dragons*

"Moe Prager is a family man who can find the humanity in almost everyone he meets; he is a far from perfect hero, but an utterly appealing one. Let's hope that his soft heart and lively mind continue to lure him out of his wine shop for many, many more cases."

—Laura Lippman, best-selling author of *Life Sentences*

"Reed Farrel Coleman is a hell of a writer. Poetic, stark, moving. And one of the most daring writers around, never afraid to go that extra mile. He freely admits his love of poetry, and it resonates in his novels like the best song you'll ever hear. Plus, he has a thread of compassion that breaks your heart . . . to smithereens."

—Ken Bruen, two-time Edgar Award-nominated author of *London Boulevard*

"Coleman is a born writer. His books are among the best the detective genre has to offer at the moment; no, wait. Now that I think about it they're in the top rank of any kind of fiction currently published. Pick up this book, damn it."

—Scott Phillips, award-winning author of *The Ice Harvest* and *Cottonwood*

“Reed Farrel Coleman goes right to the darkest corners of the human heart—to the obsessions, the tragedies, the buried secrets from the past. Through it all he maintains such a pure humanity in Moe Prager—the character is as alive to me as an old friend. I flat out loved the first Prager book, but somehow he’s made this one even better.”

—Steve Hamilton, Edgar Award-winning author of *Heaven’s Keep*

“Coleman may be one of the mystery genre’s best-kept secrets.”

—*Sun-Sentinel*

“Moe is a character to savor. And Coleman? He’s an author to watch. Make that watch and read. For this is only the beginning, folks, and I’m hitching my wagon to this ride.”

—Ruth Jordan, *Crimespree Magazine*

by Reed Farrel Coleman

Dylan Klein novels
Life Goes Sleeping (1991)
Little Easter (1993)
They Don't Play Stickball in Milwaukee (1997)

Moe Prager novels
Walking the Perfect Square (2001)
Redemption Street (2004)
The James Deans (2005)
Winner of the Anthony, Barry, and Shamus Awards.
Nominated for the Edgar, Gumshoe, Macavity Awards.
Soul Patch (2007)
Winner of the Shamus Award.
Nominated for the Edgar, Barry, Macavity Awards.
Empty Ever After (2008)

Writing with Ken Bruen
Tower (2009)

Writing as Tony Spinosa
Hose Monkey (2006)
The Fourth Victim (2008)

Edited by Reed Farrel Coleman
Hardboiled Brooklyn (2006)

Short Stories
"Kaddish", *Plots with Guns: A Noir Anthology* (2005)
"Requiem for Jack", *Crimespree Magazine*, Issue #6 (2005)
"Portrait of the Killer as a Young Man", *Dublin Noir* (2006)
"Killing O'Malley" (writing as Tony Spinosa), *Hardboiled Brooklyn* (2006)
"Requiem for Moe", *Damn Near Dead* (2006)
"Bat-head Speed", *These Guns For Hire* (2006)
"Due Diligence", *Wall Street Noir* (2007)
"Pearls", *Expletive Deleted* (2007)
"Accidentally, Like a Martyr", *The Darker Mask* (2008)
"No Roses for Bubbeh", *Brooklyn Noir 3* (2008)
"Jibber Jabber", *Once Upon a Crime* (2009)

WALKING THE PERFECT SQUARE

by

Reed Farrel Coleman

Busted Flush Press
Houston 2008

Walking the Perfect Square
Originally published in 2001 by The Permanent Press.

This edition, Busted Flush Press, 2008

Cover design: Jimmy Jack Bottlestop
Bar sign photo: PunchStock

ISBN: 978-0-9792709-5-6
First Busted Flush Press paperback printing, June 2008
Second printing, June 2009

BUSTED FLUSH
PRESS

P.O. Box 540594
Houston, TX 77254-0594
www.bustedflushpress.com

FOREWORD
By Megan Abbott

I come at *Walking the Perfect Square* backwards. Having discovered Moe Prager in *The James Deans*, Reed Farrel Coleman's critically acclaimed third novel in the series, I continued on with *Soul Patch* and *Empty Ever After*. Now, I turn to the originary novel and it is like a haunting—one of those dreams where you walk into a strange house only to discover it is your childhood home, aching with nostalgia and loss. The experience is doubly poignant, as all the sorrow that hangs in every corner of *Empty Ever After* begins here. It recalled for me nothing more intensely than back to back readings of Raymond Chandler's *The Long Goodbye* and his first Philip Marlowe novel, *The Big Sleep*. You see the darkness beginning to spread at the end of *The Big Sleep*, as Marlowe, tainted by his case, famously bemoans, "Me, I was part of the nastiness now." But you would never anticipate the gorgeous melancholy, the retreat from the world that marks *The Long Goodbye*. The beginnings and ends resemble each other, but don't fully reveal the plummy depths to which the reader will go in following our heroes. As readers, we don't emerge unscathed either.

The connection to Chandler is only natural. The Marlowe tradition is inevitably burned in all PI novelists' brains. The anxiety of influence: do I embrace or reject the gimlet-soaked father? Coleman makes the smartest choice of all, and the most rewarding for readers. He gives us a detective deeply aware of his forebears, vigilant against clichés (but never afraid to play with them) and very much his own man. While many of Chandler's "children" operate on the surface of the Marlowe tradition, Prager speaks to something deeper and more resonant in the detective's character. For instance, it is commonplace that post-Marlowe PIs walk into any situation with wisecracks at the ready, but Marlowe's deeper, wryer humor is at root a study of human nature, and a knowing tribute to its foibles and peculiarities. Consider Moe Prager describing a first dance with a woman:

> To call what we did by one name would have been a stretch. It was an amalgam of the Lindy, the tango and a half-assed polka. In spite of how we must've looked, we liked it. I liked holding her. She liked being held. I liked the way she touched me. My knee was blind to her charms. When we were done, we received a round of applause. New full glasses awaited our return. We toasted to Arthur Murray.

There's a warmth to the humor (not to mention a Chandlerian rhythm to it), which stems out of awareness of the pair's awkwardness in the moment, hesitant interest, a wariness but also a gentleness. It draws us to Prager and there are a hundred moments like this in as many pages. It is of course hard to imagine Marlowe having such an uncomplicatedly pleasurable moment with a woman. The Marlowe novels are bristling with the sexual anxiety that kicked into life classic noir. But Prager's world is not that world. It's a world of families, friendships, close ties, intimacies. Betrayals can and do occur, but Prager's relationships—romantic, familial, collegial, fraternal—are as central to this novel as Marlowe's solitariness is to his.

Marlowe's famous isolation, which grows as the series continues, extends in large part from his sense that he is an anachronism, a knight without meaning. The world around has changed, curdled, gone to rot. But while Marlowe is a man whose moral code is at odds with his times, Moe Prager's emerges from his, is born from it, accounts for and takes its strength from an understanding of the complexities of his culture. His sensibility, and his strength as a detective, are informed by the complexities he ponders, parses and only after great, nearly Talmudic deliberation, will dare to pass judgment on. Prager, in 1998, can recall how shocking the Son of Sam murders once were, saying, "But serial killing was a nascent industry then and its purveyors didn't seem to grow on trees the way they do now." But the mood is not one of hermetic retreat from a twisted world. He remains engaged, feels he has no choice. He will not abandon a world that includes his family, his child and the score of striving, essentially good people he comes across, to the looming darkness.

For all these differences, however, *Walking the Perfect Square*'s abiding theme is also deeply Chandlerian: the slipperiness of identity. The missing-person case at the heart of the novel sends Prager on nothing short of an identity quest. Slowly, through the stories shared about him, through the evidence Prager uncovers, he "builds" Patrick Maloney, the young man whose face he stares at on the posters taped to mailboxes and lamp-posts around the city. But the question of how close he can ever get lingers. Much as Marlowe habitually, obsessively returns to the decadently adorned Geiger house in Chandler's *The Big Sleep*, Prager circles back literally to Pooty's, the bar that marks the last place Patrick was seen, and to the image of the missing-person poster itself, which reminds him of the famous Magritte painting. "The point is," he tells us, "It wasn't a pipe. It was the painting of a pipe. And the poster I was looking at wasn't Patrick Maloney"

The closer he comes, the more the photo blurs, breaks apart before his eyes. Patrick is that elusive figure we see so much of in Chandler: Velma Grayle, Orfamay Quest, Terry Lennox, that shape-shifter we seek to know even as we secretly realize we will always come up empty. It is in this illusory pursuit for meaning that the core of the private eye narrative is laid bare. The blurry fear that encompasses Prager at the climax of *Walking the Perfect Square*, that moment when he looks in the rearview mirror and cannot fathom his own eyes, is the quintessential Chandler dilemma: What if there is no there there? In Chandler, that possibility broods over the novels. It's all phoniness. It's all illusion. Hollywood, Los Angeles, women, friendship, connections, meaning. It's all smoke and mirrors.

In *Walking the Perfect Square*, however, the promise of authenticity remains, if only in the far corners. Its final, ruminatory pages carry us through the varied fates of the novel's characters (one cannot imagine this in Marlowe's isolated world), opening up vistas of personal histories that entwine with popular culture (*Mystery Science Theater*, VH-1) and give us a longer view of these characters who play bit or minor parts in the central drama of the novel. It is a generous gesture, and it speaks to Prager's expansive nature but also to the larger view of history he has. *Walking the Perfect Square* is built on a structure of expansion and contraction, of flight and return. The novel circles back and forth between 1978 and 1998, with glimpses in between, demonstrating time and again that no life is solitary, that we all, for better or for worse, are linked and we'd best hold on to each other, and hold on tight.

But the more we move away from Philip Marlowe, the closer we come to him. Because, for all Moe Prager's warmth, his efforts to understand and make meaning, to find the solid ground beneath his feet and be assured that one can fix things, make them better, this is a novel steeped in a deeply Chandlerian melancholy—a melancholy that never lifts as we move through all the Prager novels. A melancholy that haunts the reader as surely as the detective-hero. He may find authenticity, the solid root of things, the beating heart of the matter, and that is comforting. But he also realizes that if there's anything worse than a world built on illusion and deceit it's the understanding that while we may find real connection—the authentic self, intimacy—it will not last. It is fleeting. It breaks apart in our hands. That is when we realize that we have one up on Prager. He has no permanence, no anchor. But we do. We have him.

Megan Abbott
New York, NY
February 2008

Megan Abbott is the Edgar Award-winning author of *Die a Little*, *The Song Is You*, and *Queenpin*. She also edited Busted Flush Press's female noir anthology, *A Hell of a Woman*. Her *Damn Near Dead* (Busted Flush Press) short story, "Policy," was the basis for her Edgar-winning novel, *Queenpin*. She has a Ph.D. in English and American literature from New York University. Visit her online at www.meganabbott.com.

For my big brothers, Jules and David

ACKNOWLEDGEMENTS

I am grateful for the love and support of my wife Rosanne and my kids Kaitlin and Dylan. I could not have written this book without the technical advice of Mitchell L. Schare, Ph.D. or my NYPD buddies: Billy Johnson, John Murphy, Jim Hegarty and Tom McDonald. I would also like to thank Ellen W. Schare for her editorial input.

To be is to be perceived
—Berkeley

I hold a picture up
everybody thinks it's me
I get a thrill out of tampering
with the atmosphere
Hey baby, I'm out of favor
You can't always be
the right flavor
Just seems that no matter
what you do
Someone somewhere
Someone's got to punish you

Nobody hurts you
harder than yourself
–Graham Parker

Hofstra University
Theater Department
Acting 2.1 Professor Stroock
Dramatic Monologue

The Lie of Wetness
by Patrick M. Maloney

<u>Setting:</u> Boardwalk. Nighttime. The sky—moonless, starless. Waves of an unseen ocean are heard crashing ashore. The solitary figure of a young man—his image illuminated by a lone, flickering streetlamp—leans over the sea air-ravaged railing. Contemplating a final walk into the womb of the ocean, he speaks . . .

You know what it's like? (pause) I'll tell you. You ever been to one of those fancy amusement parks like Busch Gardens or Hershey Park? (cups his ear) Oh, you have. Then you'll know what I'm talking about. At these parks they have these huge flume rides. Now, I don't mean the little cute ones with the fake logs. I mean they have these really big ones. They go like ten stories straight up in the air, swoop around a curve and then come flying—(gestures with his hand) I mean flyin' down into a big basin of water. You know the ones I'm talking about? The boat slams (smacks fist into other palm) into this water and boom! This freakin' wall of water soaks everything and everybody for like hundreds of feet around. Well, it's like that. Not the ride, exactly, but the waiting on line.

So you're standing there waiting your turn as this big line snakes around (gestures S shape) and you're watching big boat after big boat go up that freakin' ramp and come splashing down. And there's like these signs everywhere: (points to wording on imaginary sign) "Be aware: You WILL get wet." It's not like you need those signs either, because everybody you see getting off the damn ride's so wet they could wring out their sunglasses and make a puddle. But see here, this is the point I'm trying to make about how it is; even though you watch everybody getting soaked and there's these signs that tell you you're gonna get soaked, you tell yourself that you're not gonna get wet. Nope, not you! (thumps chest) Somehow, all of a sudden, you're fucking waterproof as Jesus in plastic slipcovers.

But then it's your turn. And you stick your foot into the boat and there's like six inches of standing water there and you're up to your ankles in it. Then it dawns on you: the signs weren't lying. And unlike Jesus, the water's gonna walk on you. So you look at the bald guy next to you and his toothless girlfriend or the mom and her frightened kids two rows up or the fat retarded guy in the tight tee shirt sitting alone behind you and you wonder how many other people getting on that ride with you told themselves the lie of wetness. Well, that's my point, you see. It's like that; just like that. We don't come with slipcovers, so we lie to ourselves instead. Christ knows I wish we didn't have to, but we do.

I have to go now.

Direction: Young man moves slowly out of flickering light; his footsteps can be heard walking down wooden steps. When footsteps stop, flickering light snaps off.

August 6th, 1998

THINGS THAT HAPPENED on August 6th: In 1945, Colonel Paul Tibbets at the controls of a special B-29 named after his mom, Enola Gay, dropped the uranium bomb, Little Boy, on the city of Hiroshima—the bomb they dropped on Nagasaki, Fat Man, was a plutonium bomb, but since both killed Japanese pretty damned well, it's not a detail most people bother with and since the second bomb was dropped on August 9th that doesn't really count, not here, not for our purposes. My daughter Sarah was born on August 6th. God, I can still remember watching the crown of her head appear, red curls even then, and how for once, just briefly, I understood about reasons for being. I'd have to call her later.

Now I was on my way to Mary the Divine Hospice of New Haven to meet Tyrone Bryson. Until today I'd never heard of Tyrone Bryson and from what the sister told me, we wouldn't have much time to cultivate a relationship. Mr. Bryson, it seemed, had taken to heart the mission of Mary the Divine and was doing his level best to make his bed available for the next poor soul to die in peace. Apparently, the "in peace" part of the equation is where I came in.

I assured the sister several times that I knew Tyrone Bryson only slightly less well than I had known Chairman Mao. At least I had seen Mao on TV. I said I couldn't ever quite recall seeing Mr. Bryson on the tube. That was, unless he had starred in a summer replacement or a short-lived sitcom. Sister was not amused, explaining that Mr. Bryson had already said we had never met. I asked if we could just clear this all up over the phone, but the sister said that was a no-go on two counts; it took a monumental effort for Bryson to speak above a whisper and, she was afraid, even if he could belt out a tune like Pavarotti in the shower, Bryson had insisted upon seeing me in the flesh.

When I expressed to sister that relatives, let alone people who didn't know me, were in no position to insist, she bit into me, hard: "Lord, Mr. Prager, he is a dying man. Haven't you some sense of charity?" She paused long enough for the guilt to start working on me. "And there is the magazine clipping and an old slip of paper with your name and a disconnected phone—"

"What clipping?"

"It's quite brittle, so I imagine it's rather old. He only showed it to me after I explained you might be unwilling to come visit a total—"

"Yes, sister," I cut her off. "The clipping, what's it about?"

"A missing man, a Patrick—"

"—Maloney."

"Yes, that's right!" Sister was impressed.

"Late this afternoon is the best I can do," I heard a voice that sounded like mine tell the nun. I think she offered me directions. I'm not sure what I said to that. I do recall hanging up.

THE ONLY THING is, I don't remember what inning it was. Maybe it was the fifth, for some reason the fifth sounds right. Whatever inning it was, it had to be the bottom half, because Ray Burris was on the mound for the Cubs and Lenny Randle—who was more famous for beating the shit out of his one-time manager Frank Luchesi than he was for his ball playing—was at the plate for the Mets. I remember Jerry Koosman was pitching for the Mets, but that's neither here nor there, because he didn't get to pitch the top half of the next inning that night.

It was the summer of 1977, July 13th, I think, and I'm sitting with my buddy Stevie in the upper mezzanine at Shea on the third base side. As Randle steps into the batter's box, I notice whole chunks of Flushing and Whitestone going dark over the outfield fence. All the Number 7 trains pulling in and out of the station across the street from the stadium stop dead. The buzz in the crowd is starting to build. Not because Randle got a hit or cold-cocked the third base coach, but because a lot of other fans are beginning to see what I'm seeing; the city going black one neighborhood at a time beyond the 410 sign in centerfield.

Meanwhile, the players and the umps are totally oblivious. There's a three and two count on Randle and . . . Snap! The lights go out in the stadium. There's an immediate announcement:

Everyone stay calm. We're working to correct the problem. Please stay in your seats. Blah, blah, blah . . . Next thing you know, Jane Jarvis, queen of the Shea Stadium keyboards, starts playing Christmas songs on the organ and people are singing and I'm singing and we're all happy. Then, boom, these red auxiliary lights come up.

I look down on the field and the players are still at their positions, but Lenny Randle's not in the batter's box. He's standing on first base. The fucking guy had run to first in the dark. He was still one ball away from earning a walk, yet there he was, trying to steal first base. Even Frank Luchesi, I thought, would have appreciated Lenny Randle's ingenuity at that moment. I'll never forget the night Lenny Randle tried stealing first base in the dark.

My other memories of that year, as I imagine they are for many New Yorkers who lived through it, are bleak. Though they are as vivid to me as the sight of Randle on first, they are more akin to the reminiscences of an amputee reliving his last few steps before his right leg was crushed beneath the wheels of a city bus. I could have told you about the record snowfall that year and how on February 17th me and my partner found an old black couple frozen to death, huddled in their bed. My partner thought it was funny that they'd have to thaw the bodies out to untangle them. Somehow, I didn't see the humor in it.

That summer was also the summer of Son of Sam. Not before, not since, have I seen the city quite so panicked. Even the looting that came in the wake of the blackout felt like a day at the shore compared to the grip of the .44-Caliber Killer. As night fell the whole of the city would hold its breath, exhaling only at the warmth of the morning sun on our cheeks. But serial killing was a nascent industry then and its purveyors didn't seem to grow on trees the way they do now.

My last shift on the job, I was working crowd control when they brought Sam in. If you look hard at the old news footage, you can see me standing just over Detective Ed Zigo's right shoulder and Berkowitz's left. Honestly, I was just as surprised as everyone else that this chubby postal worker with the wiry hair and goofy smile was Son of Sam. To me, he looked like a cross between an overgrown bar mitzvah boy and a Macy's Thanksgiving float. Christ, maybe Jack the Ripper looked like Humpty Dumpty.

With all that went on that year it's understandable, even excusable, that few New Yorkers would recall the disappearance of

Patrick M. Maloney. We were a tired city; the city that never sleeps needed rest. The local rags and electronic media ran with it for about a week, but by Christmas Eve, Patrick Maloney had been consigned to the name-sounds-familiar-didn't-he-win-the-Heisman-Trophy? bin in most people's minds. If he had been a little boy like Etan Patz or a teenage girl, maybe the press would have milked it a little while longer.

Looking back, I'm not certain I had heard of Patrick Maloney's disappearance before being brought into the matter. That's one of the slippery slopes of piecing history back together. Sometimes I'm sure I must've read about it in the papers or heard of it on the tube. Surely I must have seen one of the thousands of posters his parents put up around the five boroughs. In my life I have seen millions of flyers posted on every blank space New York City has to offer. Yet for all the wives of the Sultan of Brunei, I don't think I can describe a single one.

I just don't know. I was far too busy feeling sorry for myself after my second knee operation in three months to be certain of much of what happened that December. Back then, arthroscopes and MRIs weren't standard operating procedure. The docs cut me up pretty good. All of a sudden I had great empathy for the sliced lox my parents ate on Sunday mornings. When people ask why I had to leave the job, I tell them I had a severe case of knee-monia. It gets a laugh. The answer I give as to how I hurt the knee is inversely proportionate to the amount of alcohol I've consumed. Sober, I tell them I was hit by a flaming arrow shot by some schizophrenic junkie from a housing project roof in Queens. Two drinks, I tell them I injured the knee catching a baby thrown from a burning building by its frantic mother. Shitfaced, I tell the truth; I slipped on a piece of carbon paper in the squad room. That's me, Moe Prager, nobody's hero.

So anyway, the department handed me my limping papers—during the financial crisis, every job cut brought the city a little further away from the brink of fiscal collapse—and sent me packing. I had mixed feelings about it. I was good at the job, but never loved it, not the way the Irish guys did. It wasn't in my blood. Jews are funny that way. We have almost religious respect for the law, but tend to view the enforcers of it with great suspicion. I had taken the police exam on a drunken dare and when I received my letter for the academy, I decided it was time to stop knocking around the city university system just to maintain my draft deferment.

One year I was protesting the war, the next I was throwing protesters into paddy wagons. Though I don't suppose many would admit it, I think cops ranked a close third behind POWs and kids with high lottery numbers as the group most happy to see the war come to an end. Those "P-ride I-ntegrity G-uts" bumper stickers on our cars were horribly ineffective Band-Aids. No one enjoyed being called a pig.

For a few years prior to my fall, my big brother Aaron and I had begun pooling our resources. It was always his dream to own a family business, a wine store somewhere in the city. It wasn't my dream necessarily, but I hadn't done badly hitching my cart to other people's dreams. Besides, Aaron was really sharp with money. We always joked that he could plant a nickel in the soil and grow five bucks. He was also driven by Dad's past failure.

Having managed supermarkets for many years, my dad finally invested in his own. The store went belly-up and my parents were forced to declare personal bankruptcy. The task of lying to creditors about my parents' whereabouts most often fell on Aaron's shoulders. Aaron never got over the embarrassment of covering up for Mom and Dad. At that moment, however, no one could have anticipated the manner in which that embarrassment would bind us to Patrick M. Maloney's fate.

Hofstra University—Student Counseling Services

Treating Psychologist: Michael Blum, Ph.D.
Patient: Maloney, Patrick M. ID #077-65-0329
File #56-01-171
Transcription of session 11—November 18, 1976

PM: Good evening, Dr. Blum.
MB: Same to you, Patrick. You seem tense.
(approx 2 minutes of silence)
PM: I'm sorry.
MB: Sorry? What for?
PM: For not talking.
MB: Sometimes, silence is more eloquent than words. What were you just thinking about, when you were quiet, I mean?
PM: Nothing.
MB: Okay, fair enough. Last week, you mentioned you might like to write someday.
PM: I think about trying it sometimes.
MB: Good. Now, let's do a little writing. Imagine yourself in my chair looking out at a character played by you. Your character isn't talking. Write for me, tell me what he's thinking, Patrick. What's going through his head?
(approx 1 minutes of silence)
PM: He's tense. He doesn't know the rules.
MB: Are the rules important?
PM: Always.
MB: Always?
PM: How else would he know?
MB: Know what?
PM: How to be a good patient.
MB: Is being good important to him, your character?
PM: More important than anything. What could be more important than being good?

January 28th, 1978

I GUESS MY romance with snow died when I wasn't looking. Then, all romance is like that, isn't it? I remember I was watching the snow out my apartment window, thinking what hell it was going to be to get around. Luckily I didn't need crutches any longer, but walking with a cane isn't easy. Try it sometime. The phone interrupted my cranky contemplation of the atmosphere.

"I found it!" Aaron, usually upbeat as a hunk of lead, gushed in my ear.

"Good. I knew it was you who lost it."

"What are you talking about?"

"That metal comb I lent you when I was twelve."

"Will you shut up with that already?" he yelled as he did every time I mentioned that comb. "I never borrowed your damn—"

"Okay, okay, I'm sorry," I said. "I'm not in a good mood."

"What's the matter, your knee?"

"What else is new? So . . ."

"So," he repeated. "So what?"

"Yutz! You're the one that called me, remember?"

"Right. Listen, I think I've got the perfect store for us."

"You've got my attention."

He was almost right. The store was perfect. It was on the Upper West Side of Manhattan on Columbus Avenue a couple of blocks north of the Museum of Natural History. The area, Aaron had checked with several sources in the real estate industry, was being highly touted as the next hot spot in the city. The lease was cheap—for Manhattan—and assumable and covered gobs of room for expansion. The place was already a wine shop and the owner was willing to sell us the fixtures for next to nothing.

"Don't you see?" Aaron barked at my silence. "We wouldn't have to sink a big chunk of capital into construction right away. That does two things. First, it gives us more money to put toward the purchase of the business. Second, it buys us some time to develop a loyal customer base of our own while building on the one the current owner has."

I ended my silence: "How much?"

He hemmed and hawed, cleared his throat a few times and then gave me the news. Like I said, the store was perfect. The two of us, on the other hand, were still several thousand dollars short of mercantile bliss.

"Are you sure Miriam won't help us?" he asked about our younger sister.

"It's not her," I told him for the umpteenth time. "She would help."

"I know. I know," he confessed, "it's Ronnie. Why'd she marry him anyway?"

"She loves him. He's handsome. He's sweet and he's a doctor."

"I mean besides that," Aaron joked. "Listen, this guy's willing to give us a few more weeks to come up with the money. Let me know if you think of something. Love ya."

I thought of something: jumping out the window. But not enough snow had accumulated to soften the fall. Frustrating news heaped on chronic pain leads a man to entertain funny thoughts. One thing being off the job had allowed me to do was think. I hadn't done much of it since college. No, I'm not saying cops are dumb or don't think. What I am saying is that once you've learned the ropes, uniformed police work is a matter of routine, determination and reaction. Along with the joys of pain, I found I was rediscovering my long muted inner voice. The process of that rediscovery was interrupted by a second call.

"So how's the knee?" the gruffly affable voice of Rico Tripoli wanted to know.

Rico Tripoli was my oldest buddy from the department. We were in the same class at the academy, but didn't know each other then. When we got posted to the Six-O in Coney Island after probation, Rico and I took to each other right away. Both of us Brooklyn boys without a hook—a friend or family member already on the job with some juice, someone who could get you a plum assignment or help you when you got jammed up—we sort of watched out for each other. We still did. Even after they split us up six years ago, we would meet for dinner every few weeks.

"The knee would be a lot better if I didn't have to keep getting up to answer the god damned phone. How you doing?"

"I'm breathin'," he said.

"How's the Auto Crime Task Force working out?"

"I stepped in shit. We're workin' a career maker. A year from now," Rico bragged, "I'll be polishin' my gold shield."

"Get the fuck outta here. With the city's budget, you could solve the Lindbergh kidnapping and the riddle of the Sphinx and they wouldn't make you detective."

"We'll see."

"Yeah, yeah. So listen, buddy, about dinner, I—"

"That's not why I'm callin'," he cut me off. "Besides, wife number two isn't so thrilled with our little nights out."

"Why not? You met her on one of our nights out," I reminded him.

"That's right," he said, "when I was still married to wife number one."

"I guess I see her point. So what's up?"

"How short are you and that wop-hatin' brother of yours in the cash department?"

"Come on, Rico," I chided, "not this song and dance again."

For going on three years, Rico had tried to buy into the partnership with Aaron and me. Even after the divorce settlement, he had the finances to do it. His maternal grandfather had willed him a bundle. In fact, if we took only a quarter of the cash Rico had offered, we could sign the lease tomorrow on Aaron's perfect store. But in spite of all my arguments on Rico's behalf, Aaron refused to let anyone from outside the family in on the deal.

"I know," Rico said, "Aaron doesn't hate all Italians, only me."

"That's not right. He hates everybody, but especially you. So why'd you bring up the—"

"Patrick M. Maloney."

"Who the fuck is Patrick Maloney, another investor my brother'll say no to?"

"Patrick *M.* Maloney," he corrected.

"Jesus, Rico! Who the fuck is Patrick *M.* Ma—"

"What's a matter, you don't read the paper no more? You don't watch TV?"

"Rico, you don't stop this bullshit, I'll shoot you before you get that gold shield."

"He's a college kid that disappeared in the city about six, seven weeks ago. Don't you have eyes? His picture's on every lamppost, traffic light pole and bulletin board in the city."

"You'll have to excuse me. These days I walk around with my eyes on my legs, trying to make sure I don't trip over my cane and fall on my ass. Anyway, what's this got to do with the store?"

"I'll tell you tomorrow over lunch at Molly's. You know, that little place up by me." He hesitated: "Say one, one-thirty."

"You want me to drive all the way up—"

"It'll be worth it. What else you got to do with that knee a yours? In the meantime, go to the library and read some old newspapers. *Ciao*!"

RICO WAS RIGHT about one thing. Patrick Maloney's smiling countenance adorned the first lamppost I saw as I left my apartment building. And like a man with a new car becoming acutely aware of similar cars passing on the road, I began noticing Patrick Maloney's face everywhere. Maybe, I thought, I *had* seen him before; when I was in the hospital, perhaps, on one of the news broadcasts. Given the amount of pain medication I had ingested during the month after my surgery, I probably could have convinced myself I had seen a vision of the Virgin Mary dancing the Latin Hustle with John Travolta.

Maloney was a good-looking kid with a Hollywood smile; all square white teeth, rich lips and charm. His skin was clear and clean-shaven but for a trim moustache. His thick hair carefully coifed, not too shaggy or short. It was dark. Complexion too, I'd guess. How dark I couldn't say. The poster shot was grainy black and white. His clefted chin was squarely perfect, but his slightly crooked nose played off nicely against it. Dressed in a tuxedo as he was in the picture, he looked like a happy, handsome boy on the way to his brother's wedding.

All the papers showed the very same picture. I had no reason to believe there was anything unusual in that. All the stories said pretty much the same things. Patrick Michael Maloney was a twenty-year-old junior at Hofstra University on Long Island. An accounting major, he was a popular if unremarkable student who was a low-ranking member of the student government.

On December 7th, a Tuesday night, the student government and several other student groups held a fund raiser at a Manhattan bar. Patrick had bartended during the early part of the evening. After his stint behind the sticks, he joined friends and other members of the student government for drinks. At approximately 1 A.M., after noticing his friend Christine Valentine wasn't looking well, Maloney offered to drive Miss Valentine back to campus. Miss Valentine accepted Maloney's offer and they made their way through the thinning crowd to the door. Before they reached the door, however, Miss Valentine felt herself getting ill and ran for the bathroom. Patrick, she recalled, had shouted after her that he would meet her outside when she was finished.

When Christine Valentine emerged from the restroom and exited the bar, Patrick M. Maloney was nowhere to be found. She made a few inquiries as to his whereabouts, but no one seemed to have noticed him. She simply assumed Patrick, a little drunk himself, she remembered thinking, had grown impatient and left. Though leaving without a word was very un-Patrick-like, she was quoted as saying, Miss Valentine didn't give it a second thought until several days later. She was too drunk and nauseous at the time and there were plenty of other available rides back to campus. Of the other students who had attended the fund-raiser, none could recall seeing where Patrick had gone. The trail was already pretty cold when, two days later, the NYPD was alerted to Maloney's disappearance by his worried parents.

I would like to say I spotted something unusual in the newspaper accounts of Patrick Maloney's disappearance, but I couldn't. I had read similar stories before. As a uniform, I'd worked cases that, but for a change of name, sex or hair color, were nearly identical. The cold fact was that, short of a magician's hat, New York City was about the best place in the United States in which to vanish. Sometimes people vanished by choice. Sometimes not. There was one thing in the articles, though, that caught my attention: the Maloneys were from Janus, N.Y., up in Dutchess County. That sort of gave me a clue as to Rico Tripoli's involvement.

In 1975, Rico, like a lot of New York's Finest, had fled the city. Most moved over the Queens' border to Nassau and Suffolk Counties on Long Island. Some moved beyond the Bronx to Westchester and Rockland. A few pioneering types had gone even further north to discover the rustic charms, relative crimelessness and better real estate values in Orange and Dutchess counties. Want to guess where Rico had fled? But clarifying Rico Tripoli's role as facilitator in this did not help me understand what he had in mind for me.

January 29th, 1978

THEY WERE ALREADY sitting there when I hobbled into Molly's. Like all cops, Rico sat facing the door. He acknowledged my arrival by making a gun of his thumb and forefinger and shooting me hello. He began to get up to help me, but the anger in my eyes made him reconsider. The anger ran quickly out of my face. It was hard to stay mad at Rico.

Rico, a dead ringer for the young Tony Bennett, seemed tired. His boyish good looks had started to fray a bit around the edges. There were purple bags under his eyes and deep creases where gentle folds had once marked the outlines of his face. His gut was just beginning to creep over his belt. This was exaggerated, of course, by the tight fit of the shiny print shirt he wore beneath a hideous double-knit suit. I don't know which I hated more: disco music or the fashion it inspired.

As I approached the booth, though, my attention turned to the man seated opposite Rico. He didn't share my curiosity. His bald head never turned to look my way, not even after Rico had stood to greet me. He simply continued cradling a white coffee cup just below his chin. Rico and I embraced for a long few seconds, kissing cheeks before letting go. Out of the corner of my eye, I snuck a peek at the bald-headed man's reaction. From the sour look on his puss, I figured he disapproved. Either that or he'd swallowed a live goldfish with his last gulp of coffee.

"Hey, *paisan*," I slapped Rico's cheek, "you're looking good."

"I look like shit, you lyin' Jew bastard. This Auto Crime case is gonna get me a shield, but the hours . . . *mah—ron*! They're gonna kill me. At least," he smoothed the wide lapel of his suit jacket, "I get to work plainclothes."

I raised my eyebrows. "You got a peculiar definition of plain clothes."

Rico laughed. "I know. I'm wearin' so much polyester I'm afraid to light a friggin' match."

Baldy cleared his throat.

"Sorry. This," Rico said, gesturing to the seated man, "is—"

"—Francis Maloney," I completed the thought, offering my right hand.

Maloney took it and tried squeezing the life out of it before giving it back. He had a ruddy, freckled complexion, an unsmiling mouth and blue eyes like cracked ice.

"You're Prager," Maloney scoffed in a voice as cold as his eyes. "So you've guessed my name. Pardon me if I don't applaud."

He wasn't impressed by my powers of deduction. He wasn't the type to be impressed by much. Maybe, I thought, if I pulled a silver dollar from behind his ear . . .

"I can read a paper and put two and two together," I said, finally sitting down. "Is there a reason I should be trying to impress you?"

Rico ordered me a coffee, a Molly's meatloaf platter and attempted to strike up some diplomatic chitchat. Francis Maloney wasn't having any, his thick impatient fingers tapping out a message for Rico to get on with it.

"The Maloneys want your help," Rico said.

"How can I help?" I wondered, staring at Maloney's clothes. Maybe it was the neat creases in his impeccably ironed work shirt, I don't know. Whatever it was, it seemed to me he wore his clothes like a uniform.

"Angela . . . that's Mrs. Maloney," Rico said, "she heard about you finding the kid that time in –"

"Christ!" I threw up my hands, "is *that* what this is about?"

Marina Conseco was the seven-year-old daughter of a divorced city fireman. On Easter Sunday 1972, her father took Marina and his four other children to Coney Island. When the father returned from buying hot dogs at Nathan's Famous to where he had left his kids, he saw that Marina, the youngest, was gone. Three days later, she was still gone.

Coney Island was a very dangerous place for a seven-year-old girl. Beside the potential human predators, there was the ocean, a filthy canal, abandoned buildings, dilapidated rides, a bus depot and a confluence of subway lines. And if she had been used to satisfy someone's twisted obsession, there were miles of dark boardwalk and elevated highway under which the body of a little girl could be buried in amongst piles of bald tires and broken glass.

By the fourth day, the cops and off-duty firemen who'd volunteered to search, had pretty much stopped calling Marina's name. The hope of finding Marina alive had silently mutated into a determination to find her corpse. After my shift that fourth day, I went out with a crew of two firemen from a ladder company in the Bronx. As we rode down Mermaid Avenue toward Sea Gate, I found my eyes drifting upward. Probably because I was so tired, my eyes were rolling up in my head.

I slammed on the brakes and jumped out of the car. When the two firemen followed me out of the car and saw what I was pointing at, they shook their heads in agreement. I wondered how many of those old wooden, rooftop water tanks there were in Coney Island. We agreed to count; one rooftop at a time.

We found Marina Conseco at the bottom of the fifth tank in half a foot of dirty water, alive! Her skull was fractured, as were her right arm and left ankle. She was in shock and suffering from hypothermia. She had been molested for two days and thrown into the tank to die. But as her family had said, Marina was a willful girl, and wasn't about to cooperate with her attacker's plans.

Finding that little girl was the only outstanding thing I ever did on the job. At another time, in another place, I might've gotten my shield for saving her. I wouldn't have wanted to make detective on the back of Marina Conseco's misery and on the strength of a lucky guess. The medal they gave me was embarrassing enough. One of the geniuses in my precinct took to calling me Truffle. That lasted for about an hour. When I informed him that truffles were fungi that pigs rooted out, the nickname lost its appeal. It's funny, cooking shows make me remember that stupid nickname. But then, I also think of Marina Conseco.

"Hey," Rico motioned for me to calm down, "Angela is my wife's cousin. She's a superstitious guinea like me. I told her the story about the Puerto Rican kid and—"

"Look, Mr. Maloney," I shook my head, "I'm really sorry about your boy, but I think my buddy Rico here sold you a bill of goods. I found the girl six years ago and it was a lucky shot at that."

"Luck, Mr. Prager, is all we've got left," he admitted.

"But—"

"Listen, Prager," he dispensed with the niceties, "I've neither the time nor the temperament for bargaining. I know you people like to bargain and if it was up to me alone, I wouldn't have any of your kind involved."

Rico buried his head in his hands. It didn't take a code breaker to figure out which people Maloney was referring to. Maybe if I'd been brought up in a different era or if I hadn't been a cop, I might've reached across the table and introduced Francis Maloney to my left hook. But race baiting within the ranks of the NYPD was an Olympic sport and I'd been as willing a participant as any officer with whom I'd served. I suppose the least I should have done was leave. I didn't.

"You always this charming when you want someone's help?" I asked, my voice calm.

"If it wasn't for your kind," he continued his screed, "this country wouldn't have the trouble with the niggers we do. But that doesn't matter to me now. I'd kiss your rabbi and the starting lineup of the Knicks on their balls if it would relieve my wife's grief."

Other than the obvious tastelessness of his words, I found something about them both horrifying and intriguing. Maloney didn't give me time to explore the matter.

"Here's my offer," he said. "Rico tells me you and your brother are looking for a liquor store in the city and that you're short on scratch."

"A wine shop, but yes."

"If you help me on this and any information you come across leads to the boy's whereabouts, you'll receive a tax-free reward," he touched his index finger to his nose, "for the amount of money you need for the store. Second—"

"Hold it! Hold it! Look, I'm not an investigator. I never even made detective. And my bet is you've got a lot of other people more qualified than me working this. All I did was get lucky once. Don't you think I'm kinda low on the food chain to be making me an offer like—"

"First of all, boyo, don't you worry about my ability to make good on my word. Second, a desperate man plays even the low cards in his hand when the picture cards aren't winning. And last, you haven't heard the entire offer. Now show me the courtesy of hearing me out."

I nodded. "You've made your point. Go ahead."

"I want you to be clear on this, Prager. If you throw in with us and I'm convinced you really put your heart in it, I'll smooth the way for your liquor license whether or not you find the boy. You know, I'm certain, how hard it can be to obtain a liquor license in this state. The hurdles are enormous. Why, many is the man who has the money, but can't get the license. You get my meaning?"

"I'm not sure whether you're asking me to help or threatening me," I said.

"I'm not asking you for anything," he stood abruptly from his seat. "I'm making you a proposition. Think about it. Rico will know how to reach me."

I watched the fireplug of a man march out Molly's door without once looking back. Even then I knew Maloney wasn't the sort of man to look back, not at anything nor anyone. Rico started to explain, but I asked him to wait until after I'd had time to digest what had just transpired and a few bites of meatloaf.

"So," I said, gazing up from my plate, "what the fuck was that all about?"

Rico shrugged. "The guy's desperate."

"More angry than desperate."

"I guess," Rico agreed. "Look, I didn't know he was gonna get all weird on ya. Me and the wife was over their house a week ago for a family thing and I'd had a few and I was tryin' to give Angela some hope. You know how it is. We were in the kitchen, just me and Angela, and I told her the story about the Conseco girl. I swear on my mother I wasn't anglin' for an in on the wine store. Truth is, until Francis called me up two nights ago, I didn't know Angela had repeated what I told her. When he did call me up, I figured it wouldn't hurt to get him to help you and your brother. I hope I didn't do wrong."

"I don't blame you, but you know I woulda helped if you just asked me."

"Yeah, I know," Rico confessed. "But I figured I could do you a little good for your trouble."

I was skeptical. "Can Maloney really deliver on his word?"

"You wanna know if he can deliver? Come on. Come with me."

We got into Rico's car and drove a few miles to a VFW Hall. We parked across the street and watched a crowd of about twenty people gather out front. They were equally divided in gender, all middle-aged or older. A coffee truck pulled up and the driver handed out coffee, sandwiches, whatever. Strange thing, though, no money changed hands. About five minutes after the coffee truck pulled away, a charter bus pulled up. The crowd piled in and the bus moved off. During this whole series of events, Rico shushed me whenever I began to ask a question.

"Take a guess what that was all about," Rico said as the bus vanished in the distance.

"I don't know, a church outing?"

"Those people are volunteers," he explained. "Every day at this time a busload of people go down to the city and search for the kid. At ten at night, the bus brings 'em back. How do you think all them posters got put up? And the coffee guy gets paid out of a fund that's been established in Patrick Maloney's name."

"Not for nothing, Rico, but Francis Maloney isn't exactly the type of guy to inspire this kind of loyalty from me. What's he, connected?"

"In a way," Rico winked. "He's sanitation commissioner for the county. You don't get that kinda job unless you're wired into the political machine. And, baby, let me tell you, our boy Francis is wired in. That's how come he can snap his fingers and get you that liquor license. It's like the job, everybody owes Maloney favors. Shit, Moe, this guy's even got a hook in New York City Hall."

"Get outta here," I scoffed.

"Listen to me. Francis Maloney's the best fuckin' fund-raiser the county machine has. A part of every county worker's paycheck finds its way into the party's coffers. Every purveyor that does business with the county manages to get family members to contribute. There's not a Democratic politico in this county that doesn't owe a part of his office to that coldhearted little donkey prick. Believe me, Moe, he's got the juice to deliver on his promises."

"Who's his hook in the City?" I wanted to know.

"Joe Donohue, the mayor's top advisor on police affairs. He and Maloney was on the job together."

"Maloney was on the job?"

"For a few years," Rico said, "but he got jammed up and they showed him the back door."

"What'd he do?"

"In pre-Knapp Commission days, who knows?" Rico frowned. "Anyway, Maloney's not loose-lipped on the subject. We're not exactly kissin' cousins, ya know."

We rode back to Molly's in relative silence. I didn't thank him. I don't think he expected me to, really. We hugged and made vague promises about next month's dinner. As I approached my car he called out to me. He said that he would square things with Maloney if I didn't want to get involved. I told him we'd see, that I'd dip my toes in the water and let him know. He shrugged his shoulders the way he always did when he got an answer he didn't like. That was okay. I didn't much like the answer either.

January 30th, 1978

TRIBECA'S STREETS HAD that old New York feel, paved as they were in potholes and cobblestones and old factory buildings. TriBeCa real estate was hot. There was enough available loft space in the old factories to take up the runoff from SoHo. First the artists and dancers and galleries would come, then the limousine bohemians.

Pooty's was a corner bar on Hudson Street. It had floor tiles like a tenement bathroom and grout as black as my mechanic's fingernails. Cracked and splitting, neither the wooden booths nor once majestic bar had seen a dust rag or coat of lacquer since the Rosenbergs took one in the face for their team. Pooty's was the kind of place where people were encouraged to gouge their initials into the tables with keys. Old poets went there to die. It wasn't typically the kind of place a cop would know about, but I knew Pooty's.

Pooty's had two things going for it: the best jukebox in the city and Beck's Dark on tap. A date, an actress named Susie, took me there after the movies once. I think she got off on the idea of me being a cop, but when I showed up at her apartment door out of uniform it sort of ruined her fun. At Pooty's, surrounded by a contingent of her wannabe friends, Susie kept trying to engage me in cop talk. *Oh come on, show us your gun. Can I touch it? How do dead bodies really smell?* You know, that sort of thing. I wasn't into being on display and I was more interested in the jukebox, anyway. I think Susie went home with a photo-realist painter disguised as a busboy.

Although I hadn't been there in months, nothing but the bartender had changed. Somehow, I had trouble reconciling a bunch of student government nerds from a commuter college out on

Long Island with Pooty's. Pooty's, of all the thousands of bars in the five boroughs and on the Island, seemed to be as unlikely a place for a college fund-raiser as I could imagine. The bartender, Jack, a handsome but jaundice-skinned playwright from Ohio, agreed.

"Those losers stuck out around here like Malcolm X at an Emerson, Lake and Palmer concert. Man, they were so unhip," he said, drawing my Beck's, "they almost had style."

I wasn't sure what that meant, but I kept my confusion to myself. He volunteered that he had worked the night of Patrick Maloney's disappearance. He was just there to help in case any of the guest bartenders had trouble mixing up a sloe gin fizz or Tom Collins. But it had gone pretty smoothly, he said, mostly beers and white wine spritzers. He uttered the words with such disdain, it was difficult for me not to smack him with my cane. I asked him if he knew how the fund-raiser came to be held at Pooty's.

"Ask the boss," Jack shrugged, pointing to a door at the end of the bar. "Go on, I'll call down."

The office was the size of a double-wide coffin. A rotund little man sat at a metal desk, smoking a cigarette and punching numbers on an adding machine.

"Yeah," he said without looking up.

I showed him the replica of my badge I had made before leaving the job. He looked at it and shook his head.

"So what, I got one of them, too." He took it out to show me. "You here about Maloney's kid?"

I said that I was. He told me his name was Pete Parson, offered me his right hand and a seat. I took him up on both offers. He too had been hurt on the job, a broken shoulder: "I got between a pissed off husband, his wife and a Louisville Slugger."

He said he had lost count of how many cops, ex-cops, private investigators and volunteers he had spoken to since the night the kid vanished. Because I seemed like a good guy, he confided, he'd go over it with me again and he'd let me waste the bartender's time. It was just like they said in the paper; no one saw or heard anything unusual. I said I thought it was pretty unusual for a cop to own a place like Pooty's and for a place like Pooty's to host a fund-raiser.

"I'm the boss," he answered, "not the owner. I've got like a ten percent stake in the place. The majority owners are two ex-hippies from my old neighborhood. They thought bringing in an ex-cop would help smooth out some of the bumps in the road, if you know what I mean."

I knew exactly what he meant. Responding to bar fights ranked just below cats stuck in trees and just above complaints of off-key opera singing on the NYPD's list of priorities. If an ex-cop put in the call, however, that priority jumped up several notches. Having an armed cop to cash out and make bank deposits was good business. It also discouraged potentially sticky-fingered employees from sharing the profits. And when greedy city inspectors, carters and connected purveyors came sniffing around, there was a built-in discount for cops.

"Since that fucking Maloney kid disappeared," Parson was agitated, "there have been a lot of bumps and I can't smooth any of 'em. I got an appointment with the fuckin' state tax auditors next month and the Liquor Licensing Board is breathing down our necks. I wish I never let him book the damned thing here."

"Him?" I let it hang for a second.

"*Him*, Patrick fucking Maloney. He booked the party. He came in, offered me a fifteen-hundred-buck guarantee for a Monday night in early December and I jumped at it. This ain't Cleveland. We don't get a big *Monday Night Football* crowd in here. The only staff I had to pay for was—"

"—Jack." I pointed up. "He told me. But why'd Patrick Maloney pick Pooty's?"

"Who the fuck knows? And no, before you ask, none of the employees remembers seeing him in here before that night. He wasn't a regular as far as I can tell. Right now, I wish he'd picked any other bar but this one."

I was properly sympathetic and said I hoped things went well with the state. He wasn't optimistic nor, in my silence, was I. Francis Maloney had obviously spoken to some of his friends and was punishing Pooty's for his son's vanishing act. I had no difficulty believing that in the absence of a truly responsible culprit, the elder Maloney would lash out at the most convenient target.

Upstairs again, I had a brief conversation with jaundiced Jack. I asked him the same questions every other investigator had asked him, questions he answered with the practiced boredom of a churchgoer saying amen. He did guiltily confess to one thing I found interesting, if not exactly useful. Jack said he couldn't remember anyone being at Pooty's that night who looked like the picture of the Maloney kid. I didn't stay to argue the point. There was no shortage of witnesses to Patrick's presence that night. While apparently not the type of guy to claim he had seen a vision of Jesus in the bathroom mirror, Jack did strike me as the sort of fellow who liked the occasional vein load.

Leaving Pooty's, I felt much as I did after my college statistics classes; more confused on the way out than on the way in. But that was less Jack's and Pete Parson's fault than mine. My first step was a misstep. I could see that now. I was a bloodhound with no nose for blood. My forensics training was rudimentary at best. I wasn't going to find a magic carpet fiber or blood splatter. There was nothing at Pooty's for me to find that any of the other investigators, most far more experienced than myself, wouldn't have already stumbled upon. Maybe that's why they hadn't gotten anywhere. Sometimes, I thought, experience gets in the way. Even if I was wrong, it sounded good.

I found myself staring at a Patrick Maloney poster pasted to the mailbox next to my car. "**HAVE YOU SEEN THIS MAN?**" the bold block letters wanted to know. It struck me that I hadn't, not really. I remembered a slide of a Magritte painting from my Introduction to Art History class—I guess I had college on my mind that day. It's funny what you think about. Anyway, the painting was of a tobacco pipe and the artist called it *Ceci n'est pas une pipe.* In English I'm pretty sure that translates into "This is not a pipe." The point is, it wasn't a pipe. It was a painting of a pipe. And the poster I was looking at wasn't Patrick Maloney. I guess that's what hit me.

I didn't know squat about Patrick M. Maloney other than he was an unremarkable student at Hofstra University. In spite of his ubiquitous posters, I wasn't certain I'd recognize him unless I tripped over him and then only if he were wearing a black tuxedo and that charming smile. Enlightened self-interest aside, I wasn't even sure why I was looking for him. Marina Conseco was one thing; an innocent little girl lost in one of Brooklyn's many doorways to hell. But what was Patrick Maloney to me? Nothing more than a grainy photostat. Christ, I knew more about his father than I knew about him.

As I sat in my car, I thought about Francis Maloney, about how he had offered no insights into his son. I remembered the day before at Molly's, how something about the elder Maloney's manner had caught my attention, but I'd never gotten a handle on it. Only now I realized it was his abject coolness, a sort of angry detachment. Francis Maloney had never once referred to Patrick as his son. It was "*the* boy," not "my boy." The grief wasn't his, but his wife's. The word love had been remarkable by its absence.

My surgical knee was throbbing a warning of coming snow as I pulled into traffic. A yellow cab cut me off, nearly taking my right fender as a memento. The cabby and I took a moment to exchange middle fingers. He rolled down his window and inquired as to my mental well-being: "Are you fucking crazy, or what?" I showed him my badge. He was much more impressed by it than Pete Parson had been and moved on. But long after I had crossed back over the Brooklyn Bridge, the cabby's question rang in my head.

MY KNEE WAS more accurate than the goddamned weatherman. It was snowing again, heavily.

I had drifted in and out of sleep several times since taking a pain pill. Now I was up, sipping a cup of coffee, watching snow fall against the black of night. Normally, I wouldn't have fought so hard to try and keep awake, but I had put a call in to Rico and wanted to be somewhat coherent when he called back.

I can't say what it was exactly that made me change my mind. My visit to Pooty's had been a cold slap in the face. It helped me see how out of my depth I would be. And having heard about Pete Parson's travails with the state tax people and liquor authority, I wasn't sure I was willing to risk Aaron's dream on Francis Maloney's good graces. We would get our wine shop one day, with or without the help of that arbitrary little bastard. One thing I was certain of: the more I thought about Francis Maloney the less I wanted to know about his son. As a Jew I had a sort of genetic X-ray vision for tragedy, and tragedy was all I could see coming. We would all of us be better off, I thought, if Patrick Maloney stayed only a grainy photostat to me. The phone rang.

"Rico!" I shouted into the phone.

"Moses?" Only my sister Miriam called me Moses. "I need . . . I need to talk," she sobbed.

"What's the matter, kid? You all right? Is it Ronnie?"

"Will you please shut up?" That was better. "I'm fine. I'm just a little low, is all."

"You missing Mom and Dad? This weather always makes me—"

"Are you expecting a call?"

"It can wait. So . . ."

"I don't know if I can do this," she whispered.

"Do what? And why are you—"

"Ronnie's sleeping. I don't want to wake him up. He's been at the hospital for thirty-six hours straight."

"Okay, that's why you're whispering," I said. "But what's it you can't do?"

"I don't think I'm cut out to be a doctor's wife. I can't take it, Moses."

"The hours are killers, I know, but he's almost done with his internship. You're almost there, kiddo."

She started crying again. "It's not the hours. They suck, but it's not the hours. It's just that sometimes when he comes home and tells me things . . ."

"What things?"

Ronnie must have been zonked, because Miriam was crying so furiously now we barely needed the phone. I didn't bother to repeat the question or try to calm her down.

"He was in the ER," she choked out before the next wave of tears.

Uh-oh, the ER, that pretty much explained it. Uniformed cops get real familiar with the ER. Most of the time they're hitting on nurses, but that's less a function of pheromones than defense against the panic-in-the-butcher-shop atmosphere of the place. Working the ER was like operating inside a tornado, a tornado where blood and desperation squeeze out all the oxygen. Civilians always assume the worst part of the job is dealing with dead bodies. After a while, at least for me, the dead body thing wears off. You can distance yourself from a body, but I never got used to the ER.

There was a little baby boy, she said, the police had found naked in the snow. The snow was red with his blood. Because of the boy's condition and the bad weather, the cops decided they couldn't wait for an ambulance and rushed him to the ER. Ronnie and the other doctors tried to save the baby, but it was useless. There was no pulse. His skull and face were crushed, his spine severed and his arm bones splintered. One of his legs was broken and his abdomen was distended with blood. When the cops asked Ronnie to guess at what had caused all the damage, he said he thought someone had probably thrown the baby out a window. The cops left in a hurry, Ronnie didn't understand. He thought there'd be a lot of paperwork.

I understood and I had a sick feeling I knew what was coming, but I let Miriam tell me anyway.

"About an hour later," she was fighting back tears again, "the same two cops brought in a man with a broken jaw. A gift from the cops," she said. "It was the baby's father. He was a kid himself, Ronnie said. The cops told Ronnie the father had confessed to throwing the baby out the window. It cried too much. He just said it cried too damned much." I opened my mouth to say something, but she cut me off. Her tone turned suddenly cold, angry: "When Ronnie was treating the father, he realized he recognized him. He asked one of the cops for the name. Ronnie had helped deliver the baby a few weeks ago."

"What did Ronnie do?"

"What could he do?" Miriam's voice was shaking again. "He helped set the man's jaw. He's not a cop. He's not like you. He was still crying when he came home and locked himself in the bathroom. I can still smell the vomit. I've never seen him cry before. Do you cry anymore, Moses?"

My silence was answer enough. She couldn't hold back any longer. In between breathless sobs, Miriam asked me a lot of questions about God and man I was in no position to answer. They were questions I'd heard asked a thousand times, questions smart cops stop asking themselves pretty early on in their careers. You learn soon enough that cruelty is the one thing in the universe to successfully defy the law of conservation. Cruelty is an unlimited resource. There were days on the job I wondered why it didn't rain crying babies.

Miriam cried herself out. I don't know that I said anything of value at all. I was barely awake by the time we hung up. And when the phone jarred me back to consciousness, I couldn't say how long I'd been asleep.

"What?" I growled.

"Hey," Rico said, "you called me. What's up? My wife said you told her it was important."

I hesitated. I knew the words I had meant to say, but they would not roll off my tongue. In a movie, the director would have cut back to me asleep in my chair, my head jerking side to side. My face blurs. I'm dreaming. Crying babies plummet through the night. I run feverishly, trying to catch each one as it falls. It's snowing. The cement is slippery. At first, I save them, but more and more begin to fall. My feet lose traction. Some hit the pavement, their skulls and the concrete cracking. Soon the baby storm stops. The snow still falling, I kneel beside one of the little corpses, turn it over and there, smiling up at me: Patrick M. Maloney. I race from corpse to corpse. They all have his face.

Life is no movie. Just ask my brother-in-law Ronnie. I hadn't dreamed, not so as I could remember.

"Earth to Moe. Earth to Moe," Rico prodded.

"I'm here."

"So what d'ya want?"

"Can you get me the name of the Missing Persons detective?"

"Mike Sullivan," Rico answered almost immediately.

"I bet they call him Sully."

"What can I tell ya? You know what they say about the Irish: great drinkers, great thinkers, great writers, great fighters."

"And bad nicknames," I laughed. "I'll let you know what I find out."

I hadn't dreamed, but I can't say that Miriam hadn't gotten under my skin.

January 31st, 1978

IN-HOUSE DUMPS are part of the natural evolution of any large bureaucracy. It's one of the means by which those bureaucracies protect themselves from external scrutiny. It is safer to eat your mistakes than to admit them. And naturally, as the beast grows, so do its dumping grounds. The NYPD was no different. Most of the 30,000 or so men and women of the NYPD chomp at the bit to do a good job. They, at least at the beginning, want to collar every skell, squash every mutt they can lay their hands on. Not all, though.

There are some that start lazy. To them, it's fifty-two paychecks a year, health coverage and a good pension. They're the types that start counting backwards from twenty years the minute they get on the job. There are the cops that get ground down by the job and the inept and the psychos. Some cops end up with modified duty assignments, better known as the rubber gun squad. They get to keep their badges, but they don't get to play with their .38s anymore. Some find their way to file rooms, storehouses and desks.

Some, though, find their niches in bureaus and squads where they do "regular" police work, but where their impact is minimized. Everybody knew, or claimed to know, that the rats in Internal Affairs were lazy, yellow cops, cops who were afraid of the street, who didn't like making cases. I wouldn't know. My less-than-stellar career had kept me out of their cross hairs. There were probably some good cops in IA, but the nature of the work made them easy targets. Another reputed dumping ground was Missing Persons. I mean, what do you really do in Missing Persons, right? Think about it.

"You Sully?" I asked, limping over to his desk.

"What d'ya want, Ahab?"

"Hey, that's good. You guys in Missing Persons must get a lot of time to read the classics. 'The white whale tasks me,' " I did my best Gregory Peck.

"Rico warned me you'd be a wiseass."

I could feel myself blush slightly. "He called, huh?"

"I wouldn't talk to you otherwise," he said. "I'm so fuckin' sick of this song and dance I could puke. I musta briefed fifty guys on this file already. It's a waste a my time."

I let that slide. From the size of his gut, I figured it was a safe bet he used the time he didn't waste educating people about Patrick Maloney, reinforcing stereotypes of cops and donut shops. He gave me a well-rehearsed and not very enlightening rundown on the case before handing me the file and pointing me to an unoccupied desk.

The file contained the same sort of valueless information I already had, only more of it and in greater detail. There was nothing to indicate Patrick had vanished of his own free will nor was there anything to indicate he was a victim of foul play. Dutifully, I took down the names, addresses and phone numbers of all the people who'd given statements to the cops. The file did contain an incident report. As to departmental procedure, it wasn't strictly kosher to fill out an incident report when someone no longer technically a minor went missing. But there were times when you might fill one out just to get a distraught parent off your back. Though nearly two months had passed since the disappearance, I couldn't picture Francis Maloney as ever having been distraught. However, given his charming personality and his connections in city hall, the presence of an incident report made perfect sense.

I brought the file back to Sully, thanked him. He shook my hand for too long, as if his mind were somewhere else. When I reclaimed possession of my extremity, it seemed to snap the detective out of his trance.

"Listen," he said, referring to his watch and checking to see if anyone else might be listening, "why don't you meet me for lunch around the corner at the Blarney Stone in about two hours?"

Normally I would have suspected him of trying to sponge a free lunch off me in return for his cooperation. Not that his cooperation appeared to be worth a damn, but I got the sense he was interested in more than the size of my expense account. No, he had something to discuss and it wasn't the religious symbolism in *Moby Dick*.

"Okay," I agreed. "Two hours."

I RAN MY index finger along the board of black buttons. There was at least one moron per dwelling who'd buzz you in without asking. That, in combination with the propensity of Manhattanites to order out, could almost guarantee you entree into any doorman-less building in the city. Apparently, someone was very anxious for his or her crispy duck with black bean sauce or this particular building had more than the usual quota of morons. I could hear the vestibule buzzer still ringing as I got into the elevator.

Robert Klingman was one of Patrick Maloney's suite mates. Klingman hadn't even been at Pooty's on December 7th, but he was the only student to both talk with the cops and list a Manhattan address. As I stood outside apartment 5C not knowing whether anyone would answer my knock, it occurred to me I might have called first. I did, however, have some time to kill before meeting Sully and since no one seemed remotely enthusiastic about rehashing their involvement with the case, I thought the element of surprise might work in my favor.

I sensed I was being watched and held my badge up to the peephole. Then, just like in the movies, I listened to rattling chains, unclicking locks and the sound of the "push-in" bar being repositioned. As the door pulled back, I introduced myself to a handsome woman of fifty. Klingman's mother was a bottle blonde with mischievous green eyes and too much make-up. By the time I stepped onto her avocado shag carpet, Pearl Klingman had told me she was divorced from Robert's father and invited me to her next est seminar. Bobby K., as she called him, wasn't home.

There was a huge sheet of paper laid over a big chunk of the green flooring. Printed on the white paper was a tangle of numbered footprints and directional arrows. In the background a man's smarmy voice spoke over some dreadful KC and the Sunshine Band song.

"Do you hustle?" she flirted, then noticed my cane. "No, I suppose not."

"Another time."

She popped the 8-track out of the stereo and got us some coffee. She never asked me what an on-duty cop was doing with a cane. I returned her kindness by not volunteering that I was no longer a cop, on duty or otherwise. As we sipped our coffee, she gave me a brief history of the twentieth century as it related to her.

"So you kept your husband's last name," I said, leading her to where I wanted the conversation to go.

"I hate my ex, but believe me, I hate my maiden name more. Pearl Klingman doesn't exactly roll off the tongue, if you know what I mean, but it beats the pants out of Pearl Feigenbaum." I was forced to agree. "My Bobby and his last name were the only good things that bastard ex-husband of mine ever gave me."

She had supplied me with a perfect segue for my questions about her son's missing suite mate. Much to my dismay, a perfect segue was no guarantor of fruitful answers. Bobby never spoke much about Patrick, she said. She thought most of her son's other suite mates had been over to her house for dinner, but couldn't remember if Patrick had attended. She was sorry she couldn't be more helpful, promising to give my phone number to her son when he called.

"The world's not a fair place," Pearl uttered with unexpected seriousness as she showed me to the door. "We lie to our kids and ourselves about level playing fields and justice. But it's all just bullshit. We're all just pretense and bullshit. We would be better off if we could just accept it and move on."

Against my better judgment, I wondered what had led her to such a cynical view of the world.

"Do you think it's cynical?" she sounded surprised. "It just is what it is. You don't get it, do you?"

"I guess not."

Once again, she offered to take me to an est seminar. It would help me get it, she said. I left it at that, thanked her, shook her hand. Moving toward the elevator, I was once again treated to a muffled serenade by KC and the Sunshine Band. est, disco and shag rugs—it almost made me pine for Freddy and the Dreamers.

SULLY WASN'T AS easy to find as I thought he'd be. He had selected a corner two-top in the darkest nook of the Blarney Stone. He was working over a bottle of Bud and a roasted half chicken when I hobbled to the table. The peas and carrots on his plate were so devoid of color, I thought they might've been steamed in chlorine bleach. The poor chicken didn't look much better. I wasn't that hungry anyway. I had the waitress bring me a scotch.

Once Sully and I got done nodding hello, he slid a color photo across the table to me. It was a group shot; four men and two women, all about twenty, all wearing the blue and yellow of Hofstra's Flying Dutchmen. None of the faces looked immediately familiar. I guessed they were friends of Maloney's.

"Yeah, so . . ."

"Second guy from the left," Sully said, showing me a mouthful of chicken.

"Holy shit!" I blurted out at the precise moment the waitress brought my drink.

"Hey, I brought your drink as fast as I—"

"No, no, no. I'm sorry, it's not that," I apologized, tipping her more than the cost of the drink.

Sully smiled. "Same reaction I had first time I saw it."

"*That's* Patrick Maloney?"

"The same," Sully confirmed. "Don't look much like that poster the rest of New York City is lookin' at, does he?"

Staring carefully now, I recognized Maloney, but his hair had been buzzed to boot camp length. There looked to be a silver cross earring dangling from his left ear and a tattoo—I couldn't make it out—on his right forearm. His moustache was gone and he seemed thinner than the poster picture would have led me to believe. That charming smile was still there, yet there was something odd about the set of his eyes. It was as if his mouth were in the moment, but his focus was set on something no one else in the picture could see. I wouldn't say it was a glassy, drugged stare. It may have been. I don't know. If the photo wasn't sharp enough to let me make out his tattoo, it was silly of me to try to interpret his expression.

"When was this taken?" I demanded.

"September '77 at a student government picnic in Eisenhower Park on the Island."

"Before or after the poster pic—"

"After," he said, finishing his beer, "by a few years. That poster picture's from his high school prom."

I took my scotch down in a gulp and flagged the waitress for another round. "So—"

"That's right," Sully anticipated me. "There's a million fuckin' wanted posters up around this city and not one of 'em looks like the kid we're lookin' for. Now you're gonna ask me why. And I'm gonna tell ya, I don't know."

"How'd you get this?" I asked, waving the photo at him.

"Anonymous. Found it lying on my desk one day last week. No prints. No ransom note. No call. I figured it was finally a lead, ya know, a little crack in the ice, somethin'. So we bring the parents in, quietly. We don't wanna get their hopes up or nothin'. So I show the picture to the old man and he goes fuckin' apeshit on me: Where'd I get the picture? I better not use it. I should do my work and find the boy. I'm a lazy ass like the rest a the mutts in Missing Persons. He'll have my badge. Ya know, pleasant stuff like that there."

"So?"

"So," Sully smiled, clinking his fresh bottle to my glass, "fuck him. He brought the case to us. I'm gonna work a case my way, right?"

"Right."

"Wrong." He shook his head. "Dead wrong. I get called into the captain's office and get told to not use the picture, to not bother the parents and to check with him before making any decisions on the case."

"The brass?"

"Who else? My captain don't talk to me unless he has to. I guess someone told him he had to."

"Ask Isaac Newton, shit runs in only one direction and it ain't uphill."

"Tell me about it. So the father's got a hook, huh?" he asked.

"Joe Donohue."

"The mayor's—"

"That's him."

"Francis Maloney, that little shanty cocksucker." Sully was incredulous. "You wouldn't figure him to have that much juice."

"I agree, but he does."

I finished my scotch, he his chicken and beer. We didn't say much, both of us waiting for the other to ask the two big questions: If the Maloneys had gone to the trouble of busing volunteers in and out of the city, hiring outside investigators and calling in favors from powerful allies, why had they knowingly distributed a poster of their son which was so clearly out of date? And when the poster photo was discovered to be inaccurate, why had they fought so hard to keep an updated picture out of our hands?

My third scotch did the trick. "Why?"

"There's a lot a whys. There's a lot a answers. Take your pick. But I'm no dummy," he leaned over the table and whispered. "The kid split. The father knows that. It's a big charade for the wife's benefit."

Too big a charade, I thought, though you could make a good case for Detective Sullivan's opinion. They say Einstein was so brilliant because he could reduce complex phenomena to elegantly simple formulas. I saw a special on channel 13. But family dynamics ain't thermodynamics and Sully wasn't Einstein. There had to be more to this than a charade for the wife, there just had to be.

I didn't argue the point.

THE FLATLANDS SECTION of Brooklyn was not the stuff of picture postcards for the folks back home in Kenosha. If, on the other hand, you were on a pilgrimage to junkyard nirvana, this was the place. Flatlands was where the men who boosted other people's cars brought those cars to be harvested for spare parts or for subsequent shipment overseas. Hence the neighborhood was irresistible to cops, particularly the ones who populated the Auto Crimes Task Force.

Rico was surprised to see me. Surprised, not necessarily pleased. Apparently, there was a very active Mafia chop shop down the street. Didn't I know better, he wondered, than to tap on his surveillance van's back door? I told him that three scotches and getting jerked around by my best buddy tended to make me stupid. He excused himself, telling the other three cops in the van he'd be back before anything was likely to come down.

The Arch Diner sat at the corners of Ralph and Flatlands Avenue and was as good a place to get coffee as any other. Rico laughed, saying the wiseguys who ran the chop shops down the road frequently got their coffees at the Arch Diner. I wasn't laughing. Nor did I find it amusing when he described how the snot had frozen onto his moustache earlier in the day.

"I had lunch with Sully," I said. "He showed me a picture."

"Yeah, and so what happened?"

"It was of Patrick Maloney."

Rico's expression soured. "That's what you dragged me off a stakeout to tell me?"

"The picture didn't look like the one on the poster."

"Jesus Christ, Moe! Who looks like their picture? You take a look at your departmental ID lately? You probably look like Wolfman Jack."

"So you really didn't know?"

"Know what?" He was losing patience.

I explained about the dated picture and the new picture and how the Maloneys had refused to release a more recent photo. I also said I found it pretty suspicious that Rico had somehow neglected to mention anything about this to me.

"It's news to me," he said as he held his hand to his heart. "You think I know what this kid really looks like? I think I met him once, at my wedding. You were at the wedding, do you remember what he looks like?"

"I guess I see your point."

"It's not like the Maloneys are my wife's closest relatives. It was the father that reached out to *me*. The last time we were over their house, when I told Angela about you and the little girl, was the first time we were over there."

I apologized to Rico. He understood. Walking back to the diner parking lot, carrying coffees for the other cops, Rico reminded me of something.

"Remember what the Homicide guys used to joke about? Sometimes when they'd catch a case and the stiff would be like a thirty-year-old, ten-buck-a-trick hooker with a smack habit and a sheet as long as the double yellow lines down Ocean Parkway and they'd go and notify the mother, do you remember what the mother said every time?"

"But she was such a nice girl."

"Exactly my point, Moe. The Maloneys wouldn't be the first parents to not wanna see their kid the way the rest of the world did."

He dropped me back at my car, his words still ringing in my ears. In the ten years I'd known him, it was the wisest thing he'd said to me. What, I couldn't help wondering, did the Maloneys not want to see?

February 1st, 1978 (early)

THIS TIME I was dreaming when the phone rang. About what, I couldn't say. When I opened my eyes, it was gone.

"Yeah," I mumbled, staring half blind at the red 3:20 A.M. on the clock radio.

"It's Sully . . . Detective Sulli—"

"I know," I yawned. "I'm a little slow on the uptake after three. What is it?"

"We've got a floater. Sounds like it could be the Maloney kid. Emergency Services is fishin' him out as we speak."

"Where?"

"Gowanus Canal, by the Cirillo Brothers' oil tanks."

"I know the place," I said. "You can see it from the expressway."

"That's it. Listen, if you hurry you should be able to get there before they cart him away."

I already had my pants half on as he spoke the words. I wasn't certain to what end. I wasn't family, so I couldn't make a positive ID. I wasn't a licensed investigator and, even if I were, I had nothing in writing to prove I was connected to the case.

"Hey Sully," I wondered, "why call me?"

His answer was less than cosmic: "You bought me lunch, didn't ya? None of the other pricks sprung for so much as a freakin' cup a coffee."

He hung up. I wasn't sure I bought his explanation. Come to think of it, I hadn't exactly believed Sully's story about the kid's picture. Anonymously left on his desk, my ass! If I knew Rico, he'd probably promised Sully a share in the wine shop. Before Rico was through, Aaron and I would have more partners than Bialystock and Bloom. If you don't understand the reference, try and catch *The Producers* on the Million Dollar Movie some night.

I made good time. As I worked my way up toward the filthy water of the Gowanus Canal, it occurred to me that I'd never seen a floater, not in the true sense of the word. Sure, when I worked Coney Island we had a few drownings, but no bodies that had been in the water for any extended length of time. From what I'd heard, the water could do terrible things to a body. Old-timers always had stories about how bloated and grotesque floaters could be. If the body had any tight belts or jewelry on when it went into the water, its features could be terribly distorted.

"Think of it like this here," a retired cop from Emergency Services once told me at a Christmas party. "You take a full balloon, draw a face on it, then twist a rubber band real tight around where the neck would be. With that fuckin' blue-white skin, I can tell ya, it ain't pretty."

The same guy also told me about a floater that had been pushed from one precinct to another almost three quarters of the way around the island of Manhattan. He said they only pulled it out of the water when the brass caught wind of cops betting on how long it would take the floater to complete its circumnavigation. I wasn't sure I believed that story, but I had been a member of the NYPD long enough not to simply dismiss it out of hand.

I got through most of the cops without flashing tin. As I moved closer to the water's edge, however, it would take more than just acting like I belonged to gain access to the body. I found the detective in charge, explained about my knee-monia and how I was working for the Maloneys. He was unimpressed, but didn't figure I could do any harm by looking. The body'd been in the water awhile, he said, and there were no obvious signs of foul play. He didn't have a strong opinion one way or the other as to whether the body was Patrick Maloney.

"Male Caucasian, deceased, swollen," was how he put it. "Is it Maloney? You tell me."

As we approached the body bag, I felt light-headed, almost nauseous. It wasn't that I'd become unexpectedly squeamish. If anything, I was buzzed. Suddenly, I was being torn in several opposing directions. Part of me realized I missed the job more than I let on. At the core, I was deeply disappointed that I, unlike Rico, would never get the chance to earn my gold shield. That being there in the raw cold, my nose filled with the stink of No. 2 heating oil, was as close as I was likely to get to a real crime scene ever again. On the other hand, I was a little bit disgusted by that very same rush of excitement and the jealousy I felt for Rico.

The detective gestured for the technicians to unzip the body bag. As they began to open the bag, the tug of conflicting emotions intensified. If it was the Maloney boy, the Maloneys could start getting used to life without their Patrick and I could get my life back, whatever that meant. If my few days on the case had given me perspective on anything, it was that I was woefully ill-prepared for the time ahead of me. I had come to see the wine shop, even if Aaron and I could scrape the money together, as his dream, alone. Oh, I would never back out on him. I just couldn't picture myself sitting behind a counter all day discussing the relative merits of Merlot versus Beaujolais.

But as much as I wanted the body to be Maloney's, there was double the desire that it not be his. I suppose I could fabricate some plausible rationalization as to why I had my fingers crossed that it not be him. The truth was, I had gotten curious. What was it that made Francis Maloney tick? What was it that the Maloneys couldn't bear to have the rest of the world see about their son? What had happened to Patrick M. Maloney and why? If the body there was the kid's, some of those questions might get answered, but not by me. As wholly nonsensical as it was, I wasn't ready to share the fate of Patrick Maloney with the cops or the coroner.

"It's not him," I heard myself say in a confident voice that did not belie my relief.

"How can ya tell?" the detective was doubtful. "You can barely tell he's human, so how the—"

"No tattoo on his right forearm."

The detective pulled a sheet out of his pocket, using his finger as a pointer to help scan it thoroughly. He shoved the form at me: "Doesn't say anything about identifying marks, nothing about a tattoo."

"Hey," I held my hands up, "I've got no official standing. Take it up with the family."

He didn't like that and the look on his face told me I'd worn out my welcome. I thanked him, turned, walked away. Halfway back to my car, I spotted Francis Maloney coming my way through the maze of cops. I grabbed him by the arm to stop him. Like the detective's face, Maloney's was a billboard.

First, he didn't quite recognize me. His icy little eyes seemed to bark: "Who the fuck are you? And get your paw off me." Then, when the light of recognition clicked on, his bottom lip jutted out, his head tilting and bowing ever so slightly as if to say: "Now you've impressed me, you sheeny bastard. How'd you find out before me?"

All of that was nothing compared to his expression when I gave him the news about the body. I conveyed the message using more conventional methods: "It's not Patrick."

His face went blank, but within a millisecond it was tearing itself apart; relief fighting desperately not to reveal powerful, guilty disappointment. Relief winning a narrow victory. Strangely, I couldn't bring myself to blame him for his disappointment. Bad news really is sometimes better than no news at all. Even if there were issues between Maloney and his son that I didn't understand, the weeks of living in limbo must have been hell for his family.

"How can you be sure?" he asked.

I rested my cane against my good leg, held up my right arm and tapped my left index finger against it.

He played dumb: "What's that, Prager, the bunt sign?"

"No tattoo. And though it was hard to tell, I didn't see the earring either."

Again he seemed impressed, angry too, as he pushed past me. How had I found out about the tattoo? What else did I know that he wanted kept secret? Had he come right out and asked, I wouldn't have told him. To have leverage with a man who so coveted control and secrecy, I would have to keep secrets of my own or at least pretend I had them to keep.

Rushing in to fill the void Maloney's abrupt departure had created, came a dark-haired woman in a sailor's peacoat. About thirty, she stood 5'6" or so with pleasant blue eyes, a triangular face and too-thin lips. Her ringless left hand shook terribly, the ashes from the cigarette it held blowing onto the hem of her Navy coat. As she had been standing several feet behind and to the left of Maloney during the whole of our brief exchange, I had been vaguely aware of her presence. Even so, there were no grounds for me to have assumed a connection between the two. Now she demanded more than a fleeting cruise through my short term memory.

"Are you sure?"

I didn't have to ask about what. "Pretty sure," I said and started to explain: "But I didn't really know—"

She didn't let me finish. Putting her right hand on my forearm, she thanked me, smiled and ran toward the water.

Something about her smile got to me; her touch was electric, magnetic.

It was going on 4:30 when I got back to my car. I decided not to go directly home, choosing instead to drive on toward the Brooklyn Bridge. I picked up some coffee at a bagel shop, parked the car in Brooklyn Heights and found a park bench on the promenade. And though the skyline of lower Manhattan spread out before me like a glorious deck of badly shuffled cards, I could not stop thinking of that woman's smile.

August 6th, 1998 (late afternoon)

I GUESS IF the New York Jets and Giants could play in New Jersey and if Cincinnati's airport could be in Kentucky, it was kosher for the Mary the Divine Hospice of New Haven to be in Hamden. At least it was still in Connecticut, right? The hospice, like many of the huge Victorians along Whitney Avenue, was exquisitely detailed with gingerbread turnings, a wraparound porch and a variety of patterned shingles. The pumpkin, brown and hunter green color palette didn't exactly thrill me, but given its proximity to what I guessed was a lake and lush parkland, I could see why the diocese had selected this sight for a hospice. I told the woman at the front desk as much.

"Oh," she said, "it was serendipity, really. A wealthy Yale alum willed this property to the church a few years back. Before that, we were located in New Haven between a crack house and an abandoned supermarket."

That explains it, I thought, but didn't bother her with my meanderings about NFL franchises or airports. When I did get around to asking for Sister Margaret, the receptionist's face took a decided downward turn. "Are you Mr. Prager?" she wondered.

I could feel my heart sinking into my shoes. "Is he—"

"No, Mr. Bryson hasn't left us yet, but . . ." she trailed off in a less than reassuring tone.

"So he's all right."

"No one here is all right, Mr. Prager."

"I'm sorry. That's not what I meant."

"I understand," she said.

I doubted it. I repeated my request to see Sister Margaret, the nun who had called me earlier that day.

"She's in with Mr. Bryson and Father Izzolino."

"Last rites?"

"I'm afraid so, yes. But you've got to have faith, Mr. Prager."

I restrained myself from laughing. "Maybe," I suggested, "if Mr. Bryson knew I was here, he might hang on a little longer. Can I—"

"Sorry, but that's impossible." Rubbing her chin, the receptionist pondered how to proceed. "Sister!" she flagged down a woman in a blue habit with a simple kerchief-type wimple.

"I'll see what I can do." The nun put her hand on my arm. "It may take several minutes. We have a small chapel through that door, if you'd like to reflect."

"Thank you, Sister," I smiled, "but no. I wouldn't want to be disrespectful. I'm Jewish and—"

"So was he," she said, pointing to a crucifix. "Let me go see if I can get Sister Margaret."

I asked the receptionist if there was a quiet place where I could use my cell phone. There was a lounge, she said, just past the chapel. She thought I would be fine there.

The empty lounge looked out onto a lovely sloping lawn, a flower garden and the water just beyond it. I punched my daughter's number in. As I waited for the connection to be made, I noticed the wall clock, checked my wristwatch to confirm the time. 4:50 P.M.; in another four minutes it would be exactly eighteen years since Sarah's birth. As I listened to her phone go unanswered for a third ring, it struck me that a hospice was a pretty macabre venue for phoning in birthday wishes. Then again, maybe not. Maybe it was the perfect place.

Someone rapped on the wall behind me. "Mr. Prager?" a woman's voice called my name.

I clicked the phone off and turned. "I'm Moe Prager."

"I'm Sister Margaret. So nice to meet you." She pumped my hand. "Thank you for coming."

"Same here," I mumbled. "I mean, I'm glad to have made the trip." I think I was taken aback by the fact the sister was dressed in a pale blue nurse's uniform.

She took note of my confusion. "Yes, Mr. Prager, I am fully qualified. Some of our guests call me RN squared; real nun and registered nurse. Just a little hospice humor. You need that, that and faith."

Sister Margaret was built like a snowman with penny copper eyes and button nose. Though she wasn't smiling, exactly, she did exude a sort of calm that seemed to fill the room. I guess that's a valuable asset in a place where the folks have been at, knocked on and passed most of the way through death's door.

"How's Mr. Bryson?"

"Not very well," her eyes frowned. "The cancer has spread to most of his vital organs. Though he hasn't shared his burden with me, I suspect he's got something he needs desperately to share with you before leaving us. I think it's the only thing that's kept him alive these last few days."

"Can I go see him, sister?"

"Unfortunately, he was in such pain we had to load him full of morphine. He's lost consciousness for the moment. It could be hours before he comes to. If—"

"—he ever does regain consciousness," I finished her thought. She suggested I get something to eat. The New Haven area, Sister Margaret proudly assured me, was famous for its brick-oven pizza. There were several wonderful pizzerias within a short driving distance. There was even one I could walk to, but she didn't recommend it. Their cheese was too salty. She would take my cell phone number and call if Mr. Bryson's condition improved sufficiently to allow us to speak.

I hesitated.

"Can I ask you something, Mr. Prager?"

"Certainly."

"I've read the article Mr. Bryson keeps with him about Patrick Maloney, but I'm not clear about your connection. I confess," she blushed slightly, "to being more than a bit curious."

"And I'm probably more curious about Mr. Bryson. Tell me, sister, does the RN squared get a dinner break? Because if she does . . ."

"I'll call and order the pizza. What's your phone number? I'll leave it at the front desk. We can be back here in five minutes. Oh," she turned back after I gave her the number, "what do you like on your pizza?"

"Anything but anchovies."

She gave me the thumbs up and fairly ran to the front desk. I punched in Sarah's number once more, the real anniversary of her birth having passed unmarked some minutes before. Just as before, the phone went unanswered.

February 2nd, 1978

WORKING AGAINST THE coffee, it took a three-jigger visit with my bottle of Dewars to put my head to the pillow. When I was on the job, I'd taken great pains to guard against falling into the bottle. Now, between my lunch with Sully and this morning's nightcap, I'd consumed more hard liquor in two days than in the last few months. Over the years, I'd seen old John Barleycorn take down more good cops than all the bombs, bullets and bribes combined. And by a long stretch, too. The pattern was pretty much the same: one drink to unwind after a shift became two, became three. Soon, the line between the shift and the unwinding became a drunken blur.

It was closer to dinner than to lunch when I did get up, that stale smell of scotch and coffee on my breath. Again I was vaguely aware of having dreamed, but of what or whom I couldn't say. I can say that my first thought was of the smiling woman in the peacoat. I elected to believe I dreamed of her. Better her than the floater.

I'd tried Rico several times at the task force office without any luck. Finally, I risked a call to his home and got the second Mrs. Tripoli on the phone. Initially, she sounded about as happy to hear from me as from an oncologist. I don't think she hated me necessarily, but I suspect she regarded all of Rico's cop friends as threats. We managed to get through the conversation without exchanging hostilities. She wondered if I'd made any progress in finding Patrick. I told her it was hard to know. She even asked about my knee.

Rico, she said, had been sent down to Florida to pick up a fugitive who was willing to shed light on the task force's case. She couldn't tell me exactly when he'd be back. Two or three days, she thought. Before hanging up, I asked for the Maloneys' address and phone number. She hesitated, curious about why I didn't already have that information. I considered telling her the truth, but reconsidered. After all, I was a big boy now. My mom didn't have to cut my steak for me anymore. I think maybe I was a little embarrassed.

"I lost the piece of paper with that stuff on it."

"At least you're honest." She was unwittingly ironic, slowly dictating the information.

Now I hesitated, wanting to ask Rico's wife if she might know who the woman in the peacoat was. Not sure how to phrase the question and not wanting to push my luck, I didn't ask. She promised to have Rico get back to me if he called in from Florida. I thanked her.

I sat staring at the envelope on which I'd written the Maloneys' address and phone number. I thought about driving up there. I knew in my bones I would have to go sooner or later. Later, I decided. It was late and cold and my knee ached. But the more deeply involved in the case of Patrick Maloney's disappearance I got, the more convinced I became that where he had come from had something to do with where he had gone to.

February 3rd, 1978

IF IT WASN'T for the fact that the New York Jets football team trained there, most non-alums wouldn't know of Hofstra University's existence. And with the way the Jets had played since their '69 Super Bowl victory over the Colts, most non-alums, like myself, were seriously invested in trying to forget. I think the school was founded by a Dutch immigrant family who'd made their fortune in the logging industry in Michigan's northern peninsula. As to why they picked Uniondale, Long Island, NY, for the campus, your guess is as good as mine. None of the students I asked seemed to know or care. They were having enough trouble giving me directions to the dorm suite Patrick Michael Maloney had once occupied. Marijuana Studies must have been a popular major.

The south part of the campus was actually quite attractive, very Ivy League. But like most schools that had expanded to meet the Baby Boomer explosion, Hofstra had suffered the indignities of late '60s and '70s architecture: nearly windowless concrete boxes that looked better suited to protecting German machine-gun nests along the Normandy coast. Patrick Maloney's suite was located on the side of the campus where the Jets maintained their facilities, in one of four white dormitory buildings that dwarfed every other structure as far as the eye could see. Very tasteful. I think maybe at night they put a crossbar between the towers so the Jets' kicker could practice field goals in the dark.

I thought I could have talked my way past the security guard at the lobby desk, but showed him my badge instead. Unlike most square-badgers, this guard was highly unimpressed. He shook his head no at my advance towards the elevator.

"NYPD issuing canes these days?" he wondered. "Must be new since I got off the job."

"Special issue for the gimp squad. We chase the ambulance chasers," I said. "How long you off?"

"Five years in April. Haven't looked back a day since I put in my papers."

Yeah, right. He hated the uniform so much he was willing to go back in the bag to guard coeds and potheads for four bucks an hour. I didn't feel like arguing the point, so I turned the discussion to Patrick Maloney. Maybe I could use his cop's instincts to my advantage. Apparently, this wasn't a very original idea.

"You're the first guy to show up in weeks. First month, we had every off-duty cop on the planet running in and outta here. I was givin' out numbers like the deli counter at Waldbaums. I was gettin' interviewed every ten minutes."

"How about one more time?"

Surprisingly, he said he remembered Maloney. The old cop said Maloney stuck out from the other students because he was always really polite and impeccably dressed.

"Always had a good morning or good evening for me. Called me sir. My own kids don't call me sir," the security guard lamented. "And the creases in his pants were so sharp you could cut paper with 'em. The rest of the kids around here dress like bums and the best I get out of 'em is a grunt. It's the uniform. They got no respect for the uniform. Draft card burnin' mother . . . If I had my way, I'd—"

I cut him off before he got started critiquing President Carter's neutron bomb policy. In a way, the old cop's rantings served as a reminder. You had only to scratch the surface just a little to hit raw nerve. Sure, we were doing the bump through the decade with OPEC and the Symbionese Liberation Army to distract us, but we weren't so far removed from the Tet Offensive or Selma or Dallas that we had forgotten. There were scabs forming on the wounds, but there was still fresh blood beneath the scabs. I'd keep that in mind.

As I rode the elevator up to the eighth floor, I thought about what the security guard had said about Patrick. I wasn't certain, however, how much credence to assign his statements. Maybe he was saying what he thought I wanted to hear. Cops are as guilty of that as anyone else. Maybe the Maloneys had gotten to him and given him some incentive to spout the family line. Or it might not have been anything so sinister. Over time, he might have woven what he'd read in the papers and heard about the Maloney boy into his memory so that he could no longer distinguish between what had actually occurred and what had been suggested. Still, I could not dismiss what he had said. It rang true, especially about the creases in Patrick's pants. It was too obscure a detail for someone to fabricate. And I couldn't help remembering the military creases in the elder Maloney's clothing when we'd met at Molly's.

While the hallway didn't exactly reek of marijuana, its earthy sweet perfume hung in the air like a happy ghost. Put out to pasture, I could finally admit to loving that smell. I ran a finger along the wall. It was sticky with resin. The desperate kids, I thought, could probably lick the walls and catch a buzz.

I found Patrick's old room, Led Zeppelin blasting on the other side of the door. The bass line ignored the door, massaging my feet through the soles of my shoes. The smell of pot was more intense here than in the rest of the hall. I gave the door a good rap to no avail. Given the volume of Robert Plant's falsetto, I could understand why. I knocked again, harder. No response. I gave my foot a try. No luck, I was batting 0 for 3. Finally, I tried the door. It was unlocked and since no one would invite me, I let myself in.

The kid seated in front of the stereo had his back to me. As loud as the music was, I was surprised his ears weren't bleeding. I guessed he was further distracted by the skull-headed bong he was busily sucking on. Before approaching him, I stopped to admire the art. No silly blacklight posters here. Each wall had been painted with meticulous reproductions of popular album covers. To my left was the prism on black of *Dark Side of the Moon*. To my right was the grasshopper of Steely Dan's *Katy Lied*. Behind me, Aqualung gave me dirty looks. Aaron always thought it immature of me to keep up with rock music. Maybe. Then again, Aaron thought Woodstock signaled the coming apocalypse.

I didn't even bother trying to announce my arrival and simply tapped the kid on the shoulder. That gave him a start. He spilled some bong juice on his jeans and the grass in the bowl on the floor.

"Hey, man!" he screamed. "What the—"

Deciding to cut past the bullshit, I showed him my badge.

"Oh man, oh man," he lamented. "I'm fucked now. My parents'll—"

"Calm down. Take it slow. This isn't a bust," I said. "Lower the stereo. I only wanna talk."

Dutifully, he turned down the volume. I thought he was going to kiss my ring. That was good. I hoped it would make him want to cooperate.

"What's your name?"

"Mitch," he squeaked, "but everybody calls me Doobie."

What a surprise. I scanned the list of Patrick's suite mates. No Mitch. No Doobie. I read the names aloud and asked Doobie if any of them were around.

"They're outta here, dude," he said, the tension going out of his voice. "After that weird Maloney guy did the Houdini thing, those guys trucked over to other dorms. I guess they were getting hassled too much."

I wondered why everyone, including the ex-cop downstairs, had neglected to tell me Patrick's roomies had scattered. While I fumed quietly, my eyes drifted back to the album cover walls. Doobie noticed my admiration.

"Pretty cool, huh?"

"Your work?" I wondered.

"No way, man," he laughed. "I have a hard time with stick figures. They were here when we moved in. There's a Moody Blues in the bathroom. Too bad he didn't do any Zep or Zappa."

"Yeah, too bad. Do you know which one of the roommates did—"

"Houdini, man. Patrick. Look, he initialed them in the corner."

Doobie was right. PMM appeared in the lower left-hand corner of each mural. It wasn't exactly the ceiling of the Sistine Chapel, but I was impressed. The detail was amazing.

"You looking for him?" Doobie asked.

"Me and everyone else. You called him weird before. Why?"

"I didn't mean nothing mean by it," Doobie said defensively. "I used to live down the hall and we didn't really talk or anything more than a hello. You know? But he was just weird. I don't know."

"Try."

"He was . . . I mean, he was kinda . . . You ever see that movie with David Bowie in it?"

"*The Man Who Fell to Earth*?"

"That's it! You know for a cop, you're—"

"Thanks, but let's get back to the movies."

"Right. Sorry, dude. So, yeah. You know how Bowie was like an alien. Patrick, he was kinda like that. He didn't fit in. He lived on the hall, but he was apart from us."

I was losing patience with the Doobster and praying he wasn't pre-med. "Can you give me an example?"

He pointed over my shoulder at the snarling Aqualung. "He painted all of these, right. But from what the guys told me, Patrick never listened to this music. Well, no . . . they told me he pretty much hated head music. He would split or lock himself in his room whenever the tunes came on. They said he painted the walls to like kiss their ass. It was like a trade, you know?"

"A trade for what?"

Dobbie thought about that: "For putting up with him, I guess. If they went out to a bar or to an Islanders' game, they'd include him."

"If he didn't fit in here, why didn't he just switch roommates?"

"I guess he was like tired of doing that, man. Bobby told me—"

"Robert Klingman?" I asked. The mental image of Klingman's mother teaching herself the hustle popped into my head.

"Yeah, Robert Klingman. He said that Patrick had changed roommates every term since freshman year. See, that's what I mean, he was just a weird dude, dude. He also smiled too much, you know?"

I didn't know. All I could tell from what Doobie had shared was that Patrick Maloney was desperate to fit in. As a Jewish cop, I could empathize. I'd been willing to take a lot of shit in order to be accepted by my peers. I kept pressing Doobie for other examples of Patrick's eccentricities, but he just shrugged his shoulders a lot and said he was getting munched out. Yet, I got the sense he was hiding something from me. I put on the full-court press, reminding him of the badge in my pocket and that a relatively small quantity of his preferred smoke could get him a free room in Attica courtesy of the Rockefeller drug laws. He acted hurt. I wasn't playing fair. I'd promised him there'd be no bust. There wouldn't be, I said, if he would just stop holding back.

Doobie threw his hands up in surrender. "Okay, dude, you win. But like word got around campus to not . . . you know. I mean what if the guy's dead or something. It's not right for me to—"

I told him I understood, but that there was no proof Patrick was dead. Maybe, I said, what he had to tell me, no matter what it was, could help me find Patrick.

"One night I came over to borrow a Yes album from Bobby Klingman." Doobie's tone was suddenly very serious. "I just let myself in. It was cool, the front door was always open. No one was in Bobby's room, but I heard someone else in the suite. I figured I'd smoke a j with whoever it was. And then I like see that

Patrick's door is open a crack, so I look in. I was gonna say something, but it was just like weird man, weird."

"What?"

"Patrick was in his underwear and he was walking backwards in like a perfect square. He kept doing it over and over and the whole time he's like looking over his shoulder to make sure his feet are landing in the same spots on the floor. I didn't know what to do. I didn't wanna embarrass the guy, you know. And shit, I was pretty stoned and I was getting into it. So when he gets done walking the squares, he gets dressed."

"So," I shrugged, "he gets dressed."

"But not like I get dressed. He starts counting backward from twenty out loud, sorta whispering to himself like, and takes all the shit folded on the bed and gets it on before he's at zero. Then he starts counting again, but forward this time, and gets undressed. Folds everything back up and does it again. What I notice is he does the right side first; right sock, right pants leg, right sleeve. When he takes the stuff off, it's like backwards. Everything from the left. It was spooky, man, and I didn't feel right about watching anymore. So I start tiptoeing out and Bobby like comes in the front door and drops a book on the floor."

"Patrick saw you, didn't he?"

"Yeah," Doobie bowed his head. "Our eyes like met. I felt shitty, man. I never said anything about it, not even when all the cops came around."

I held my right hand out and shook Doobie's. I thanked him and told him I respected him for keeping Patrick's rituals secret. Before I left, I suggested he start locking the suite door. You never know, I said, who might be watching or who might let himself in.

Originally, I'd meant to track down as many of Patrick's roommates as I could find, but suddenly that strategy had lost its appeal. Doobie's cannabis-hazed recollections had turned my scheme on its ear, for he had breathed life into Patrick Maloney. I could no longer treat Patrick as an abstraction, a poster, a means to my brother's ends. Patrick was human to me now, a man with pain and quirks and secrets. Doobie had done more to motivate me than all the carrots and sticks Francis Maloney could muster. I was going to find Patrick, me, no one else, no matter how long it would take.

As I left the dorm I could hear the ex-cop/security guard call after me. For his lack of candor about Patrick's roommates, I rewarded him with my ignorance. There was a philosopher once who said something like, to be is to be perceived. I hoped the security guard would reach the very same conclusion.

OUTSIDE AND WALKING toward the student center, I figured I had two options: I could find the student government offices or try to locate the health services building. Since I was certain Patrick had been a member of the student council, but hadn't a clue as to whether Patrick had sought help for his . . . I don't know, his rituals, I guess I'd call them, I opted for the sure thing.

The door to the student government offices was wide open. Here, too, I was greeted by music. Joni Mitchell, this time, and not so loud that I was in danger of permanent hearing loss. I smiled sadly. It had never before occurred to me that the older one gets, the less one's life is accompanied by music. I remembered my parents' house and how music was confined to an hour of show tunes on Sunday mornings. Even for me, news radio had begun replacing music as the soundtrack of my life.

Inside, a long-legged girl in cowboy boots and white painter's pants danced with the file cabinet. She had square shoulders, a waterfall of curly brown hair and a profile that featured impossibly high cheekbones. I stood for a few seconds, watching her lip-synching the tense elation of newfound love. Then, recalling Doobie's guilty voyeurism, I knocked my knuckles against the door: "Hello!"

She turned right around, smiling, not a hint of embarrassment showing on her pale, strangely Victorian face. Her name was Maria. She didn't look like a Maria, she said. We agreed that I looked more Italian than she. Most everybody did. Eventually she got around to asking me what I wanted. Patrick Maloney's name chased the smile off her face and ruined her appetite for Joni Mitchell.

Yes, she knew him. No, she didn't like him. He did his work on the council, but he had no enthusiasm for it. He was a phony, a user.

I told her I'd gotten a very different impression of him.

"Sure you have," Maria said, "but . . ." She stopped herself, her pale skin turning bright red.

I pressed her. "But what?"

"I'm just sick of the bullshit," she hissed, anger contorting her face. "All that stuff in the paper is . . ."

"Did you date him?"

"Date him? No. He would never have asked me and I wouldn't have gone."

"Why?" I wondered.

"Why what? Why wouldn't he have asked or why wouldn't I have gone?"

"You pick."

"He wouldn't have asked because I was too pretty," she said without a hint of self-consciousness.

"And if he asked . . ."

"I thought he was creepy even before . . ." Again, she stopped herself. "He was just odd, that's all."

"Before what? Look, Maria," I said, showing her my badge, "I'm not this kid's press agent. I want to find him, not nominate him for sainthood. If he's a schmuck, he's a schmuck. It's not for me to judge. If you've got something nasty to say, say it."

"It's not my story to tell." She walked away from the file cabinet over to a desk and wrote something down on a sheet of pink memo paper. "Here," she said, "go talk to her."

I took the paper. "I apologize, Maria. I didn't mean to upset you. I think you knocked me off balance. No one ever said I looked Italian before."

She smiled at that a little, just a little. As I walked back down the hall I listened for Joni Mitchell's voice, but it never came.

The address Maria had given me was off campus, way off campus. Again I thought about finding student health services. Only now I was on shakier ground than when I'd left Doobie's. And even if I could have found some shrink or social worker to answer my questions, I wouldn't have known what questions to pose. Apparently, Patrick Maloney was not only human, but a complex one at that. We humans do have that unfortunate tendency. Poster pictures were easier on the soul, not many tics or quirks, no enemies to deal with.

THOUGH SOUTH OF Glen Cove, Brookville was still, I think, considered part of Long Island's Gold Coast. While it was no longer the exclusive playground of the obscenely wealthy, the zoning board wasn't exactly busy approving variances for trailer parks. I don't suppose you would designate any of the houses spread out along Route 107 as mansions, per se. I mean they were big, bigger than most of the houses in Brooklyn, but you couldn't hangar anything more substantial than a Boeing 737 even in the largest of the bunch.

Nancy Lustig's house, if it was her house—her name and this address were on the memo paper Maria gave me—was a stunning red brick colonial that sat at the end of a beautifully cobbled driveway. Set against the snow-covered grounds, the place looked like a scene out of a Christmas beer commercial. I parked the car alongside a red Porsche, probably the gardener's car.

As I hobbled up the front steps, I could make out a pair of eyes behind the leaded glass panel in the front doors. They marked my progress, which, given my lack of skill with a cane and the slickness of the granite, must have been more entertaining to watch than the clown car at the circus.

The door swung open. A squatty girl dressed in the best L. L. Bean had to offer, ran to take me by the elbow and help me to the landing.

"Thanks," I said as she ushered me through the door.

"You're the policeman?" she asked.

"Maria called you? I figured she would. You're Nancy Lustig?"

"I am. And you are . . . ?"

I told her as we shook hands. She took my coat, told me where to put my wet shoes and showed me into an adjoining room. She excused herself, saying there was tea water on the boil in the kitchen.

The house was less museum-like than I would have expected. All old leather couches and throw rugs, the room I'd been consigned to was cozy enough. The fire in the stone hearth reinforced that feeling. Various family photos covered the walls, but the roughly carved mantle was reserved for photos of Nancy. From birth to bat mitzvah to the present, not the best of them made Nancy look more than plain. To have even called her a cute baby would have required some bending of the truth.

"Lemon or milk?" she screamed from the kitchen.

"Just sugar," I called back.

"What do I call you: Officer, Detective Prager?"

"Moe works. You know, I'm not a cop, not anymore. I'm retired. I'm—"

"You're looking for Patrick." Nancy Lustig appeared, carrying a silver tea service on a clear Plexiglas tray. "I hope you find him."

"You do? Given Maria's reaction, I thought—"

"Maria's protective of me." Nancy poured my tea. "Help yourself to sugar. She was my roommate for three years. Somewhere in there she sort of appointed herself the big sister I never had. Really, I saw it more as her George to my Lenny."

She was testing me. Was I just a dumb cop? If she was going to tell me her story, whatever that story was, was I going to get it? Would I understand her pain? I decided to take her head on. I got the feeling she'd shut down at the first sign of bullshit.

"Nancy—can I call you Nancy?" She nodded that I could. "A lot of cops, maybe most, couldn't name a thing John Steinbeck wrote, but don't mistake a lack of education for stupidity. Most of the other cops I worked with were pretty smart in their ways. Besides, you're too short and bright to be Lenny."

"Maria's beautiful, isn't she?"

"I'd hate to have her pissed off at me."

Wrong answer. "That's not what—"

"She's pretty sexy, yeah."

"I'm not." Another test.

"I don't suppose you are," I said.

"If you were at a keg party and saw Maria and me hanging out at the edge of the dance floor, who would you ask to dance?"

"In this hypothetical do I have two good knees?"

She liked that. "Sure, two good knees and moves like Superfly."

"I guess I'd ask Maria."

"Not Patrick," she said, trying to suppress something that might have been a smile. "He asked me. And he meant it. It wasn't on some bet or dare. He wasn't stoned or drunk, though I don't think it would have mattered if he were. He really wanted to dance with me. Me! I waited my whole life for a boy who looked like Patrick to ask me to dance. I know it's silly, but . . . can you understand?"

"I think I do."

"And Maria . . . God, it was worth it just to see the look on her face." Now, as she relived the moment in her head, her smile was in full bloom. "Poor Maria, she didn't know what to do. You know, Mr. Prager, I've had people be jealous over my father's money, my car, my GPA, but the jealousy that flashed across Maria's face . . . No matter what happened with Patrick after that, I'll never forget that moment."

"I think we all have moments like that." I gave her a blow-by-blow description of the first time I beat my brother in one-on-one basketball. And I agreed with her, the look on Aaron's face was something I wasn't likely to forget. "He was proud and angry all at once."

"Exactly."

I had passed her tests. She recounted for me how Patrick had asked for her number, how sharply dressed he had been when he showed up for their first date: Adonis in Jordache jeans. They went to the movies and to some disco out on Sunrise Highway. He had been a perfect gentleman, she said in an oddly disappointed tone.

"You know, there's a lot about that night I know I should remember but don't. My head was just swimming. I was watching other girls watching us."

But what had started out on such a high soon settled into a strange, repetitive pattern. There were movies, lots of them. Dancing, always dancing and the occasional dinner. No double dates. Then there was a kiss goodnight at the dorm door. Never an invitation to spend the night.

"Oh, we made out sometimes." She got defensive. "He'd rub my . . . Ah, he—"

I told her I understood. He didn't seem very experienced. A good Catholic boy, she guessed. He didn't sound like the good Catholic boys I knew.

She would do most of the talking when they were out. She talked about everything, about her family, her life. Patrick, on the other hand, never discussed his family. School, mostly. They could have gone on for years, she thought, and she wouldn't have known him any better than the night they met at the keg party.

"He was a good listener then," I prodded, "like a sponge."

"No," she said, "like a wall. It was like he wasn't listening at all. I don't know how to explain it. He didn't ignore me when I spoke. He faced me. He seemed interested. I just got this feeling."

She told me that she'd started seeing a therapist at Hofstra. Nancy admitted she could have afforded to go to any shrink in the tri-state area, but didn't want her parents to know or to control the purse strings. In any case, Nancy and Patrick's relationship had been a hot topic during her therapy sessions.

"We talked about how I wasn't really satisfied with how the relationship was going, so we worked out a strategy for me to talk to Patrick about it. It was to be all very calm. We even rehearsed. I'd made up my mind that I was going to say something the next time we went out. But I was still really, really nervous."

"I can understand that."

"Do you? Look, I want to be clear. It wasn't that I was nervous about being with a man. I was no virgin. Getting laid wasn't the issue. You know the old joke. With one of these," she bowed her head toward her groin, "a girl can get as many of those," she pointed to my lap, "as she wants. Even girls like me. That's right, Mr. Prager, I know the look."

"The look?" I puzzled.

"The look the morning after when the boy rolls over, sees me and wonders just how much he had to drink the night before."

Out of my own guilt, I let that slide. "So what did happen?"

"I don't know," she laughed nervously. "What I mean to say is I don't know what got into Patrick. That night when he picked me up at my dorm, he asked if Maria was around. When I said she had already split, he . . . well, we . . ."

"He took the initiative," I offered.

"Yes, he took me and the initiative right there on the dorm room floor. Whether he'd gotten the sense I was going to say something or whether it was coincidence, I can't say."

Though the earth hadn't exactly moved for her—Patrick had reached the finish line before Nancy had gotten fully out of the gate—it was progress. Enough progress, she thought, to not want to set things back by airing her dissatisfaction with their relationship. All the lines she had so carefully rehearsed with her therapist went unsaid. But the progress just got incorporated into the routine. Now the dancing, dinner and movies came to include sex.

Sometimes, she said, the sex got rough. Not abusive, no S&M, just rough, desperate almost. She never understood why and he didn't volunteer any explanations.

"I never complained. I wasn't being a martyr or anything. It was just that he'd let me try different things when he was in that mood." She blushed slightly. "It was more . . . satisfying for me."

He still made himself unknowable. And the sex, rather than improving things, had given her more to be unhappy about. When I asked her what her therapist had said, Nancy hesitated. She confessed she had begun skipping sessions soon after she and Patrick had slept together for the first time, eventually stopping therapy altogether.

"It's called resistance," she explained. "I didn't want to confront what I knew in my heart, so I avoided dealing with it. I knew, maybe from the first date, that Patrick and I had nowhere to go. But I just couldn't let go of that night at the keg party. Even now I . . ."

"You stopped going to therapy. What did you do?"

She started crying: "I made an ass of myself." Thankfully, I didn't have to ask how. I don't think I could have. "I tried a solution out of some stupid women's magazine," she said after regaining her composure. "I asked Patrick if he wanted to go—No, that's a lie. I asked Patrick to take me to Club Caligula. It's a—"

"I know what it is."

Club Caligula, like Plato's Retreat, was one of the sex clubs that had recently opened in New York City. Such clubs had always existed, usually as underground establishments catering to a very specific clientele. One drive through the meat packing district after dark and you'd know these clubs were nothing new. What did set these clubs apart, however, was their more mainstream appeal. Rather than attract patrons through coded whispers in the dark, these clubs advertised in *New York* magazine. As such places went, Club Caligula had a bit of a wilder rep than Plato's. Maybe that's why she'd picked it. I didn't ask.

"It was couples only and single girls the night we went," she was quick to say. "Once you got inside the rules were simple: You had to strip completely or wear a toga and everything had to be voluntary. Other than that . . ."

She went on to describe all the different rooms. There were hot tubs and saunas, jungle rooms and beach rooms, even a dungeon. You could rent play toys, buy drinks. There was one guy selling loose joints. The smell, though, was something Nancy said she would never forget. She could smell it now.

"It was overwhelming, so raw. Dirty and sweet in the same breath." She was almost wistful.

"And you and Patrick?" I wondered.

"The same, only he seemed even more distracted. Then a couple came over to us and . . ." Nancy started clearing her throat furiously, blushing beet red. "Before we could say no, she—She kissed me. Oh God. I ran. I ran to the locker room, changed and got a cab back to school. I think I brushed my teeth and gargled for an hour. God, what an ass I was and such a baby. What did I think was going to happen in a sex club?"

"I don't know," I said, "maybe that's why you went. What happened to Patrick?"

"We didn't see each other for a week after that. To paraphrase Humphrey Bogart, I pretended to be sick and he let me pretend."

I could see she was embarrassed by the whole thing, so I dropped it. Besides, the club had been her idea, her faux pas, not Patrick's. No, there was something else. Maria's anger had been too real. She couldn't have sent me to Nancy for this. Whatever the trauma was, its roots had to be deeper than a night of ribaldry gone wrong.

"I missed my next period."

"Pregnant?"

"Either that or the rabbit committed suicide and they tried to pin it on me."

Neither one of us found that particularly amusing.

"So," I said confidently, "he acted like a jerk, right? He didn't want anything to do with it. Told you he was too young to get married and said he'd find a good safe clinic with you. He'd pay, of course, and he'd even go with you."

Now she was crying so hard her body shook. She ran upstairs. I didn't follow. After my indelicate pronouncements, I assumed I was the last person on earth she wanted to be comforted by. I was about to go on a treasure hunt for my coat when Nancy reappeared. In her left hand she carried a framed drawing or photograph. As she kept its back to me, I couldn't tell which. To my amazement, she apologized.

"If only he had acted that way, Mr. Prager," she said, falling back into her stuffed leather chair, "you wouldn't be here now."

"I'm not sure I understand."

"Do you know what Patrick did when I told him I was pregnant? He got down on his knees and cried. He took the back of my hand and rubbed it along his cheek. Then he kissed it, stood up and told me he loved me. He loved me! In the eight months we dated, he'd never even said he liked me. And when he kissed my hand, it was the first sign of real affection he ever showed."

From that moment on, their relationship bore little or no resemblance to what had come before. Patrick was with her constantly, showering her with gifts. He wanted to meet her family and had finally discussed his own, if only tangentially or in passing. But now it was Nancy who became the silent partner.

"At first, I sort of enjoyed it. God, who knows, maybe if he had been more like that when we started . . . But it got creepy. It was almost as if he had planned, well maybe not planned, but hoped, for this all along. One night he came to my room and gave me this." She turned the frame toward me. In it was a nude sketch of Nancy with a child at her breast. "It's beautiful, isn't it? He made me look beautiful. I should have thrown it away, but I couldn't."

She had broken down when he unwrapped it for her. Later, however, he gave her another gift, a diamond ring. He asked her to marry him.

"You know what you said before when you thought Patrick had said all that stuff about being too young and not being ready?"

"I remember."

"Okay, you were wrong. But what was weird was that he was too quick to accept things. He never voiced any concern or anxiety. I don't know anyone who doesn't get crazed at the thought of fatherhood. And here we were unmarried, still in college, different religions. But Patrick just snapped right into this father-to-be thing like he'd been waiting for it. You know what I mean?" she asked rhetorically. "I got the sense that it wasn't me he loved or even the baby. It was like we were props to plug into this fantasy he had that included a wife, a baby and a split ranch."

She confessed that she never entertained the thought of having the baby. She was too young. She wasn't ready, even if Patrick was. And when she was prepared to discuss the abortion with Patrick, he proposed.

"What did you do?"

"Like my Dad says, I punted. What could I do?" she asked, back on the defensive. "I couldn't tell him about the abortion, not then, and I couldn't say yes. I told him I was flattered and that I'd have to think about it."

"How'd he take that?"

She rubbed her hands together furiously, tilted her head to the floor and whispered: "He hurt me." Then, as if wanting to prevent my judging him, she screamed, "He didn't mean it! I . . . I mean, he . . ."

Calmly, I asked, "What did he do?"

"He grabbed my shoulders like this." She stood and placed her hands on me. "And he shook me so hard he dislocated my left shoulder. The whole time he was yelling at me: 'You can't do this to me! You can't do this to me!' Two guys in the next room pulled him off me. But before he left, Patrick took the ring out of my hand and spit on me. He spit on me!" She welled up. "The two guys wanted to report Patrick to campus security, but I begged them not to. They looked relieved and took me to the infirmary."

"But you didn't say no to his proposal," I wanted to confirm.

"No, I just said I'd have to think about it. I guess," she said, "I'd been following the script perfectly up to then. It was like he couldn't tolerate a rip in the fabric of his fantasy."

The doctors, Nancy continued, reset her arm, gave her some pills for the pain and sent her home to her parents. She told them she had gotten clumsy and fallen down the stairs. I winced at that. As a cop I'd had a hundred women repeat that same lie. Spitting blood and broken teeth at my feet, they would stubbornly cling to their stories. Even as I pointed out to them that there were no stairs in their apartments down which to fall, they would repeat their lies like a prayer. The doctors hadn't believed her either, but she refused to involve the police. It took weeks for the bruises Patrick's fingers had left to fade.

"When my folks weren't around, I'd pull my blouse down below my shoulders and stare in the mirror. I'd touch them. It was like he still had hold of me. Sometimes, I think I can still feel them or see them in the mirror," she admitted.

She had left school and moved back home. Her parents were more gullible than the infirmary staff and accepted her story about the steps without question. Unfortunately, she had to compound the lie by saying she had been very drunk. Still, she said, it was all she could do to convince her father not to bring suit against the school.

As soon as the shoulder was better, Nancy had the abortion. Maria had taken her to the clinic. Though she hadn't told her parents about the abortion, Nancy tried convincing herself through me that they would have understood.

"They know something's wrong. My shoulder's been completely healed for months and I haven't gone back to campus since last May when I . . . when Patrick hurt me. Sometimes I wish they would just ask, you know?"

I told her it was moments like these that made me glad I wasn't a parent. She said she had never seen Patrick again. He had called her the day of the abortion, crying into the phone. He hadn't said anything, but she knew it was him. He had followed her. But that was the last of Patrick until she read the papers last December. Although she claimed to be glad to be rid of him, I got the sense there were things she desperately wanted to say to Patrick.

"He taught me a lot, but I guess he wasn't trying." She frowned. "I'll never feel the same way about anything. The abortion did that, I think. In school, everything is an abstraction. It's point, counterpoint. Now it's hard for me to see things that way. All the battle lines get kind of blurry when the world is gray. But some good came of it. I think I know what's important now.

The mirror's no longer my enemy and I think I'll recognize real love next time, if there is a next time."

I agreed she would. I wondered if she'd ever been interviewed by the police or other investigators. She had, a few times, but they asked pretty superficial questions. And when they discovered that she and Patrick had broken up six or seven months prior to his disappearance, they politely excused themselves. Had she told any of them about the abortion? She hadn't.

"Why tell me?"

"It was time," she said.

I let that hang a moment before asking: "Did Patrick know you were going to therapy?"

"Absolutely, I was proud of it. I told everyone but my mom and dad."

"Did he ever, I don't know, talk about it?" I struggled. "What was his reaction?"

"It's funny you should ask," she smiled. "He was schizo about it, sort of paranoid but really really curious."

Nancy didn't know if Patrick had sought help himself. He had certainly never discussed it. She didn't know if it would help, but she gave me the name of the therapist she had seen at school. I thanked her. She repeated her wish that I find Patrick and offered to help in any way she could. I gave her my phone number and told her to call if she could think of anything she thought was important. If she just wanted to chat, I said that was all right, too. On the way to the front door, Nancy told me she'd be going back to school next September, but not Hofstra. Stanford or UCLA, she thought. She liked California.

"I picked Hofstra because it was close to home, safe. It felt good to have my parents around. You know, so they could protect me or rescue me. One more myth shot to hell, huh?"

As she walked me to the door, I asked: "The last time you saw Patrick, what color was his hair and did he have an earring or a tattoo?"

She stared at me as if I just landed from Mars, but fought back her curiosity and told me his hair was black, neatly cut and parted down the middle like a real disco lizard. No, he didn't have any tattoos and only she had worn earrings.

"When you read about Patrick's disappearance, were you surprised?"

"No," she said after a second's hesitation and closed the door.

It was dark when I pulled out of the driveway back onto 107. The big houses were harder to see from the road, some were completely cloaked in the fallen night. I thought not so much about Patrick Maloney as Nancy. She had reminded me of something that working stiffs like me tend to forget. Money is a great insulator. Let's face it, Nancy Lustig was never going to worry about food stamps or the price of gas. And sometimes money can soften the blow when you fall, but it can't stop you from falling. The pain she felt was as real as it gets and I doubt the size of her bond portfolio was much of a tonic.

I found a bar not so much because I needed a scotch, but because I needed a place to escape. On a more practical note, I needed a place with a Yellow Pages and phone. I had to find a room for the night. A return trip to Hofstra was first on tomorrow's itinerary and I didn't feel like driving back to Brooklyn.

Oddly, as the incongruous images of Patrick Maloney walking the perfect square and of his assaulting Nancy Lustig jockeyed for position in my consciousness, I became keenly aware of the taste of my scotch. I suppose I needed it more than I was willing to admit.

February 4th, 1978

SLEEP HAD COME in fits and starts. If I bothered adding my Zzzs together, they would likely add up to only three hours, tops. Maybe it was the strange bed. I can't say. What I can say is that I was in an unexpectedly sour mood.

As I sat eating my eggs at the diner across from the motel, I scribbled facts and a timeline on a napkin. From what Nancy had told me, I knew she had met Patrick at a party in September '76. They had dated until April or May. At some point, she had started therapy and become dissatisfied with their relationship. They began sleeping together and sometime in March, I estimated, they had gone to Caligula's. In April, Nancy discovered she was pregnant and Patrick warmed to her considerably. By May, he had proposed and attacked her. By the end of May, she had moved home and terminated the pregnancy. He called her the day of the abortion and after that had no further contact.

After the abortion but before September of '77, Patrick had transformed his look—getting a tattoo, an earring and cropping his hair. At some time, either during or after Nancy and Patrick's relationship, Doobie had stumbled upon Patrick's strange rituals. I should have thought to ask when, exactly. Patrick Maloney was artistically gifted, fastidious, unable to keep roommates, aloof and rigid, potentially violent. On the other hand, he craved acceptance, was willing to go to considerable lengths to be included in social plans.

That's what I knew, what I believed I knew. There were huge gaps—like the first nineteen years of his life—that needed filling in. Shit, there were huge gaps in the information I did have. But I had only limited faith that knowing more would somehow magically lead me to a satisfactory answer or any answer at all as to Patrick's whereabouts. It struck me I could learn everything there was to learn about Patrick Michael Maloney and get nowhere. There was no cosmic rule necessarily connecting Patrick's disappearance to his past.

A chunk of ice falls off a jet and crushes a woman putting groceries into her trunk. Does anybody hire detectives to check into her past? Does what she just purchased in Key Food have anything to do with what killed her? Of course not. But disappear or perish in some mysterious way and the details of your life come under intense scrutiny.

Luck being beside the point, look at what I had uncovered in one day of meaningful investigation. Not only had I stumbled across things Patrick himself and, in all likelihood, the Maloneys wanted kept secret, but what about Nancy Lustig? Did Patrick's disappearance give me license to peer into the messy corners of her life? Was everyone who'd had contact, either significant or casual, with Patrick Maloney suddenly fair game? I thought about how painful it would be for Aaron to reveal the details of our family life if I were the one to unexpectedly disappear. For the first time I had insight into why Francis Maloney had played things so close to the vest. It didn't make me like him any better, but I guess I could see his point. He was doing damage control. If Patrick was lost forever, he didn't want his family's privacy to be a secondary victim. I respected that.

I'd lost my appetite for eggs. Throwing a buck on the table, I stood to leave. I crumpled up my napkin and shoved it into my pants pocket. That was kind of silly. I don't suppose the busboy or waitress spends much time deciphering notes the customers scribble on their napkins. Only in the movies do people read napkins or notes on the back of a matchbook. I thought about heading home, leaving everyone's messy corners behind. It would be my last chance, I thought, to walk away.

I didn't, heading, instead, back to Hofstra.

THERE WAS NO need for me to shoot my way in and, for once, my badge wasn't required viewing. The receptionist listened attentively, taking me at my word. As everyone on campus was aware of Mr. Maloney's disappearance, she said she'd be willing to help me in anyway she could. That spirit of cooperation took an immediate plunge when I asked to see Patrick Maloney's records.

"We have confidentiality rules here and I can't tell ya a damned thing, but you already knew that," she wagged her finger in smiling disapproval, "didn't you?"

I said I did, but my mom had always told me that if you don't ask you don't get. Since her mom believed in the same philosophy, the receptionist was willing to give me a second chance. I asked to see Dr. Friar, Nancy Lustig's former therapist.

"She won't tell you anything either," the receptionist warned, thumbing through a hefty appointment book.

"Name, rank and serial number, huh? Call me thick-headed," I winked, "but when I ask someone for a date, I like for them, not their mom, to tell me no."

Even as she picked up the phone to call in to Dr. Friar, the receptionist was pessimistic. Unless it was urgent, the staff was usually available by appointment only. I told her to mention I was an acquaintance of Nancy Lustig's.

"She'll be right out." The receptionist was impressed. "Have a seat."

I picked up a magazine and got through two questions of an interview with Alex Haley. Last year's airing of the *Roots* miniseries, he thought, was a small step in raising the consciousness of white America. For any significant reconciliation between the races, white consciousness would have to be raised significantly higher. Smart man, that Alex Haley.

"Hello, Mr. Prager, I'm Liz Friar. If you'll come with me . . ."

Dr. Friar was a woman about five foot six and of undetermined age. Somewhere between thirty-five and forty-five was my best bet. Parted in the middle, her straight, shoulder-length black hair bounced as she walked. There was some wispy gray amongst the black. Though she wore little makeup to highlight her smiling brown eyes or slyly crooked mouth, I'd say she was an attractive woman, if not quite pretty. She dressed in designer jeans, a loose sweater and sneakers.

I followed Dr. Friar into a rather sparsely decorated room. No degrees adorned the walls, nor did any tranquil paintings of mountain streams.

"Yes, it is a bit minimal," Dr. Friar said, reading my eyes if not my mind. "But I don't think the students notice. My private practice office is more comfortable. If you would like to make an appointment to see me there, I—"

"No, this is fine."

"You mentioned a Nancy Lustig to the receptionist. Is she a friend of yours?"

"An acquaintance. She gave me your name."

Dr. Friar didn't say anything to that. I hadn't even gotten to Patrick Maloney and I was getting stonewalled.

"I'm not really here to talk about Nancy, Dr. Friar. And I realize that if I were, you probably wouldn't talk to me about her, would you?"

"If she was my patient, no, I'm afraid I couldn't possibly."

"If she was your patient, huh? Look, Dr. Friar, I'm not good at fencing, so let me lay it out for you."

"Please do."

I recounted my meeting with Maria and how she had pointed me in Nancy Lustig's direction. Nancy, I explained, seemed like a nice girl who'd gotten caught in a bad situation, but my interest was strictly limited to Patrick Maloney. I wasn't there to pry, but to try and gain some insight. In an attempt to earn the doctor's trust, I fed her details of Nancy's story that I could have learned only from Nancy directly. I mentioned the lines Dr. Friar and Nancy had rehearsed together to help Nancy confront Patrick about her dissatisfaction. That got me exactly nowhere. "I don't know what it is I can do for you, Mr. Prager. Even if I were inclined to help—which I confess I am—I still am at a loss as to how. Unfortunately, my hands are tied."

I asked if she had treated Patrick Maloney or if she knew of anyone on staff who might have. She gave me the same answer. She was bound by professional ethics. I said I understood. I wasn't happy about it, but I understood. And since I had no idea of how much time the doctor would give me, I had to come up with something pretty quickly.

"Do you enjoy games, Dr. Friar?"

Her eyes positively twinkled: "Secretly, Mr. Prager, I think all psychologists love games. Games are a useful metaphor for what we do. Our clients—or patients, if you prefer—live their lives or, for our purposes, play the game of life by certain rules. They seek our help when the game goes badly or becomes painful, unfulfilling or when they realize that continuing to play by the old rules produces diminishing or counterproductive returns. In a very real way, our task is to help our clients see that they, in fact, have the predominant hand in setting the rules. Using a host of techniques, we direct or nudge them toward a realignment in the ground rules.

Often the rules simply need tweaking. Less frequently, they need a complete overhaul."

"And if you adjust the rules just right, the game's played differently and produces more rewarding results."

"Of course," she admitted, "it's really not quite as straightforward as all that. Individual lives, like individual ballgames, have unique dynamics. And for people suffering from extreme disorders like schizophrenia . . ." she trailed off sadly. "Fortunately, the metaphor holds for most of the students we see here. But I've gone on too long. You see, I teach here and tend to slip into my professorial role without much prompting. You mentioned a game."

"It's a lawyers' game," I said, "and since their rules and your rules about confidentiality aren't so different, I think maybe it'll be, okay for you to play. It's a game of hypotheticals."

"Yes, Mr. Prager, I'm afraid I play that game at every kid's birthday party and cocktail party I attend where the other guests aren't psychologists. But in this instance I—"

"Doc! Doc! Doc!" I put up my palms like a traffic cop. "Right up front, I'll swear this has zero to do with Nancy Lustig. Zero! Not even indirectly. So please, just hear me out."

"Go on."

"For argument's sake, let's say I was walking down a hall and I peeked through a door that was slightly ajar. And through that crack in the door, I witnessed . . ."

Without naming him, I described for her Patrick Maloney's square-walking behavior and dressing rituals as Doobie had described them to me. Dr. Friar's face remained neutral throughout, as she jotted down a note here and there. I further listed the impressions I had formed about Patrick's rigidity, aloofness, inscrutablity and his seemingly paradoxical hunger for acceptance.

"This is a hypothetical construct, of course," she said when I'd finished, though her neutral expression had turned decidedly incredulous.

"Of course."

"And with this information you'd like me to do what, Mr. Prager?"

"Come on, Doc, give me a break," I pleaded. "You want me to crawl over hot coals or what? You know what I'm trying to do here. There's a missing kid out there somewhere. Maybe he's dead or maybe he's selling roses for the Moonies. I don't know. Maybe I wouldn't like him so much if I knew him and maybe I don't like his family, but—" I cut myself off when I realized I was raising my voice. "I'm sorry."

"Not at all, Mr. Prager. He's gotten under your skin, this hypothetical construct, hasn't he?"

"I guess he has, yes."

"There's that unique dynamic I mentioned," she said with a comforting smile. "It's your good fortune I'm fresh out of hot coals and I've got a class to get to in another building. So, let's see what I can reasonably say about your hypothetical construct."

"That'd be great. Besides, I left my asbestos suit at home."

"Your construct seems to be suffering from obsessive-compulsive neurosis. I could give you several hours course work on the subject, but," she said, checking her watch, "we'll see what we can do. There are two components of the disease: obsessive thoughts and compulsive behavior—the former often, though not categorically, leading to the latter. The obsessive thoughts are of an anxiety-provoking nature. The most common example is of the person who becomes obsessed with thoughts of germs and bacteria, of contamination. What did he touch? Who touched it before him? What diseases were they carrying? So, if you were obsessed with such thoughts and these thoughts began causing overwhelming anxiety, what might you do?"

"Wash my hands," I answered.

"You might wash them a lot. The compulsive behavior, Mr. Prager, becomes a comforting response mechanism for the obsessive, anxiety-provoking thoughts."

"I can see that," I admitted. "It almost seems logical. I'm hungry, I eat. I'm worried that my hands are dirty, I wash. But Pa—I mean, my construct's behaviors don't seem to have that sort of logical connection. What does walking backwards in a square or counting out loud to twenty while getting dressed have to do with anything?"

"Good question. The short answer is, I don't know, exactly," she said, throwing up her hands. "The patient himself sometimes doesn't know. You see, one of the aspects of obsessive-compulsive neurosis is expansion of behavior. Let's say our hand washer notices himself winking in the mirror as he washes his hands or catches himself thinking of a line from an old Abbott and Costello comedy routine. The winking or the silent repetition of the comedy routine can become secondary comfort mechanisms. They might replace or augment the hand washing. A year down the road, what began as simple hand washing alone might expand into a series of behaviors which would be difficult to trace back to the original behavior or antecedent anxiety. Another aspect of the syndrome is that the original anxiety, fear of contamination in my example, might itself be symbolic of a root anxiety that has nothing obvious to do with germs. Issues of self-esteem, marital discord, sexuality are only a few of the things which might cause the underlying anxiety."

"It's sad," I heard myself say.

"Sometimes it can be profoundly sad and of all the things I treat, the most ironic. A system set up as a means to gain some measure of control in one's life can, in some cases, lead to a paralytic loss of any control. You become a victim of your own devices. But," she brightened, "it isn't always so dire. We all suffer from this sort of thing to a lesser extent."

"Do we?"

"Ever throw salt over your shoulder, Mr. Prager, or have a lucky shirt? Superstition, some might even say prayer, are more socially acceptable expressions of this sort of behavior. Ever have a relative who constantly checks the gas jets on the stove or obsesses over whether he or she locked the door or left the lights on?"

"You knew my mom, huh?"

I told her about a friend of mine who refuses to watch Mets games until the top of the third inning and then only from a recliner. Given the Mets' record, she joked, maybe he should try the sofa.

We talked for a few more minutes. She said that the intensity of my construct's compulsive behavior might be related to the strength of his anxiety. She also warned that people who suffered from obsessive-compulsive neurosis could be skilled at hiding their symptoms from the world.

"On the other hand," Dr. Friar said, "if the symptoms become overwhelming, some will—"

"—isolate themselves, withdraw." I finished the thought. "They might even disappear."

"They might, Mr. Prager, but don't be seduced by simple answers."

I stood and thanked her for her time. She was, she said, glad to answer hypotheticals any time they might be useful. I promised to keep that in mind.

"Mr. Prager," she called after me.

"Yeah, Doc."

"How is Nancy?"

I thought of a few smartass answers, but opted for a safe: "I think she'll be fine."

February 5th, 1978

I'D WAITED PAST rush hour to leave, using the extra time to listen to a big-band anthology I'd inherited from my dad. As I listened, I pictured my mom, replete with curlers and ragged house dress, teaching Aaron to jitterbug and cha-cha before his bar mitzvah. My downstairs neighbor was in a less nostalgic flame of mind and banged his disapproval with a broom handle against the ceiling. Good thing for him I wasn't reminiscing about my bar mitzvah when I spent hours teaching my mom to twist and mash potato.

I called Aaron. No one was in. I called Miriam to see how she was doing since the night Ronnie had treated the dying baby. I avoided asking any direct questions about that night. After the usual small talk I asked her if, when we were growing up, she noticed that I had any weird habits.

"You're my big brother, Moses. When I was little I thought everything you did was wonderful. By the time I was ten, I thought everything you did was weird."

"And now?"

"The last time I checked," she said, "I was still older than ten."

Apparently, she had regained her equilibrium. I gave her my love and hung up. Since the meeting with Dr. Friar, I'd spent hours dissecting the idiosyncracies of everyone from my maternal grandfather to my second-grade teacher. As my Aunt Sadie used to say: "We're all a *bissel mesghuga*." We're all a little crazy. It was comforting to know Aunt Sadie and Dr. Friar agreed. When I was about a block away from my building I caught myself wondering if I'd locked the front door.

The drive up to Dutchess County went pretty quickly. The sun was bright and old drifts of snow outside the city were still beautifully white. I stopped at a family farm to buy an apple pie and wound up with two. I made a second stop at a florist shop, bought a half-dozen roses and headed for Rico's house.

I wanted to make a peace offering to Rose Tripoli. Over the years I'd seen too many friendships fall by the wayside and I was determined to not let that happen with Rico and me. I thought maybe I could build on the pleasant phone conversation we'd had the other day. If Rose and I got to sit alone together for an hour, I thought, she might see me as less of a threat. I hoped she could learn to distinguish me from what she viewed as dangerous baggage carried over from Rico's first marriage.

The fact that Rose Tripoli was a blood relative to the Maloneys didn't exactly work against my dropping by. Unlike Rico, she would have witnessed the family in action over the course of many years. Maybe she would be willing to share a word or two about family secrets. Even if she had no direct information, there wasn't a family branch in the world that didn't speculate, often too loudly, about the other branches.

From the first unanswered ring of the front doorbell, I sensed my brilliant ploy would have the net effect of adding two apple pies to my waistline and six roses to the trash. Still, I did all those silly maybe-she's-in-the-shower-and-didn't-hear-the-bell type of things people do. I rang at the front door a few more times, banged the brass knocker, rang at the back door, cupped my face with my hands and peered through several windows and rapped my knuckles on a basement window before conceding defeat.

Snowmen tipsy from thaw and refreezing marked my progress as I rolled slowly down Hanover Street. In spite of the snow and the bare-limbed trees, I could almost smell fresh cut grass, barbecue smoke and see touch football games in the road. Situated on half-acre lots, the modest houses, no two of which added together would equal the square footage of Nancy Lustig's, were of three styles: shingled L-shaped ranches, clapboarded colonials or saltbox Capes. Some of the residents of Hanover Street had done variations on the theme. One of the ranches had a second floor, white aluminum siding and solar energy panels on the roof. Two of the saltboxes sported shed dormers. Several of the colonials had added rooms above their two-car garages.

Yet, as I read the address numbers off the mailboxes, I knew the Maloney house—regardless of its style—would be untouched. No ugly solar panels on their roof, nothing showy, nothing to attract unwanted attention. Everything would be old style and impeccably maintained. The driveway, walkways, entrances perfectly clear of snow and ice and not one inch shoveled that did not have to be. Inside, there might be simple crosses on the walls, maybe a rendering of a favored saint, but they'd have no Mary on the half shell or bathtub Jesus on their lawn. Close to the vest. Everything close to the vest.

Twenty-two Hanover Street was everything I thought it would be. Even the lack of numerals on the mailbox proved me right. Pulling into the snowless driveway of the tidy ranch, its cedar shakes painted a deep, joyless green, I wondered if it had looked much different the day Francis Maloney purchased it. Only on a house so drab could rain gutters and down spouts stand out so prominently. As a small concession to brightness, there were several white window boxes adorning the front facade.

Some people might have been surprised a man like Maloney, a man who had risen to a county commissioner's post and who wielded obvious political clout, would still live in such a modest house. I wasn't. At the academy, an instructor once said that some guys became cops for the badge and the gun. Some, he said, do it for the authority and responsibility the other clowns think they get from the badge and the gun. Francis Maloney, it seemed, liked the responsibility and authority of his position. Not all powerful men need to rub it in other people's faces. That made two things about the man I respected. Still, I didn't anticipate kissing him smack on the lips anytime soon.

Hoping he was out and his wife in, I grabbed an apple pie and the roses. As I stepped up onto the little concrete slab of a porch, I saw the first hint the Maloneys actually lived here. For encircled by the aluminum filagree on the old storm door, was the letter M. And in spite of my suspicions, I couldn't bring myself to believe it was already there when they moved in. Just as I rang the bell an oil delivery truck pulled up next door. My head was still turned, watching the oil man unreel his truck's hose, when I heard her hello.

"Hi," I said, turning back around. "I'm—"

"We sort of met the other night," she interrupted. "Do you—"

"I hardly recognize you without your peacoat."

"You remember." Her face brightened.

If I hadn't remembered another thing about her, I wouldn't have forgotten that thin-lipped smile. I nodded my head at the oil truck. "It seems we have this oil tank karma."

"No dead body this time." Then, noticing the flowers and pie, her expression went numb. "Is something wrong? Did Patri—"

"No. Take it easy. No news."

She put her hand to her heart. "I'm sorry. Come in, Mr. Prager."

"Moe."

"Come in, Moe."

She emptied my hands and showed me where to hang my coat. I tried not to let it bother me that only one of us knew the other's name. I decided to not break up the momentum by airing my grievance. She disappeared into the kitchen.

"These roses are lovely. I'm just putting them in some water. Would you like a cup of coffee?"

"Great. Thanks."

"Dad's not here," she shouted above the running water. "He's in the city today. Ma's over at the church. Go on into the living room. This won't take a minute."

Well, okay, now I knew she was Patrick's sister. I'd already tentatively come to that conclusion, but she still had me at a disadvantage.

"You know," she continued as I walked into the living room, "Dad was pretty impressed that you were there that night before everyone but the cops. It's not easy to impress my dad."

Her words barely registered. I was somewhat in shock, for unlike the exterior of the house, what I saw in the living room came as a complete surprise.

"Oh," I heard her say upon seeing my face, "you didn't know. Well, welcome to the shrine. Guided tours are free."

Atop the dull green carpet, on either side of the big picture window, sat twin oak and glass display cases reaching nearly to the ceiling. The one on my left was filled with ribbons, rings, medals and trophies. It was an impressive collection, especially the trophies. There were gold-plated baseball players of various sizes waiting in eternity for pitched balls they would never hit or hit balls they would never catch. There were silver-plated basketball players, bronzed bowlers, lacrosse men, pewter hockey sticks and wrestlers. But it was football trophies that predominated.

The display case on my right, however, was, to an athlete, someone like myself who had played organized sports his entire life, far more impressive. For in this case was an assemblage of game balls the likes of which I had never seen. As in the trophy case, they were balls from many sports with football trumping the others. Trophies, medals, ribbons and rings are nice, but they're usually awarded by leagues or judges or committees. Game balls, on the other hand, are awarded by your teammates and coaches. Game balls are the ultimate gesture of respect and are therefore more meaningful than any hunk of metal. Third-string quarterbacks get Super Bowl rings, but never game balls.

"There are more packed away," she whispered sadly.

"Patrick must be some—"

"Not Patrick," she cut me off. "Those are Francis Jr.'s."

And as if my eyes had just then learned to focus, I saw that many of the trophies and game balls bore the name Francis X. Maloney or Frankie J.

"Here, Mr. Pra—Moe, turn around," she urged, gently touching my shoulder.

On a shelf above the unremarkable couch, its cushions suffocated by heavy plastic slipcovers, was an American flag bundled in a tight triangle. On either side of the flag were gilt-framed photos of a handsome, clean-shaven man in his early to mid-twenties. He resembled the poster picture of Patrick, only he had an athlete's neck, a fuller face and the icy blue eyes of his father. In one photo, Francis Jr. posed in formal Navy blues. In the other, he sported pilot fatigues. Along with the flag and photos were a watch, cufflinks, commander's bars, wings and an open medal case. The medal itself was somewhat obscured by the other personal effects. A semicircle of small flags—American, Irish, State of New York, Navy, Dutchess County—framed the shelf. It was, as she had said, a shrine.

"His F-4 was shot down over the Ho Chi Min Trail in '72, not long before the cease-fire. My parents died with him that day."

"What about Patrick?" I wondered.

"What about him?"

"Look, sorry, this is a little embarrassing. What's your name?"

She smiled at that, stuck out her hand: "Katy."

"Okay, we're even now." I held onto her hand a little too long.

"Come on," she said, leading me toward the kitchen, "let's go talk."

We stepped into the less rarified air of the kitchen, back to a place where expectation and reality were more closely aligned. The old fixtures, the black-and-white linoleum, felt comfortable somehow. The apple pie I'd brought was out of its box on the kitchen table next to a simple blue vase that held the roses. It took us a few cups of coffee to get back to my question about Patrick. First, we made small talk; the weather, my knee, the wine shop. She was thirty-two, the eldest child. Francis Jr. was a year younger. She'd gotten married a few months after he was shot down.

"Jesus," she laughed, her eyes lost in the past, "it was like a second funeral. I shoulda known right then and there Joey and I were done for. I think Ma was so cried out, she couldn't muster happy tears. And Dad . . . It was like Francis's ghost held his other arm as he walked me down the aisle. 'Taps' would have been more in order than 'The Wedding March.' "

"You're divorced?"

"It was the best thing, really," she said, the glaze of the past gone from her eyes. "We didn't have kids. Joey was a good man and a good provider. Handsome, too. But you don't marry a man because he gets the most checks in the very good boxes on a survey. At least, I've learned, you shouldn't. No, they say that marriage'll kill the passion in any couple. From my side of things, there wasn't any passion to begin with."

They had lived with Joey's parents, which hadn't exactly worked to stoke the embers of any romance between the newlyweds. After the separation, Katy moved into Manhattan. She had a sublease on part of a loft in SoHo. She worked as a graphic designer for a midtown ad firm.

"I've been splitting my time between the city and here. My company's been very good about time off." I told her I'd seen evidence that she wasn't the only artist in the Maloney family.

"I'm not half as talented as Patrick," she shook her head, "but he lacked—lacks a passion for it."

"Passion, huh? There's that word again."

I wondered if it was Katy who had first taken Patrick to Pooty's. She had indeed and was duly impressed I had figured it out. I'd be a liar to say I didn't enjoy her admiration. None of the other hordes of investigators had asked. She had always to volunteer that information. Nothing ever came of it. Katy had taken him there a few times over the years to try and encourage him.

"It's an—"

"—artists' hangout. I know. Beck's Dark on tap and a great jukebox," I said and told her I was surprised I hadn't seen her there myself. I recounted the tale of my failed date with Susie the actress.

"Her friends really asked to touch your gun? God," she slapped the table, "I think I would have been more tempted to show them the bullets, if you know what I mean."

"They weren't quite that annoying."

I told her I'd heard her father had been on the job. Before I ever got around to asking about it, she warned me right off the topic. The subject was taboo. She couldn't remember anyone ever laying down the law about it, but, she said, they all understood that to broach the subject was an invitation to a beating. As Nancy Lustig had been quick to defend Patrick, Katy was quick to say her father hadn't really made a habit of hitting them.

"Maybe Francis, a few times. Patrick . . . I think maybe once or twice. We knew he was a man not to threaten lightly."

"I asked before about how Patrick had taken his brother's death." I finally got back to where I'd started. "I've got an older brother. I told you about Aaron, right?"

"He of the wine shop to be?"

"That's him," I confirmed. "He's much better with money. He was better than me in school and all. Hell, he even skipped a grade in Hebrew school. Not that that'll get you a discount on the subway or anything. He wasn't a football star or fighter pilot, but I still felt like I lived in his shadow. I'm not that familiar with the New Testament, but did Christ have like a younger brother? Because if he did, Patrick must've felt like him."

"Patrick loved his brother."

This wasn't going to be easy. I told her I loved Aaron, but that I resented him as well. All I wanted to know was how Patrick had reacted to Francis Jr.'s death. Part of him, I offered, must have felt a sense of relief.

"I suppose I see your point, Moe," Katy admitted, grudgingly. "But on the other hand I think he felt naked and unprotected. Frank had been a wonderful big brother to Patrick, his best friend in a way. Patrick could always disguise his—I'm not explaining this well."

"Keep trying," I urged.

"Okay, it's pitch black." She waved her hand as if a wand removing all light from the room. "You look up into the heavens and your eyes catch sight of a gloriously bright star. Every night you gaze up and there's that enchanting star. You come to set your course by it. One night, though, you look up and the bright star is gone," she snapped her fingers, "its light snuffed out. Then, once the shock's worn off, you force yourself to look back up. There, just a little further east in the night sky from where the extinguished star used to shine, you notice a new star, a smaller star. Its light is pretty but not nearly so dazzling as the other's. And you realize the little star's not new at all. It's always been there, its light overwhelmed by the glory of the other."

"So," I said, "Patrick was comfortable being the little star."

"You see, until Francis Jr. was killed no one around here put much pressure on Patrick. My Dad can be a pretty fierce task master and not exactly cuddly."

"I've noticed."

"But he's not a stupid man. He never expected Patrick to follow in Frank's footsteps. Who could?" she shrugged. "And Ma had the best of all worlds for an Italian mother: a perfect son who supplied her with endless bragging material and a sensitive, quiet, devoted son who didn't object to her occasional smothering."

"But when Francis Jr. was killed, Patrick was exposed."

"I don't think my parents could help themselves. Even me, I think I was just as guilty. Suddenly he was forced to bear the weight not only of the meager expectations the world had for him, but of the enormous ones we had for his brother. Patrick went from being a voice in the chorus to lead tenor without singing lessons. So you see, unlike you and your big brother, Patrick didn't really have to compete with his until Frank was dead. Somehow, Moe, I don't think he viewed Frank's death with a sense of relief."

We went directly back to small talk from there and there wasn't much of that. We pretty much finished our last cup of coffee in silence. I asked to see Patrick's old room. Katy pointed the way and let me explore on my own.

It looked like any boy's room, maybe a little neater than most. That, I thought, probably had more to do with his mother's housekeeping than with his obsessive-compulsiveness. There was a high school pennant, a pennant from Hofstra, another from Annapolis. There were even some trophies: one for fencing, another for Little League baseball and a few for track. He'd been a miler. There was a Sylvester Stallone poster above his desk. Above his old bed, however, was a flawlessly painted reproduction of Francis Jr.'s dress uniform picture so prominently displayed in the living room. I found the initials PMM painted in one corner. Either there was nothing else to see or I just wasn't seeing it.

I found Katy still in the kitchen, staring off into space. I wanted to ask about Patrick's strange behavior, but having failed once already at playing amateur shrink, I found myself asking general, roundabout questions. They got me general, roundabout answers. Yes, Patrick was neat, a perfectionist about his appearance. What about the shorn hair, tattoo and earring? He was in college, she said, college was meant to be a time in one's life to explore new things. I was politic enough not to mention Nancy Lustig.

"Why'd your dad give Patrick's prom picture to the cops and not a more recent one?"

She seemed surprised I had to ask. "He hated Patrick's new look."

Talk about a superficial answer. I had a thick skull, but even I could tell Katy had given me all the meaningful information she was capable of giving for the day. I started to say my good-byes when Katy suggested we meet in the city for a drink.

"I'm going back to SoHo tomorrow night."

"I'd like that a lot." I could be so articulate.

She gave me her Manhattan number and took my arm as we walked to the door. I had just a few last questions for her. Of course I'd seen Patrick's prom picture, but I didn't know anything about his date that night. Did Katy know who the date was? Where she lived? I didn't know that it would do any good, but I wanted to talk to her.

"Theresa Hickey," she answered immediately. "She grew up around the corner on Dover. She cuts hair at The Head Shop on Harper Street. She's probably there now. Maybe you can catch her."

I recognized the locale. "Harper Street, that's the road Molly's Diner's on, right?"

"Best meatloaf in the county," Katy confirmed. "You know when you turn back toward the highway from Molly's? Well, go past the entrance a few hundred feet. It'll be on your right-hand side."

I thanked her for everything and told her how much I was looking forward to that drink. I offered her my hand. This time it was she who held on too long.

"Did you really find that little girl like cousin Rose said?"

"Marina Conseco? Yeah, I did."

"Find my brother, Moe. I'm worried about the little star."

THE HEAD SHOP was just where Katy Maloney said it would be. Contrary to the salon's name and promises of unisex coifs, The Head Shop looked more like a denizen for the blue-haired set than a place Ziggy Stardust and the Spiders from Mars were apt to favor with their business. Though a red and white spinning pole was nowhere to be seen, the shop fixtures were strictly Grandpa's-shave-and-a-haircut barbershop. I could feel Norman Rockwell lurking just beneath the disco ball veneer and harvest gold paint.

I stood at the vacant front desk, a poster of Patrick Scotch-taped above it. Business was slow, but Gloria Gaynor was reassuring any doubters about ultimate survival. In perfect time, two women spun, wheeled, turning tight fast circles, weaving their hands together and apart in an elaborate hustle. Another woman, a black buzzer in her hand for a microphone, swayed, spinning too, sang with Gloria note for note. What her voice lacked in power it made up with enthusiasm. Not far from me, a chubby girl with envious eyes watched the show as she robotically washed a customer's hair. Though prettier than Nancy Lustig, I figured the shampoo girl for Patrick's prom queen. As the song wound down, I got her attention: "Theresa Hickey?"

"That's Theresa over there," she pointed with her chin at the singer, "but it's not Hickey no more. She don't have an appointment for an hour yet. Sit down and I'll wash you in a minute."

Theresa Not-Hickey-No-More was tall, flat-bellied and slender with stacks of blond hair, green eyes, a perfect nose and pillowy lips. Back in high school she'd probably been captain of the cheerleaders and girl most likely to star in every sophomore boy's dream. Now, two years later, she was probably cheering for busy Saturdays and five-buck tips. More than likely married to a city cop—no, fireman—I guessed, and a year, maybe two, away from her first baby. I wondered if she'd be starring in anybody's dreams come her twentieth reunion. Yeah, I had her all figured out. Sure. She probably spoke like William F. Buckley Jr. and transplanted kidneys in her spare time.

"Oh yeah," she beamed when I introduced myself, "my husband's on the job in the city; Midtown South."

She didn't sound anything like William F. Buckley, but she was studying to be a nurse. She was glad to talk about Patrick over a cup of coffee at Molly's. Anything, she whispered, to get out of that dump. We walked to the diner.

"Sanka for me," I told the waitress. "Any more caffeine today and I'll fly home."

"Don't forget to file a flight plan, honey." She winked. "Coffee for you. Right, Theresa?"

"So what can I tell you about Patrick?" she puzzled as the waitress walked away, but didn't wait for me to ask. "We grew up around the corner from each other. We played together when we were kids. Our parents were kinda friendly and my big sister dated Frank Jr. for about five minutes before he went into the service."

"That's it?"

"That's it! Why, you wanna know if he was better at Hit the Penny than me?"

"You were his prom date, weren't you?"

"Oh that! It wasn't like we were going out or anything," she snickered dismissively. "We were covering for each other. You know how it is. I was dating Billy, he's my husband now. But I was only eighteen then and he was twenty-five. My parents would have flipped out. And to tell you the truth, being older and everything, Billy wasn't crazy about a high school prom."

"I can see his point."

"Patrick was the perfect solution," she went on. "My parents knew and trusted him. And even though we hadn't been close in forever, we were old friends. Billy knew that."

I agreed that was all to the good for her, but what, I was curious, did Patrick get out of the deal? Here, Theresa was less forthcoming, giving a wide range of answers. She didn't really know. Patrick hadn't said. Maybe he had just broken up with someone. His original date backed out.

"Come on, Theresa," I coaxed, "out with it."

"I think he was seeing somebody he didn't want his family to know about."

"Who?"

"A tramp."

"She got a name?"

"Just thinking about her makes me want to take a shower."

"I'll give you two bucks for a bar of soap," I said. "What's her name?"

"Tina Martell. Tits was what the boys used to call her. She hangs out at Henry's Hog," Theresa said, standing up to leave. "I'll tell the waitress to forget our order. A cup a coffee'll get you more than information from Tina."

UNTIL I MADE friends outside New York City, I never understood the phrase "wrong side of the tracks." In Brooklyn, subways often run right through the middle of neighborhoods where the median income and apartment size is identical whether you live on this side of the BMT Line or that, so the phrase is meaningless. When I was about eleven and saw a guy fall off the platform in front of the D train, I figured wrong side of the tracks meant on top of the rails. But if I'd only seen Henry's Hog at a younger age, any confusion would have vanished in an instant.

An old wood frame house converted into a biker's bar and clubhouse, Henry's Hog was wedged between an abandoned paint factory and auto body shop. The view out Henry's front window—if you could have seen through the yellowed glass—was of train tracks that got about as much use as the paint factory. I patted the bulge in the small of my back where I kept my .38 holstered. Gary Cooper with a cane, preparing for battle with Henry and the Hell's Angels.

When I walked in even the flies yawned. So much for *High Noon*. A trio of pot-bellied guys with scraggly beards played poker in a booth. Dressed in the filthiest jeans and jean jackets I think I'd ever seen, the three of them stopped blowing cigarette smoke in each others' faces long enough to smirk at me. One saluted my arrival by raising his can of Carling Black Label. The bartender, a tattoo of a blood-dripping rose below his right ear, interrupted his *General Hospital* viewing to ask what I wanted.

"A Black Label and a word with Tina."

If them was fighting words, the barman didn't let on. "Have a seat over there. Tina!" he shouted. "Blind date's here."

I ferried my beer over to a table by the jukebox. After a minute, I realized Henry's Hog was the first place I'd been in in days where Patrick Maloney wasn't staring down at me from his omnipresent poster. It was a pleasant change of scenery.

A woman ducked under the service bar and came toward me. She wore dusty, black leather chaps over jeans, square-toed boots and a Harley T-shirt, her huge breasts straining against the tight shirt. She was short with square shoulders and a thick neck. It too sported the bloody rose. Her bottle-black hair was cropped. Several silvery studs adorned each ear. In spite of it all, she had a sweet, doughy face.

My eyes darted from her tattoo, to her earrings, to her severe hair. I got a crazy idea in my head: "Is he here?"

"Is who here?"

"Patrick."

"Patrick who?"

"Patrick Maloney," I said.

"Hey, Hank," she called over her shoulder to the bartender. "You know a Patrick Maloney?"

"Shut up! I'm watchin'." Then a commercial came on. "What was his name?"

"Patrick Maloney," she repeated.

"Nah, I went to school with a Frank Maloney, but he got his ass shot off in Nam."

And as Hank mouthed the name Frank Maloney, a light clicked on behind Tina's cow eyes. "Why don'tcha buy me a beer, mister?"

When I brought her beer back to the table, we clinked cans and exchanged proper introductions.

"You really didn't know he was missing?" I was skeptical.

"We ain't big on current events around here, are we Hank?"

"Shut up, I'm watchin'."

"So," she asked, "what happened to him?"

I explained about the night he disappeared and gave her a brief summary of the events that had led me to Henry's Hog. I was a little more detailed about the conversation I'd had with Theresa.

"That cunt! What'd she tell ya, that they used to call me Twat?"

"Tits."

"I guess she was in a good mood. But I bet she wouldn't be if she knew her sainted fuckin' husband and his buddy double-teamed me a few summers ago in a car around the corner from that stupid hair place she works in. Bitch can have him," she sneered, waving her pinky at me. "Guy's hung like a hamster."

I let Tina vent her spleen some more before asking about her and Patrick.

"Tell me about you and—"

"There wasn't no me and Patrick. Shit, he was good lookin'. He took me to the movies and we balled a coupl'a times. I mean, he was sweet and everything, but kinda goofy."

"Goofy?"

"Yeah, he got me pregnant and he—"

"—asked you to marry him."

Her jaw dropped. "How the fuck did you know that?"

"Call it an educated guess."

She didn't persist. "It wasn't like he was the first guy who knocked me up or nothin'. Lookin' back at it now, I guess it was nice that he wanted to take responsibility. No one else ever does."

"When he asked you to marry him, what happened?"

"I thought he was puttin' me on."

I pressed her: "But what did you say?"

"Not much. First I sorta laughed at him," she said guiltily. "When he kept botherin' me, I told him to take a freakin' hike. Lunatic kept tellin' me he loved me, he loved me. He was gonna prove it to me and take me to the prom. Like I wanted to go to the prom, right? I told him to get the fuck outta here."

Tina said she had the abortion pretty soon after that, making a revealing joke about the clinic naming a room after her. Only one of us laughed. She was determined never to give literal meaning to being a motorcycle mama. Patrick had tried to see her in the interim, but she managed to warn him off. Once she had the abortion, he lost interest. That didn't exactly come as a big surprise to me.

I thanked her for her time. She didn't thank me for the beer. She started to give me a message to pass on to Theresa the next time I saw her. I told her not to bother. I wasn't likely to be seeing Theresa any time soon.

"Well fuck her and fuck you, too." She snorted and headed back under the bar.

Hank shrugged his shoulders at me. I shrugged mine at him. The three card players laughed and shook their heads. When I left, the flies yawned again.

February 6th, 1978

DISTRACTED BY THE shadows and the dance of the little flame, I realized moths were not unique in being drawn to the fire.

Not even Aaron, great scholar of the Beth David Jewish Center, had a firm grasp on the arcane workings of the Hebrew calendar. Me, I had enough troubles with the "Thirty days has September . . ." rhyme. So it was with continued skepticism that I regarded the notice from the temple of when to light my father's memorial candle. I couldn't get the image out of my head of blindfolded rabbis throwing darts at a calendar. This year the dart had landed on the fifth of February.

Of course I was supposed to have lighted the candle at sundown. However, as I was somewhere between Henry's Hog and the highway home when the sun dropped down, I'd missed the appointed hour. I was not overcome by guilt. My father was five years dead. I didn't have a *Twilight Zone* view of the metaphysical. I didn't picture my dad with angel's wings, busily keeping memorial candle lists. I pictured him in his coffin. Lists were for Santa Claus. When I visited his grave, I didn't chat with the headstone.

The phone rang. I knew it would be Aaron. Twice a year, on the mornings following the scheduled lighting of the memorial candles for our parents, Aaron would call to chastise me for forgetting. God forbid he should call me the day before so I wouldn't forget.

"Yes," I said without waiting, "I lit the fucking candle."

"That's good. Did you confess your sins to God and accept the Lord Jesus Christ as your savior?"

"Sully? Christ, I'm sorry," I answered without thinking. "I thought you were somebody else."

"No kiddin'."

"What's up?" I wondered.

"We got somebody says he saw him yesterday."

I didn't have to ask who Sully was talking about. "Where?"

He didn't answer. "I'm goin' to interview him now. Wanna keep me company?"

"What do you think?"

"There are some ground rules," he warned.

"Always the fine print. Go ahead."

"The family can't know, not until I check this guy out. All I fuckin' need is aggravation from the father if this is a false alarm. If he checks out, I tell the family. Also, I talk, you listen. You're there as a courtesy. Don't abuse the courtesy, understand?"

I agreed to his terms. If I didn't want to get shut out of the process, what choice did I have? I took down the address and directions, checked my watch and told him to give me forty minutes. He said I had thirty.

Hoboken was a long tee shot across the Hudson from Manhattan and known to the rest of the world as the place of Francis Albert Sinatra's birth. Frank Sinatra notwithstanding, I'd never been to Hoboken. For the first few minutes out the Jersey end of the Holland Tunnel, the area looked about right for Henry's Hog to open a franchise. But once in Hoboken proper, things improved. Narrow streets lined with red brick and brownstone buildings, old-fashioned candy shops and ethnic delis gave Hoboken the feel of old Brooklyn or the Bronx before Robert Moses cut its heart out.

Finding 326B 9th Street was considerably easier than finding parking. I drove past the building. Sully was out front, pacing, checking his watch. A block away, I managed to squeeze into a space that exposed my right front fender to peril in the event anything wider than a Volkswagen should try and pass.

On the ride over and now as I walked to meet Sully, I puzzled over why the detective continued to favor me with special treatment. Of all the people involved in this case, Sully had shown me the picture of the new-look Patrick Maloney. Okay, so maybe he owed Rico a favor and by sharing the picture with me, Sully figures he covered that marker. Then Sully clues me on the Gowanus Canal floater. I'm willing to believe Sully thought he owed me one for buying him lunch at the Blarney Stone. But why let me in on this? I didn't see what he owed me anymore, especially since I hadn't bothered to share any information with him.

My dad used to like to say: I may be dumb, but I'm not stupid. Intentionally or not, Sully was bearding for someone, someone who wanted to use me. But for what? I remembered the bikers playing poker and Francis Maloney's reference about playing the low cards when they were all you had left. It was weird, like Sully and me and all the other investigators on the case were sitting around the same poker table, but Sully kept showing me most of the cards in his hand. It was the cards I couldn't see that worried me. My dad never said anything about looking a gift horse in the mouth, but I thought it anyway as Sully sneered at me impatiently. I shook his hand hello.

"You're late," he chided.

"I'm sorry. You didn't have to wait."

He winked. "Ah, fuck you. Come on."

We were going to talk to Mr. Enzo Sica. Mr. Sica had called Detective Sullivan's bureau that morning, claiming to have seen Patrick Maloney the previous day at a local shopping center.

"Why you checking this lead out?" I asked. "You must get a hundred calls a day from head cases who swear they saw the Maloney kid with Elvis."

"Before Elvis died last year," Sully said, "all the wack jobs used to say they spotted so-and-so with JFK."

"But why—"

"Sica mentioned a dark blue winter coat," he talked over me. "That's what the kid was wearing. We never released that detail to nobody so we could weed out the cranks."

Enzo Sica came to the door in a sleeveless T-shirt, striped pajama bottoms and slippers. He was seventy if a day and bald as a lightbulb. Though hunched, he had the powerful build of a man who'd done a lot of heavy lifting in his time. When Mr. Sica reached for thick glasses in order to inspect Detective Sullivan's shield, our hearts sank.

"Don't worry, don't worry," Enzo reassured us. "Deeza glasses only for da close-up looking. From acrossa da street, I'm-a see like an owl."

We were not reassured. Mr. Sica led us into a pleasant living room with old but clean furniture and a beautiful tin ceiling. His citizenship certificate was framed and hung over the sofa. The walls were covered with family pictures and pictures of Sica standing next to several stone structures.

"Atsa my wife, Stella. Sheeza dead three years now." He crossed himself. "Deez are my kids an-a da grandchildren." He caught my eyes gazing at a black-and-white shot of an intricate garden wall. "Im-a build dat," he thumped his chest proudly. "I'm a stone-a mason my whole life, from da time I step off da boat in-a 1925. Look here . . ."

He gave us a brief pictorial tour of the projects he'd worked on, offered us some grappa and started smoking a cigar that looked like brown rope and smelled like shit.

"If you saw him yesterday," Sully was curious, "why wait to call us till today?"

Mr. Sica said he didn't know who Patrick Maloney was yesterday. Not until late last night, when he was returning home from dinner in Manhattan with an old friend, did he see the poster.

"In da train-a station, I'm-a look at dis picture on da pole. I say to myself, heeza look familiar. I tink about it overnight an-a dis morning, I call you."

I confirmed to Sully that I hadn't seen any of the posters on this side of the river. He shook his head in agreement. Sully asked why this young man, of all the people Mr. Sica must have seen at the shopping center, stuck in his head. The young man, Mr. Sica said, acted very nervous.

"He had in heeza hand some shopping-a bags. Dey swingin' back an-a forth. Heeza head, its-a look everywhere. Quick. Quick. You know, like somebody eez after him?" Sica pantomimed, his head darting from side to side.

The young man had worn a stocking cap, so Enzo couldn't say anything about the length of his hair. He might or might not have worn an earring; glare from the sun and the snow made it difficult to tell. And since his arms were covered by an overcoat, it was impossible to know about a tattoo. Sully laid out several snapshots on Enzo Sica's coffee table and asked the old stone mason to pick out any that resembled the young man. The thick glasses back on, he chose three pictures. One was the ubiquitous prom pose. One was the student government picnic photo. One, I would learn, was of a convicted child molester about Patrick's age who looked only slightly more like Patrick Maloney than Abe Lincoln.

Next, Sully spread out some advertisements from the Sunday papers. All the models wore winter coats. Along with the ads, the detective pulled out a color chart. He asked Mr. Sica to match the coat and color that came closest to what the nervous guy had worn. With gentle shakes of his head, Sully indicated to me that the old man was pretty close on style—a hooded parka—and several shades off on the color blue.

After a few more questions about time and location, Sully motioned that it was time to leave.

"You said the nervous guy was holding some bags," I broke my silence.

"Shopping bags like-a from da department stores."

"Can you remember, was there writing on the bags, like the name of a certain store?"

He closed his eyes tightly, trying to recall. "*Spate. Spate.* (Wait. Wait.) Writing-a . . . Si! Yes! There was-a writing, but . . ." He held his hands up in surrender. "I can no remember."

Sully thanked him again, left his direct number in case the old man remembered anything else and informed Sica he was in line for a reward if his information led to the discovery of Patrick's whereabouts.

"No! No money!" he grew agitated. "No money!"

He slammed the door behind us, hard.

When we got to street level I was anxious to hear what Sullivan thought: "So . . ."

"I don't know. I don't think he's a nut job or nothin', but those fuckin' Coke-bottle glasses, geez! He was close on the coat, but everybody wears those parkas."

"Outta the three pictures he pulled, two were of Patrick," I argued.

That's when Detective Sullivan explained that the third photo was of a child molester who didn't resemble Maloney except in age. "What the fuck, I guess I gotta give the old wop the benefit of the doubt. I think he really saw the kid."

"Me too."

"Shit, with your endorsement I guess I'll sleep better tonight."

"Fuck you, Sully."

"I'm gonna call this in," he said. "Wanna come back to the city with me?"

"That's okay. I got some stuff at home to catch up on. Thanks for the heads up."

"You know, Prager, that was a good question you asked in there. About the shopping bag, I mean."

He was right, of course. It was a good question, an elemental one. My guess is, he'd been waiting for me to ask and would've eventually asked himself if I hadn't obliged. Was he just stroking my ego, I wondered? Easier to yank my chain that way. I figured if I was going to get used, I wanted something in return. I waited for him to walk a couple of steps.

"Sully," I called to him.

"Yeah."

"You got a hook in Personnel or IA?"

He walked back toward me. "Why?"

"I want a look at Francis Maloney's old personnel file." He wanted to know why and I told him I was just curious. Nothing more complicated than that. Sully pissed and moaned about how difficult it was to get files, especially old, inactive ones. It was unethical, he reminded me, but not in those words. He could get jammed up for even trying.

"You were on the job. You know how it is."

Indeed I did. Everything he said was true. "Hey, I understand. I just thought I'd ask."

Agreeing that Mr. Sica's tip might net us Patrick in a few days and that we could then forget the Maloneys ever existed, Sully and I left it there. I watched him disappear around the corner before heading back to my car. Sitting in my front seat, I was suddenly exhausted. It struck me that I'd been working on the assumption Patrick Maloney was dead. Admitting it to myself only now, I was overcome by decidedly mixed feelings. A garbage truck blared its horn at me to move. There was no way for the driver to know how relieved I was at the distraction of his horn.

Sully had warned me not to tell the family about Mr. Sica, but when I got home I called Katy Maloney's Manhattan number. Chances were she wasn't back from her parents' home, anyway. I got one of those stupid answering machines. I left an awkwardly worded message about the day's events and asked her to call me back. After hanging up, I realized I hadn't left my number. I called back. I hated talking to machines.

February 7th, 1978

PAGE 4 OF the *Daily News*, Patrick Maloney gets a reprise on his fifteen minutes of fame. Pieces of the original stories detailing his disappearance had been cannibalized for the update. It was all there but a mention of Enzo Sica. Witness's name withheld by request, the article said. Two pictures accompanied the story. One featured my favorite Missing Persons detective holding up a replica of the parka Patrick was wearing the night he vanished and, if Enzo Sica was to be believed, the parka Patrick Michael Maloney was still wearing. The other picture, however, was a surprise. Prom Patrick had at last been replaced by picnic Patrick: short hair, earring and all.

Unfortunately, I doubted the picture would be much help. Newsprint reproductions are grainy at best, but because this one had been cropped and enlarged so severely, it was cloudy and indistinct like those silly snapshots of Bigfoot. I was encouraged that the Maloneys were willing to open up. Armed with a little hope, they were finally putting on the full court press. I wondered how many busloads of volunteers would be hitting the streets of Hoboken.

With the media coverage and the search back in high gear, I figured I could take the weekend off. It was time to shift my focus from Patrick to his sister. Still too early to call her; I put down the paper and decided to exercise my knee on the boardwalk. Though it was impossible to see the sun directly from my apartment, its light seemed particularly bright today. I don't know if that was a vestige of my school days. Sunlight always seemed brighter on Saturday mornings, the winter air less bitter. I made it as far as the lobby.

"Hey, you gimpy prick! Yeah, you with the flat Jewish ass!" a welcome voice called from behind me.

I turned to see a bronze-faced Rico Tripoli holding a box of Cuccio's pastries.

"Tough work, those extradition assignments in Florida, huh? I guess you squeezed in a few minutes by the pool."

"The beach!" He shook his head in disapproval. "You know I hate pools."

"That's right, Sicilians are just strong Arab swimmers who lost their way."

Rico smiled broadly, showing off his white teeth. "Fuck you!"

"Don't get mad at me. You're the one named Tripoli, remember?"

Back in my apartment, Rico freshened his coffee with some Dewar's. When he tried to add scotch to mine, I put my hand over the cup. I told him I couldn't, that I had a date. I played coy when he asked if it was anyone he knew. Surprisingly, he let it go at that.

"Be that way," he said, pouring even more alcohol into his mug.

"Cut it out, asshole!" I warned him. "I had a pleasant talk with your wife the other day. All she needs is for you to come home drunk from my house."

He wasn't going home, he said. He had a good twelve-hour stretch of reports to do back at the task force office. No cop likes paperwork, but I'd never known Rico to soften the blow with alcohol. It worried me a little. We chatted about his big case and the wiseguy he'd picked up in the Sunshine State, Cheech "the Stick" Russo.

"They don't call him the Stick cause he's skinny," Rico winked. "If he hurt his knee like you, he wouldn't have to buy a cane. Fuckin' guy keeps the head warm in his sock. Big dick and a bigger mouth; he was gonna get wacked and ran. Amazin' how talkative they get when it's their ass is gonna get chopped up and thrown in the Fountain Avenue dump."

I agreed. When I saw that he was finished, I started to tell him about where I'd gotten with Patrick Maloney. But just as Rico had stopped me from my stroll on the boardwalk, he stopped me now.

"That's what I'm here about," he said, pulling an envelope out of his coat pocket. "This is for you."

Inside the envelope were ten crisp hundred-dollar bills, a phone number and someone's name scrawled out on a sheet of stationery from Francis Maloney's office.

"Who's Brian Kupf?" I asked.

"When you and Aaron apply for your liquor license, give him a call. He'll take good care a ya. The little donkey said the thousand should cover the work you've done."

"What, no roses? No thank-you card?" I feigned disappointment. "I don't get it. I—They haven't found the kid yet. Isn't the father getting a little ahead of himself?"

"What can I tell ya?" Rico shrugged. "I guess he figures now that he got a good lead, he can focus his forces. Makes sense to me."

"If the lead is good."

"I heard you thought it was," he countered. So, Rico'd been talking to Sully. "Until now, Maloney's had people lookin' all over the fuckin' map."

"Even if it was really Patrick the witness saw, the kid could be a million miles away by now."

"Maybe, but it's two months already and he's still close." Rico was right, of course. "So anyways, even Francis Maloney doesn't have unlimited funds. He's trimmin' the payroll a little. I'm sure you're not the only guy gettin' shown the door."

"I guess."

"Hey, for what, a week's work, you pocketed a grand and a fast track on the liquor license. Be happy! Take the fuckin' bread and run." Rico looked at his watch. "Shit, it's late. I gotta split."

He sucked down his fortified coffee, shook my hand and headed for the door. He mentioned something about getting together for a night out. It was all pretty vague, perfunctory. In spite of the friendly, deprecating banter, I sensed a distance between Rico and me I couldn't conveniently attribute to his wife's prejudices. Even as he slipped out the door I felt him slipping away. The sun no longer seemed especially bright.

"I'M SORRY I didn't get back to you," she said breathlessly. "I just got back from—"

"—Hoboken."

"Putting up posters and asking around. We had like a hundred and fifty volunteers. Everybody was rushing. After all the discouragement, this news . . . Listen, Moe," Katy's tone grew suddenly serious, "was this witness—I mean, do you believe him? Do you think he really saw Patrick?"

"I do. Can I ask you something?"

"Sure."

"How," I was curious, "did you know I spoke to the witness?"

"You have to ask?"

I guess I didn't, not really. "Your dad."

"I think he knew before the detective called him. He's got friends, you know . . ."

"I know."

"Isn't it great news, about my brother?" she wanted my encouragement.

"Except for one thing," I said. "I'm out of a job."

There was loud silence on the other end of the phone. Then: "What? My dad fired you?"

I explained that "fired" wasn't quite the right word. "Look, he didn't exactly hire me in the first place. It was more of a trade type of thing; a favor for a favor. When I came on board, your family was grasping at straws. What harm could taking a flyer on me do? I'd gotten lucky once a long time ago. Maybe I'd get lucky again. As it turned out, you didn't need my luck. Hey, at least I got to meet you."

But she wasn't having any. "It's not right. I got a bad feeling about this."

"Don't turn superstitious on me," I said, remembering Dr. Friar. "It was a business decision."

More silence. "Can I hire you?"

"What?"

"Don't turn deaf on me. You heard me. Will you work for me?"

It was an intriguing idea. Truth be known, I wasn't happy about getting my walking papers at this stage of things. I knew too much to walk away fat and happy now. My curiosity hadn't waned. Quite the opposite. I played for time: "Can we talk about it later?"

She relaxed: "We better or I'll have to kick your ass."

"Tough Catholic girls make me nuts. Think you can fit into your old plaid skir—"

"Watch it or I'll kick you in the knee. Eight o'clock okay with you?"

"I'm afraid to say no. It's fine. Where do—"

"Pooty's," she said, no hesitation in her voice.

I seconded the nomination without debate.

* * *

I GOT THERE purposefully early. Pooty's was nearly empty, the jukebox quiet. Grimy as ever, you could almost hear the mold spores growing. Jaundiced Jack, the Shakespeare of single malts, was behind the bar chatting up some skinny peroxide girl. Maybe he was asking her to come back to his garret later so they could compare needle marks.

"Pete downstairs?"

He screwed up his face like he was getting ready to challenge me. Then, the dull bulb of recognition flickered. With supreme effort he smiled and tilted his head toward the staircase. Just as on my previous visit, Pete Parson was busy working an adding machine. I rapped on the wall outside the office. Turning, he recognized me right off. He didn't smile.

"I didn't expect a kiss," I said, "but—"

"Sorry." He offered me his hand.

"State Liquor Authority still busting your shoes?"

"With regularity," he said, holding up several pink memo sheets. "These are all messages from their investigators wanting a piece a my time."

"Here," I handed him another sheet of paper.

"What's this?"

"Give that guy a call," I said, pointing to Brian Kupf's name. "Tell him you're a friend of mine and that Maloney says to get off your back. Try not to push him. I may need his help myself someday soon."

"Why you doin'—"

"I don't know if it'll work, but try it. Did you hear, the cops found somebody says he saw the kid in Hoboken two days ago?"

"No shit!" he smiled. "Credible witness?"

"I think so."

"Hey, thanks for this." Parson held up the paper I'd given him. "Can I do anything for you?"

"I'm meeting a date here in a few minutes and—"

"I'll call Jack upstairs and take care of it. Everything's on the arm tonight. If either you or your date sees the bottom of your glass, you let me know. I'll fire that conceited prick bartender so fast it'll make his geeky little head spin. He's good but he annoys the shit outta me."

"Thanks, Pete."

"Here," he flipped me a roll of quarters. "That should keep the jukebox busy a while. And do me a favor, there's this song Jack just hates. That Bruce Springsteen song. I don't know. It's got a sax in it. Something about tramps."

" 'Born to Run?' " I said.

"That's it." He stood and clapped me on the back: "You got it. Play that song a few times. It makes Jack crazy. What's he say, playing that song makes the bourgeois twerps from Jersey feel cool? Asshole's from fuckin' Dayton, Ohio, and he's bad-mouthing Jersey? Play that song, play it a lot."

Something popped up in the back of my mind, an idea, a random thought . . . I can't tell you what, but it felt important. Something about music, maybe. Important or not, it was lost the minute Pete started talking again. He was going to come up to the bar and check on me, he said, and to see the look on Jack's face when that song came on for the tenth time.

"You okay?"

"I think I was gonna say something," I frowned, "but it's gone."

"I hate when that happens," Pete commiserated. "Feels like an itch you can't scratch."

Upstairs, Jack was just getting off the phone with Pete when I sat down at the bar. He regarded me with all the enthusiasm of a coma victim. Apparently, gimpy ex-cops were just too uncool for words. He informed me that my money was no good at his bar; the evening's tab was on the house. I played dumb. It was big of him, I said, throwing a twenty on the bar.

"How about tip money?" I coaxed. "Go ahead, take it."

He hesitated like a starving dog sniffing poison meat. I could see the wheels turning behind his eyes, the fix already cooking in the spoon. Twenty bucks in the tip jar was a comfortable way to start the night, but what if Pete found out? Was it worth getting canned? He took it.

I pointed to the beer pulls: "Becks Dark. Hey, got any ABBA on the jukebox?"

He just rolled his eyes as I brought my pint over to the juke. I pumped about five bucks worth of quarters down the slot.

110 There's A Place
    Beatles
135 Born to Run
    Bruce Springsteen and the E Street Band
140 In the Mood

Glenn Miller Orchestra
155 My Old School
Steely Dan
135 Born to Run . . .

"If I ask nicely, will you show me your gun?" Katy whispered in my ear as she snuck up behind me.

"Depends how nicely you ask," I said, not turning to face her. "What'll you have? And don't hold back. We're drinking free tonight!"

"Glenfiddich, straight up. Why, what's the occasion?"

Laughing, I said: "Your dad's doing one of the owners a favor. I'll explain later." I handed her the roll of quarters. "Play whatever you'd like as long as you play 135 every few selections."

She looked at the box. "I didn't figure you for the Springsteen type."

"He's all right, but that's not the point. I'll explain that later, too."

She joined me at the bar as the early Fab Four faded out. We clinked glasses, exchanging nervous pleasantries, saying how happy we were to be there. She said she'd punched in about ten more selections, 135 accounting for two of the ten. I explained about the bartender and Pete Parson and worked my way back to how her father was doing Pete a favor.

"Dad needed someone to blame," she said.

"I figured as much. That's why I'm doing what I am. I like this place. I'd hate to see it go under because of misplaced vengeance. So, how'd it go today?"

"It's hard to say."

Just then, a drummer pounded his skins, a sax let out a low sustained growl, a glockenspiel tinkled and a twangy guitar hummed. Number 135 filled the air: "In the day we sweat it out in the streets of a runaway American dream . . ."

"Oh, fuck!" Jack snarled. I almost spit out my beer. "Ooh, it's the Boss," he swooned. "Apocalypse on the fucking boardwalk. Did you play this?" Jack asked me.

"What can I tell you?" I shrugged. "You don't have any ABBA."

Katy nudged me. "I guess he really does hate this song."

"I have a funny feeling that by the end of the evening we're not gonna be very fond of it ourselves."

Pooty's wasn't the type of place where folks made an entrance. People just sort of drifted in off the street. It was happening now, empty bar stools filling up around us. We watched the door, trying to guess what kind of jobs the most recent arrivals were out of.

"Actress," Katy elbowed me, as a lean, hollow-faced girl came in.

"Dancer," I argued. "Look at those legs."

When two young guys dressed in Rutgers sweatshirts walked through the door and headed straight for the jukebox, Katy and I looked immediately at Jack. He cursed under his breath and started singing: " 'Dancing queen, she's so sweet, only seventeen . . .' Maybe ABBA isn't such a bad idea," he smiled, refilling our glasses.

I repeated my question about the day's progress in Hoboken. The results, she answered, were decidedly mixed. Their goal for the day had been to find at least one, hopefully two other people who could place Patrick at or near the shopping center at approximately the same time Mr. Sica had reported seeing him there.

"Right now," she said, "our optimism is like a broken stool standing on one rickety leg."

"Enzo Sica."

"And," Katy continued, "it's leaning against a wall of blind hope. But if we could find other witnesses, our optimism would stand on more solid footing and we could move it off the wall."

They had found a few people who claimed to have seen Patrick, but when pressed none of the potential witnesses panned out. Some got the time all wrong. Some the place. The ones who got those details right, couldn't swear they hadn't confused their own memories with what they'd read in the papers. None remembered the shopping bags. Again, a detail omitted to help weed out the cranks and treasure hunters.

It was the strong impression the nervous young man had left on Enzo Sica that helped convince Sully and me the old stone mason was being truthful. Today's witnesses were not so impressed by who they had or thought they had seen. Katy didn't think that made them liars, but . . .

"It's hard to tell after a while. You want so much to believe. My heart tells me to listen and my head tells me they're all just full of shit."

"I know," I said, but I didn't.

Glenn Miller came on. "Wanna dance?" we asked simultaneously.

"Jinx," she said. "You owe me a beer."

"Tonight that's not a problem."

She hesitated. "Your knee?"

"Let me worry about that."

We chugged what was in our glasses and moved out onto the tiles. To call what we did by any one name would have been a stretch. It was an amalgam of the Lindy, the tango and a half-assed polka. In spite of how we must've looked, we liked it. I liked holding her. She liked being held. I liked the way she touched me. My knee was blind to her charms. When we were done, we received a round of applause. New full glasses awaited our return. We toasted to Arthur Murray.

"So, did you find a clerk or shopkeeper who might've helped Patrick that day?" I asked, returning to the subject of Hoboken.

"One guy said he thought he remembered helping pick out a dress shirt for someone who fit my brother's description. It was the right time and place."

I could hear doubt in her voice: "But . . ."

"Shirt was the wrong size and way too businessy. Brooks Brothers-type shirt was what the guy said. The customer paid in cash and split."

I thought about asking something I'd been hesitating to ask. All along I believed the Maloneys must have assumed, as I had, that Patrick was dead. The only questions, then, were, was it an accident or foul play or suicide? And where was the body? Now that there was a chance he was alive, I wondered what the family thought. Did they think he was kidnapped? I doubted it. There'd never been any phone calls or glued newsprint notes with ransom demands. It wasn't like he was Patty Hearst or anything. Did they think he had amnesia? Nah, only in soap operas. So, given the remaining options, they must have concluded Patrick had simply checked out of his old life. But why?

"You've gone quiet all of a sudden," Katy noted. "Don't tell me you're a sad drunk."

"No, it's just that—"

"So!" A jolly Pete Parson appeared. From the smell of him, I guessed he'd been doing a little private celebrating downstairs. "How we doin'? Jack treating you good?"

Jack conveniently turned his back.

"Great," I said, relieved he had chosen now to visit.

Pete cleared his throat: "Aren't you goin' to introduce me?"

"Katy meet Pete. Pete meet Katy." They shook hands, smiling goofily at one another.

"Jack!" Pete shouted above Steely Dan. "The good stuff."

A dismayed Jack slapped a dusty bottle down in front of us. As he did so, the drums pounded, the sax wailed, the glockenspiel tinkled, the guitar twanged. Number 135 was up for its second at bat of the evening: "In the day we sweat it out on the streets of a runaway American dream . . ."

There was murder in Jack's eyes. Spotting it, Katy and I spun on our bar stools and pointed at the kids in the Rutgers shirts. "Fucking Jersey!" he hissed. "Why didn't they bomb Ho-Ho-Kus and Newark instead of Hiroshima and Nagasaki?"

"Shut up and pour," Pete ordered with great satisfaction.

It was Calvados, he said, French apple brandy. His great-grandfather was from Normandy, where the apples grew. It did taste of apples—more like butane, but a little like apples. When Pete headed back downstairs, he took the bottle with him.

By the fourth playing of "Born to Run," Katy suggested the time had come for us to take a walk and to get some food into our bellies.

"Weren't we supposed to eat first?" I wondered.

"Too late. You like Ukrainian food?"

"Pierogi is my middle name. East Village, right? Okay," I said, "let's see if we pick the same restaurant. We'll walk."

"We'll take a cab. You may not be feeling any pain now, but you might in the morning."

We agreed to take a cab across town, but to walk once we hit the Village. We said our fare-thee-wells to Jack. Jack, who was all right in the end. His venomous, running monologue was pretty damned funny and after Katy and I'd had a few, we found ourselves wanting him at our end of the bar. I hate when people do that, refuse to live down to expectations.

As we approached the exit, an unfamiliar song was just starting to spin on the jukebox turntable. It was all simple chords and backbeat, but nasty somehow, kind of like a Dave Clark Five song dressed in black. I could feel that fleeting thought I'd had in Pete Parson's office reemerging.

"Who is this?" I heard myself asking no one in particular.

"It's the fucking Ramones, man," a faceless voice shouted out of the crowd.

Katy tugged my arm. "Come on."

I didn't move. "Do you have a picture of Patrick? Not an old prom one, but—"

"Will this do?" she asked, pulling something from the pocket of her coat.

The Maloneys had printed new posters of Patrick based on the picnic photo Sully had shown me. It was better than the reproduction that had appeared in the papers, but not that much better. The accompanying description had been updated, too.

"Great," I said. "We can stop at a copy store by NYU on the way."

She shook her head. "Why, do you think Patrick's hiding under the table in a Ukrainian restaurant?"

"Maybe, but we're not going to eat just yet."

"What are—"

Now it was my turn to pull her by the arm: "There's a cab. Let's go."

ACTUALLY, IT HAD been more difficult finding an open copy center than I thought. There were any number of open pizza places for people to satisfy their marijuana munchies or thriving gift shops for tourists to purchase miniatures of the Statue of Liberty giving the finger, but God forbid your dissertation defense was coming up Monday and you had to make copies of your notes! For ten bucks the cab driver took us back to his garage and for five additional dollars the dispatcher made us twenty copies of the poster.

"That was either the most expensive short cab ride I ever took," I said, helping Katy out of the back seat, "or the most pricey photocopies ever made."

I'd been tempted to tell her my plan during our taxi safari through the streets of Greenwich Village, but I was afraid she'd shoot my idea down. If Katy could only see for herself, I thought, she might understand my inspiration.

"Okay," I said, after spotting someone who fit the bill coming our way, "close your eyes."

"The corner of East Ninth Street and Second Avenue is no place to play Blind Man's—"

I talked over her: "Humor me. Close your eyes. Eyes closed?"

"They're shut! They're shut, for Christ sakes!"

"Describe how Patrick looked the last time you saw him."

She did so, confessing she'd never really seen his tattoo. He wore the earring in front of the family despite their protestations, but none of them knew he even had the tattoo until the picnic picture surfaced. I had no trouble believing Patrick Maloney could keep a secret.

"Ready?" I asked when she was done.

"Ready."

I told her to open her eyes and spun her slowly about. "Look!"

Heading right for us was a lanky boy in his early twenties. He wore ripped black jeans, a black leather jacket that had seen better days and sneakers. His pale, sunken cheeks were clean-shaven and his short, dyed hair was nearly yellow: more crayon than Clairol. There was a sizable steel safety pin dangling from his left earlobe. Under the amber streetlight, we could make out letters crudely tattooed across the knuckles of both his hands as he passed.

"A punk," she said, "so wha—" But she caught herself.

"Do you see?"

"I think so," Katy hesitated, unconvinced.

"Think about it a minute," I said. "If he just split, for whatever reason, this would be a perfect place to hide. With the way he looks now, he'd fit right in. Christ, he'd look like every third guy walking down Avenue A. With that stupid prom picture posted everywhere, no one would have spotted him. And let me tell you something, even before the punks moved in, the people down here weren't disposed to helping the cops."

She hesitated: "I guess. But what would he live on? He hasn't touched his bank accounts or used the emergency credit card Dad got for him."

"Maybe he'd planned on this for awhile and packed away some cash. You know that thing you said before about him hiding under a table?" I said, pointing at the door of the Ukrainian restaurant ten feet to our left. "He could be doing dishes or bussing tables. Maybe he's sleeping on a different couch every night. Maybe he's got a room in a cheap dive. I don't know. You tell me. Did you ever stop to think that maybe he's had help? A friend or a new girlfriend?"

"*New* girlfriend?" she was startled.

"Later," I begged for time to continue making my case. "Anyway, there's always a way to hustle up some money in this city. Panhandling comes to mind. Maybe he's drawing tourist sketches in Washington Square for five bucks a pop."

Katy laughed joylessly: "That'd be ironic, wouldn't it?"

I thought it more likely he'd be selling nickel bags or fake hits of mescaline in Washington Square, but given his sister's reaction to the mere idea of a new girlfriend, I thought it prudent to leave mention of drugs out of the equation.

"So, if he's fallen in around here with the punks and the artists," I said, "I think we should pay a visit to the music and dance clubs. We'll leave posters with the bouncers, rope men and bartenders. They might help."

Having gone through months of letdowns, Katy wouldn't let herself be optimistic. "They won't pay any attention."

"Remember what I said to you before at Pooty's when you asked to see my gun? It depends how nicely you ask. It's been my experience that club employees grasp the value of cash incentives and future reward as well as anyone."

Almost unconsciously, she reached under her coat into a pants pocket. "I've got about sixty bucks, subway fare and an American Express card."

I frowned. "I don't think bouncers take American Express."

"But this restaurant does," she said, pointing at the blue and white American Express decal on the door. "My head's spinning. I've gotta eat something."

I looked at my watch. It was late for dinner even by Manhattan standards, but very early in clubland. Rubbing my belly, I nodded my consent. As I opened the door for her, Katy stopped in her tracks. "What about Hoboken? Do you think it was really Patrick?"

I let the door close, took hold of Katy's shoulders and turned her to look down East 9th. "If Manhattan from here to the Hudson suddenly became invisible, what would you see west across the river?"

"Jersey City?"

"Don't be such a *vance*," I said, playfully rapping a knuckle on her head. "Besides Jersey City, what—"

"Hoboken."

"A short subway ride or walk to the PATH train and from here you'd be across the river in fifteen minutes."

"Don't be so proud of yourself," she punched my arm. "And what's a *vance*, anyway?"

"It's Yiddish for wiseass woman who wants to be kissed."

"You're right," she said, "I'm a *vance*."

With eyes shut, her lips no longer seemed thin to me.

August 6th, 1998 (evening)

SISTER MARGARET WAS right on. The pizza was incredible. The crust was crispy but pliable, the sauce sweet and the mozzarella fresh . . .

"It's not easy to impress a Brooklynite with pizza, but if I had a hat, I'd tip it."

The nun, a bit embarrassed, I think, by her pride, bowed her head. She regretted, she said, not being able to have a beer with me. Beer made the experience complete. But she would be on duty when she got back to the hospice.

"Like a cop," Sister Margaret shook her head, "no drinking on duty."

"Sister, don't believe everything about cops you see on TV."

"Are you a policeman, Mr. Prager?"

"Was, Sister. A long time ago."

"Is that how you came to be involved in the disappearance of Mr. Maloney?"

I tried putting her off: "It's a long story."

"Well, there's a lot of pizza and I don't think Mr. Bryson is going to come around before we're finished."

I wondered if curiosity was a bad thing for a nun. Sister Margaret told me that curiosity usually wasn't encouraged in the order, but as a nurse in a hospice she'd found her natural curiosity a gift.

"Many of our people have hidden things for years. I believe in many cases their guilts and stresses over these unspoken things have contributed to their suffering. It's not a very scientific analysis, I know, yet I believe it."

"Shouldn't they confess to priests?" I asked.

"Don't believe everything about the Catholic church you see on TV." She happily goaded me. "Some in our care aren't even Catholics. Mr. Bryson, for example. And frankly, the dying have the right to tell what they want to whomever they want. Surely I have heard some dark tales over the years. Rapists and molesters have unburdened themselves to me. But mostly people just share things with me they had wanted to say to a long-gone relative or friend they did wrong to as a child. Sometimes, Mr. Prager, the thing that haunts the dying most is an old unkindness to a stranger.

"I think knowing death is coming for you is a mixed bag, a blessing and a curse. For the family of the dying, it's a blessing, I'd say. Things can be put in order, grudges forgiven, balance restored. And when death finally comes, it comes as a relief. The mourning is shorter lived, because the loved ones have been grieving all along. For the dying, though, it can be brutal. And I'm not talking about the physical pain here. I had a waitress friend tell me once that she could barely remember the customers who'd given her her biggest tips, but she could describe with crystal clarity the people who'd stiffed her. Impending death can be like that, it can amplify your sins so that everything else is background noise. I think Mr. Bryson has a ringing in his ears. Now, I'm not sure what he has to say, but he's made it abundantly clear that in this instance, you're the only one he's prepared to say it to."

"Don't tell me you're jealous, Sister."

She held her right index finger and thumb about an inch apart. "Maybe just a little. Are you married, Mr. Prager?"

"Separated." I swallowed hard. "What's that they say, all roads lead home? The reason my wife and I are apart is because I kept an old secret. It's funny that that's what we were talking about."

"I'm so sorry. An affair?" Sister Margaret asked boldly.

"Nothing that simple, I'm afraid. I think she could forgive me that. You know how there are some guilty secrets you can own up to at any time? Because their time for pain has passed? Like a few years ago at Passover seder, I told my brother Aaron that I used to watch him and his girlfriends make out through a hole I found in the wall. We all laughed about it and I rated each old girlfriend on a make-out scale from one to ten. But there are some things that grow worse with time. You have a narrow window of opportunity to share the pain or admit your guilt, but once that window closes . . ."

"I don't mean to pry," Sister Margaret said, placing a comforting hand on mine, "but if you'd like to share it with—"

"Thanks, Sister. It's nice of you, but no, not now. Maybe when everything shakes out, we'll make a date for pizza and we'll talk about it."

"It's a date. Do you have children?"

"A daughter," I said, producing Sarah's high school graduation picture. "She's eighteen today."

"Oh that red hair, she's beautiful."

"She's supposed to be going to the University of Michigan in a few weeks," I said with equal amounts of pride and anger.

"Supposed to . . ." she parroted. "There's a problem?"

"A boy. Listen, Sister Margaret, can we get—"

"Absolutely."

There was a moment or two when the only noise at the table was chewing, but eventually I got around to asking about Tyrone Bryson: How had he come to the hospice? How long had he been there? What did Sister know about him and his past?

The answers were straightforward if not very enlightening. Bryson had come to the hospice after being treated at one of the diocese's hospitals. He had been at Mary the Divine for only three weeks. Sister Margaret didn't know much about Mr. Bryson other than he had been living on the streets of New Haven. His only possessions were his ill-matched clothing, the slip of paper with my name on it and the newspaper article. He was a New Yorker. He'd shared that much with her and from the day he'd arrived at the hospice, Mr. Bryson had begged for someone to track me down.

I began to give the nun some background about my involvement with Patrick Maloney, getting only as far as that first call from Rico when, as if on cue, my cell phone chirped.

"It's for you." I handed the phone over to Sister Margaret.

"He's conscious," she said, "but I don't know for how long or that he will ever be again."

I threw too much money on the table before catching up to sister. Part of me regretted not having the leftovers wrapped to go. It's funny what you think about.

February 7th, 1978 (late night)

FIRST KISSES ARE a revelation, so uncomplicated and so unlike firsts in bed. Somehow, the awkwardness of first kisses adds to their beauty: Which way should I tilt my head? Will she mind if I cup her chin in my hand or should I hold her in my arms or should I touch her at all? Will she close her eyes? Should I look to see? Will she part her lips? If she does, should I follow her lead? And when, in the end, in spite of your considerable calculation, you bump noses, it's funny and the tension burns off like fog.

Dinner was eaten in splendid silence, each of us lost in contemplation of consequence and possibility. Driven to distraction by the sweet perfume of onions frying in butter and chicken fat, my mental riffings were under attack by the vision of my Bubby Hana, dressed in black grandma shoes, hairnet and housedress, standing in her kitchen and grinding chicken livers. I was such a romantic. I wondered if Katy was under similar attack. What would Freud have said? Pass the rye bread and chicken schmaltz, probably.

"What are you laughing at?" she asked, as we finished splitting a piece of strudel.

"Nothing," I lied. Try as I might, I couldn't think of a graceful way to weave Freud, my maternal grandmother, chopped liver and the curves of Katy's breasts in a coherent sentence that wouldn't insult Katy or make me seem certifiable. Though I suspected the both of us would have forgiven most anything at that moment, I wasn't willing to risk it.

Agreeing that twenty bucks a man would properly motivate the people whose help Katy and I were about to solicit, I talked the restaurant manager into cashing a personal check. Getting a personal check cashed in New York City is an accomplishment on par with finding the Holy Grail and winning at Three Card Monte. The badge helped, but it was the poster of Patrick and Katy's sincerity that turned the trick. As thanks we offered a twenty to the manager. He refused and set about taping Patrick's poster to the door.

"I hate banks," Katy said, as we began walking downtown. "They have our money twenty-four hours a day, but our access to it is confined to six hours, five days a week. You shouldn't have to beg someone for what's yours."

"They're experimenting with cash machines in other parts of the country," I told her. "Banking hours are good for impulse control. I'm not sure letting people at their money all the time is such a great idea. Even level-headed people make some pretty stupid decisions with a bellyful at three in the morning. I don't think adding ready cash to the equation is bound to help."

"I can see what you mean."

"Plus the bad guys'll love cash machines. Muggings will skyrocket and drug dealing will become a real growth industry."

"You still think like a cop," Katy observed.

"I'll take that as a compliment," I said, before kissing her again.

LOCATED OFF BROADWAY, below Canal Street, in a part of Manhattan that was not unlike Pooty's neighborhood, Dirt Lounge was our third stop after CBGB's and The Vatican. This area, however, was still heavily commercial and unlikely to go completely artsy-fartsy any time soon. Dirt Lounge played the dance hall equivalent of the anti-Christ to Studio 54: no glitz, no neon, no paparazzi. If not for the black leather and spandex crowd milling about at the short flight of steps outside the little factory building, you might miss the place altogether.

I showed my badge to one of the motorcycle-jacketed bouncers at the rope and asked to speak to the man in charge. The bouncer grunted. Turning, he whispered to someone who must have been standing directly behind his mountainous body. Stepping around to the bouncer's right came a slender little man with a magenta mohawk, sickly white skin and black lipstick. His ears were so littered with studs, safety pins and dangling razor blades that if he were to stand between two strong magnets his face would peel off. Betraying all the metal and makeup, his droopy eyelids and downturned mouth lent him the bearing of cultivated boredom more closely associated with eighteenth-century French aristocrats than punk rockers.

"Badges don't get you an entree here," he said, looking past me and pointing to people in the crowd. "And what's with the cane, new undercover squad?" He almost smiled.

That joke was getting old fast. "I'm not looking for an in," I said, "just two minutes of your time."

"Please," Katy pleaded over my shoulder. "Please."

"Okay, I need a break anyway. Bear, you can handle it for a few," he told the bouncer before turning back to us. "This way."

The bouncer unhitched the ratty velvet rope, letting us and three or four other people through. Poorly lit and shabby, the place smelled like the bathroom of an Irish bar on St. Patrick's Day, only not as sweet. But the music was loud and snappy, even if the snippets of lyrics I caught were as dark as the lighting. Some of the dancers—mostly kids just jumping up and down like palsied pogo sticks—smiled in spite of themselves. Dancing makes alienation a tough mask to wear.

The mohawked aristocrat led us past the caged ticket window, down a long hallway and up a flight of stairs. The office was lined with album covers literally stapled to the walls and ceiling. The albums covers of bands like Yes, Pink Floyd, the Moody Blues, Emerson, Lake, and Palmer, Jethro Tull, the Strawbs, Gentle Giant, Genesis and some I'd never heard of, were defaced in one way or another, mostly with rude graffiti. "Fuck" and "suck" comprised the bulk of the Magic-Markered criticism. Some of the defacement was pretty skillful, however. "Days of Future Past" had been sliced into razor thin strips and reconstructed into a nonsensical but striking square of blues, yellows, blacks, whites and reds. It did not escape me that two of the album covers featured here had been reproduced—minus the Magic Marker—on dormitory walls by Patrick Maloney.

"Adolescent white boy music," the little aristocrat shook his head disdainfully, resting his cigarette in a vinyl record heated and perverted into a scalloped ashtray. "Pretentious, bankrupt bullshit."

"In ten years someone will be saying the same thing about the Sex Pistols," Katy spoke up.

"We'll all be dead in ten years, so what the fuck?"

This was all too profound for me. I decided to get to the point before anyone mentioned Camus or Nietzsche. I gave him some posters, asked him how much scratch he would need to spread around with his staff and wondered if there was anything we could do for him personally. He dismissed the offer like his cigarette ashes, with the flick of the wrist. Throughout my presentation, his ennui seemed to deepen and set like concrete. Then, for a reason I couldn't immediately grasp, his face brightened.

"You know, you look familiar. You from Brooklyn?" he asked.

"Sheepshead Bay, but I went to Lincoln."

"You're shittin' me, right? You know Tony Palone?"

"Tony the Pony, the best second baseman in South Highway Little League history? Nah," I winked, "never heard of him. Who do you think used to dig his throws outta the dirt at first base?"

"I'm his little cousin, Nicky."

We rehashed old times in the neighborhood, talked about how Tony was doing down in Florida with his construction business. I was careful not to point out how the Sex Pistols and Dead Kennedys might consider talk of baseball and Brooklyn adolescent white boy bullshit.

"Don't worry about your brother." He threw his arm around Katy like she was family. "If he's around, I'll hear about it. Moe, gimme your number. I'll spread the money around to the right people and I'll tell you later how much you owe. Keep your bread for now."

Katy thanked him and asked to use the bathroom. Nicky hesitated: "The Dirt Lounge bathroom is kinda like Berlin before and after the war," he said, "only worse."

Nature's call blinded her judgment. "If I spot Dr. Mengele, I'll call Simon Wiesenthal."

When Katy was down the steps, Nicky began to whisper: "What if I find this guy, but he don't wanna be found? You know half of the losers downstairs got a habit. Maybe this Patrick kid's got one, too?"

I told him he was right to guess Patrick didn't want to be found and that I was counting on the community's taste for heroin to help us along. "Junkies would sell their sisters for a fix. You think they'll hesitate to give this kid up?"

Nicky agreed. If Patrick Michael Maloney was involved in this scene, his life incognito would soon be drawing to an end "I better get back out front," he said. "We'll meet Katy on the way."

She was waiting for us at the bottom of the stairs. Nicky was curious to hear her reaction to the Dirt Lounge bathroom.

"You didn't tell me there was only one bathroom for everybody," she wagged her finger. "The only thing missing was

Joel Grey and the Hitler Youth singing 'Tomorrow Belongs to Me.' I was the only one in there actually using the toilet for anything but puking. There was a threesome in one corner who were so entangled they looked like a bowl of leather spaghetti. One guy had a needle stuck between his toes and three girls were doing lines of coke off the top of a urinal. You should sell T-shirts that say: 'I survived the bathroom at Dirt Lounge.' "

Nicky was horrified: "T-shirts!"

"Bankrupt bullshit!" Katy and I harmonized.

Nicky shook my hand and kissed Katy on the cheek. He handed me six passes to the place to use at my discretion. I almost gave them back, but didn't. Even if I were in no shape to use them, I thought they might come in handy. Miriam liked to dance and Ronnie, that tight-assed husband of hers, could set up a practice in the bathroom.

It was close to 3:00 when we got out of there, the crowd in front bigger than before. Without asking her if she was up to it, I pulled Katy into a cab that had just dropped off a couple of girls so drunk they nearly ran down the sewer. They had left two vodka bottles in the backseat as souvenirs. I gave the cabby a familiar address on Hudson Street.

There was no crowd milling about Pooty's and no one, not even my new buddy, Jack, was inside. Only a rather green-at-the-gills Pete Parson remained, mopping the floor. He didn't exactly click his heels when he saw someone knocking at the door, but summoned up a smile for Katy and me. He unlatched the door for us and made no excuses about the lateness of the hour or his flourishing hangover.

"A nightcap?" was all he said.

"Two Grand Marniers?"

Katy nodded her approval. As Pete walked back around the bar, I said I'd take pity on him and not demand the orange brandy in heated snifters.

"Demand away," he laughed. "You won't get it."

After placing our drinks on the bar, he apologized for not joining us. If he were any less green, we might have been insulted. Katy and I clinked glasses. I kissed her, savoring the texture of her lips and the citrus burn of the alcohol.

"Mopping, huh? You're gonna ruin this place's image. Next thing you know, you'll dust the booths."

"Never," he said proudly.

Katy then regaled him with stories of her trip into the realm of unisex bathrooms.

"Sounds kinky," Pete feigned a chill. "I gotta get me one of those."

That reminded me; on the cab ride over I'd decided to give two of my Dirt Lounge passes to Jack. It seemed more his kind of place than anyone else I was acquainted with. Even if he hated the place, it would be worth it just to listen to his sarcastic rantings.

"Where's Jack? What'd he pick up some ballerina and ask to go home early?"

"Jack?" Pete packed a lot of distaste into that one syllable. "Not old Jackie boy, he's as queer as the Queen of France."

Katy took the pronouncement in stride. My first inclination was to debate the point. Then it dawned on me that I'd sound like my Aunt Sadie the time she heard cousin Artie was dating a black woman: "A *schwartze*, not my Artie!" And trust me, Aunt Sadie knew my cousin Artie a lot better than I knew Jack. Jack's homosexuality also went a long way toward explaining Pete's hostility. I didn't figure it stemmed from Pete's love of the Jersey shore. Cops and gays had a long history in New York, kind of like the Turks and Armenians but not as loving.

"Well," I fumbled for something to say, "do me a favor. Leave these passes for Marie Antoinette and tell him we had fun tonight. And let me know how the Liquor Authority thing shakes out."

Pete just shrugged, promising I'd be the first to hear after his partners. He thanked me again and locked the doors behind us.

"Give me a dollar," I demanded as we approached my car.

Confused, Katy said: "What?" But even as she did so, she reached into her pocket and fished out four quarters. "Here."

"It's official," I announced.

"What is?"

"That I'm working for you now."

"You want to keep your new job?" she asked coyly.

"I do."

"Then you're going to have to sleep with the boss."

I opened her door. "I guess I can force myself."

"I'm counting on it." When I slid in next to her, she said: "Let's go to Coney Island."

"Coney Island's closed."

"Then I guess you're gonna have to kill some time making the boss happy."

If I hadn't turned the ignition key at that moment, it would have turned itself.

February 8th, 1978

IT HAD BEEN long since I'd drifted into sleep with a woman in my arms instead of a pillow. Warm bodies were never the problem. Dating is easy for cops, single or otherwise. Early on in my career I learned never to underestimate the power of the uniform. In the middle of an antiwar demonstration at Brooklyn College, a girl asked me out as I walked her back to the paddy wagon. When I declined, she called me a pig. And, of course, there was always Suzie the actress, so disappointed by my appearance out of the bag. Uniforms were makeup for men. For some reason, the uniform got your looks bumped up from coach to business to first class in the eyes of certain beholders. Rock stars aren't the only ones with groupies.

Exhausted, sleep is all we did. By the time we got upstairs to my apartment and made our trips to the bathroom, it was past 5:00. When I came out of the bathroom dressed only in pajama bottoms, Katy was waiting for me in the living room. Nude beneath her shirt and sprawled across the couch, I saw her eyes were shut only as I reached her. She startled and, like a trooper, stood right up, pushing her body close to mine. Tilting my head down, I kissed her lightly and led her into the bedroom. I kissed her again, stroked her hair back and whispered the word "later."

Years had passed since I'd felt comfortable enough not to force my hand, not to say yes when my disinterested heart stood by. And when those hungry moments were past, there was often too much embarrassment and self-loathing left on the sheets, poisoning the air for intimacy. For me, taking all I could get was no prescription for love. That's what I could say later to Katy, because I had faith somehow there would be a tomorrow for Katy and me that allowed sleep to come to us without coming between us.

We woke up on opposite ends of the bed. This wasn't TV, after all. But when we did wake up, Katy slid across the sheets to me, her back against my chest, my arms around her.

"You know that night we met at the canal," I whispered, "you smiled at me."

"I did?"

"You did. And when I got back to my car and closed my eyes, I could see your smile. It means a lot when I can see something with my eyes closed. Not that I closed my eyes much that night. I couldn't get you out of my head."

I kissed her neck and she spun around in my arms to face me. "Why does it mean so much?" she asked.

"Because I have a good memory for words, for details, not images, for names, not faces. Well, that's not a hundred percent true. I can remember a face, but it's hard for me to visualize a face. When my life flashes before my eyes, it'll be in text, not pictures. Christ, am I making any sense? Just stop me before I make a complete ass of myself."

"Ssssh," she put her finger across my lips. "You know yourself, that's a good thing. Not many men know who they are. I'm a little embarrassed," she said, pulling herself so close to me her breathing sounded like the wind.

"Don't be embarrassed, not here. What is it?"

"No one's ever liked my smile before. My lips are too thin and my teeth—"

"I can see my father's face with my eyes shut," I stopped her, "but I have to look at a picture to really see my mom. And I remember Andrea Cotter's smile. Before you, hers was the only smile to ever stick in my head."

"An old girlfriend. I think I'm jealous."

"Old maybe, but not a girlfriend. Andrea was a year ahead of me in high school. You know how some people aren't beautiful to look at or anything, but there's this energy about them or the way they carry themselves that just makes you want to be close to them?"

"I think so."

"Andrea was like that. She was a little stocky and her legs were too thick, but she was a cheerleader. She was the lead in *Sing*. She was editor of the school newspaper and she wrote great poems. I was just in awe of her, not in love exactly. Don't get me wrong, I used to imagine us together. I think every guy in school tried to imagine being with Andrea. She never made herself unapproachable or acted above it all, but I just couldn't ever bring myself to talk to her. Then in my junior year I wrote this poem—"

"You write poetry?"

"Wrote! Wrote! One poem, and it got published in the school magazine."

"Do you have a copy?" Katy asked excitedly. "Can I see it?"

"Someday maybe."

She kissed my cheek. "I'm sorry. I interrupted. Tell me about Andrea."

"There isn't that much more to tell, really. The last week in May, the week the magazine came out, I was cutting a class and went to hang out on the boardwalk with my friends. By the time we were almost there, it got cloudy and they turned back. I went anyway and sat on a bench and stared out at the beach. 'Excuse me,' someone said, and I looked around. It was Andrea Cotter. 'You're Moses Prager, aren't you?' I said something stupid like, yeah, the last time I checked. 'I love your poem,' she said. 'I wish I could inspire someone to write like that.' "

Katy covered my mouth with her hand. "The poem was about her, wasn't it?"

"Yes."

"Now I really want to read it. Do you think she knew?"

"I don't know. I was afraid to ask," I confessed.

"What happened?"

"She took a copy of the magazine out of her bag and asked me to autograph the page my poem was on. I said I would only if she would autograph her poems in my copy. We exchanged books. When we handed them back, she just smiled at me for a second. That was the smile that stuck in my head. I'd seen her smile before, you know, but never at me. I wished her good luck in college and she told me something goofy like keep on writing. When she was out of sight, I looked at the page she had signed."

"You were hoping she left her phone number."

"Can't blame a guy for hoping," I said. "But she didn't. She just signed her name."

"So, is she famous? Did she marry rich?" Katy actually sounded jealous.

"She died that summer in a fire in the Catskills with two other girls from school. They were up there waitressing to earn money for college. Some drunk moron was smoking in bed in the employee quarters . . ." I snapped my fingers. "Seventeen people died."

"Oh my God, Moe, I'm sorry."

"That's okay," I said. "It was a long time ago and now I have someone else's smile to dream of."

Katy was crying, more for Patrick, I think, than for Andrea Cotter. When she calmed down some, I kissed her mouth, her neck. Tears on a woman's neck are intoxicating. I worked my lips down her body until I turned her crying into coos.

FOR ALL MY bravado and confidence, I kept listening for the other shoe to drop. When would she quietly get out of bed, shower—maybe not even shower—collect her clothes from the living room and dress as quickly as she could, begin her makeup job in the hallway mirror only to decide to finish in the cab or subway car and call to me as she walked out the door: "Thanks, Moe, I'll call you," or "Call me." I liked it better when they said nothing at all or stayed for coffee.

And Katy did get up, walking quietly to the bathroom. I could hear the shower running. I prayed she took short showers. I hated lying silently in bed waiting for them to go. But Katy refused to buy into my history.

"For chrissakes, Moe!" she screamed above the shower, "if you don't get in here soon, I really am going to do this by myself."

I didn't quite set the land speed record.

If there were any lingering doubts after our marathon shower, Katy removed them by using my toothbrush. It's amazing, isn't it, how two people can spend hours moving in, out, over, around and through parts of each other's body but refuse to share a toothbrush in a pinch?

"What do you want to do?"

"I'm too sore for that," she said, looking up from her coffee. "But I do remember saying something about Coney Island."

I pulled back the curtains and informed her that the white stuff falling past my window wasn't ash from the building incinerator and that with most of the rides closed until Easter, Coney Island wasn't exactly America's garden spot.

In an eerily accurate aping of her father's voice, Katy said: "Tough shit, son. You work for me now."

"I surrender. I surrender. Come on, I'll take you to Nathan's."

After we'd both inhaled our hot dogs and fries and washed them down with orangeade, she told me how her dad used to take the kids to Coney Island on Sundays. Her dad was from Brooklyn originally.

"He never stopped missing it," she said. "He used to say how taking us kids to Coney Island was his duty, but I think he enjoyed it more than we did. There are plenty of amusement parks between here and Dutchess County."

"You mean your father really is human."

"I've never checked his pulse, but I love him."

I quickly dropped that line of conversation. When I made a move to leave, Katy mentioned Marina Conseco, but not by name.

"Can you show me where you found the little girl?"

I tried to laugh it off. "Cut it out, will you? What is this, an episode of *This is Your Life*? Next thing you'll want to do is meet the rabbi who circumcised me."

"Please show me the building."

What could I say? The snow was barely falling now and it was a short walk. I could see it was important to her. All the optimism over Hoboken had drained out of her. The weeks of false leads and unfulfilled hoping had worn her down. Maybe she just wanted to touch the bricks, to stand before a shrine to answered prayers. Whatever her reasons, she didn't need to explain them to me.

"This is it," I said, pointing to the dilapidated building. "They took the water tank down years ago. Good thing, too. It was a rickety old piece of shit. I'm amazed it didn't collapse in on us."

The snow had stopped completely. Katy stood silently, looking up at the roof, shielding her eyes from a sun that wasn't there.

"I heard the story from my mom who heard it from my cousin Rose's husband," she finally said, eyes still fixed on the roof.

"Rico, yeah, he was in this precinct with me then."

"So I heard how you found her . . . What was her name? I know you told me, Maria, Ma—"

"Marina," I corrected.

"I'm sorry, Marina. I heard the story of how you found her," Katy said, looking straight at me, "but maybe because I heard it third-hand, I don't know how she disappeared in the first place."

"No one ever asks me about that part. Everyone just assumes that because she was abused and someone left her to die up there that she was abducted," I said, looking away from Katy.

"She wasn't?"

"Yes and no. She was upset about her parents' divorce and she thought if she could scare them by running away . . . you know how kids think. Then she got lost and disoriented. I guess she picked the wrong guy to ask for help."

Katy said she was finished here. She thanked me for putting up with her insane requests. Still, something had changed. Her tone was formal, her words measured. Although part of me was panicking about the change in her, wondering what I'd done wrong, I resisted the urge to interrogate her. Saying my knee had had all the exercise it could bear, I asked if we could take the bus back to my building.

"Of course," was all she said.

Hoping a few minutes of quiet reflection and the bus ride would shake her out of her mood, I tried coaxing Katy into staying for dinner, maybe even for breakfast. No, she said, she was tempted but there was work in the morning and a long-neglected project due by midweek. And more importantly, though she never said the words, there was guilt. I'd been a fool not see it. I'd miscalculated her reasons for wanting to visit the building where I'd found the Conseco girl. I imagined I could hear her berating herself: Patrick was out there alone somewhere, hurting or dead or, like that poor little girl, waiting for death to come. How could I have let myself enjoy myself under these circumstances? How can I want to be with a man I would have never met if . . .

Jews know guilt. We can smell it on your breath. We can read it in the lines of your face because we've looked at it in mirrors for thousands of years. Guilt is like a witch's spell. Once cast it cannot be reasoned away. No, Katy would have to let the guilt rattle around in her head and heart awhile before she could remove the curse.

"This is us," I said, pulling the chord to let the driver know we wanted to get off.

She seemed relieved to hear we didn't have to go back up to my apartment. I'd drive her straight home if that's what she wanted. That was what she wanted, but, as it turned out, I couldn't keep my word.

We snaked our way through the parking lot to my assigned spot. We found the charred carcass of what used to be my '76 Plymouth Fury surrounded by a moat of filthy water and foam. The acrid vapors of burnt tires hung in the air, tearing at our throats. The stench really seemed to get to Katy, who was turning an ugly shade of green.

"Fuckeeng keeds!" Jose, the building's head maintenance man, said, seeming to appear out of thin air. "Dee firemen have gone fifteen minute ago, Meester Prager. Dey stop it before dee gas tank go. Cops leave a number inside for you."

"A report number," I mumbled, "for insurance."

"*¿Que?*"

"Forget it."

Reluctantly, Katy came upstairs to put herself back together. I offered to call her a cab and pay her fare home, but she insisted on taking the subway. She was a big girl, she said, and needed the time to think. Though still not completely relaxed, she had softened somewhat, even managing a smile and agreeing to let me walk her to the subway.

At the station, she hugged me, kissed me on the cheek. But when she dropped her token in the slot and pushed through the turnstile, she stopped and looked back.

"I'm sorry about this afternoon," she said. "Last night was unbelievable. I like you, Moe, and—"

"You don't have to apologize," I interrupted. "I know it's hard for you. It must get in the way of everything, what's going on with your brother. I'd hate for it to get between us."

She walked back to the turnstile. "Me too," she said and, bending over the turnstile arm, grabbed me by the collar and kissed my mouth. "Call me in a few days."

In Jose's office now, waiting for the maintenance man to find the police report number, he repeated his accusations about the neighborhood kids. Thanking him and taking the slip of paper from his hand, I didn't bother arguing the point. It may have been kids like Jose thought, but I didn't like it. My car was in an exposed spot. The kids I knew usually operated under cover of darkness. Why pick my car to torch in the middle of the afternoon?

But by the time I got to my apartment door, I'd calmed down. Jose was probably right. I was just being paranoid. I'd had too much to drink last night, didn't get much sleep and Katy's moods had left me a little punchy. I should be happy, I thought, slipping my key into the lock. It wasn't a Porsche 911 they'd roasted their marshmallows over. It was a Plymouth Fury, for Christ sakes! Chrysler would probably be bankrupt in a year and the car would've been worthless. Take the insurance money and run.

The phone started ringing as I opened the latch. I wasn't particularly in the mood to chat, so I let it ring. After ten rings, my wish was granted. But almost as soon as it had stopped, it started again. I surrendered and picked up.

"You've been warned," an unfamiliar man's voice droned in my ear. "The next time it won't be your car."

Click. He hung up before I could ask what I'd been warned about. So, Jose was wrong. Sometimes it's no fun being right.

February 10th, 1978

I STARED AT the phone, started to dial her number, stopped, put the receiver back in its cradle. I ached to hear her voice, but things were more complicated now. For the last two days, whether on the phone with the insurance company or at the car rental office or during dinner with Miriam and Ronnie, the threat gnawed at me: "You've been warned. Next time it won't be your car." Only fools laugh off threats and I wasn't laughing. This threat wasn't issued by some schmo in the schoolyard who was mad because I pitched him inside or some mutt I arrested for petty larceny. No, this guy wasn't playing. He'd risked serious jail time and, if my gas tank had exploded, other people's lives to make his point.

The fact he was willing to put innocent people in harm's way is what really worried me. For even if I were inclined to call his bluff, there was no guarantee I'd be his target. As I sat across from Miriam and Ronnie at dinner on Monday night, I couldn't get that thought out of my head. What about Aaron's family? Would Cindy turn the ignition key one morning and blow herself and the kids all over Bay Parkway? The thing about it was, the guy on the phone had neglected to mention what it was I'd done or was doing or should stop doing to get the sword of Damocles put back in its sheath. Unfortunately, the only answers I came up with held very little appeal for me. That's why I didn't fear for Katy and why things were so complicated. The devil was on my shoulder and I didn't know how to brush him off.

I finished dialing this time and was more than a little relieved to get her machine. The relief was short lived. Katy picked up when she heard my voice.

"Hey," she said, a smile in her voice, "I was hoping it was you. I missed you yesterday."

"Me too. What are you doing tonight?"

"Meeting you for dinner, I hope. Is everything okay? You sound—"

"I'm still in mourning for my car," I deflected. "You okay?"

"I don't know. I feel a little weird about how things went Sunday."

"We can talk about it later. Listen . . ." I hesitated, "there's some other stuff we have to talk about, too. It might be a little unpleasant, but I didn't want to hit you with it cold."

"Is it Patrick? You heard something from Nicky and it's not good. Tell me now, Moe. Don't make me—"

"I heard from someone," I said. "It wasn't Nicky and I'm not sure it's got anything to do with where your brother is. I swear."

She didn't believe me, but guessed correctly I wasn't going to discuss it over the phone. We set a time and a place and quickly ended the conversation. Given my warning about the evening's agenda, making small talk would have been like misting plants before a storm.

Patrick Maloney had disappeared again, only this time it was from the pages of the daily papers. Nothing came of his being spotted in Hoboken, so he was out, sent back to the bench until someone else saw him strolling with Elvis. Even then it was unlikely Patrick would get another shot. There were just too many murders, oil embargoes, terrorists and dirty wars to go around. So much blood and so little space! Only the sports section seemed to have unlimited growth potential.

The phone rang.

"Yeah," I said tentatively, worried about who might be on the other end.

"Geez! You always this cheery?" It was Pete Parson. "You must be real popular at wakes."

"Sorry, Pete, I've had a rough few days. What's up?"

"On behalf a me and my partners, I just wanted to say thanks. They called off the hounds."

I was surprised: "So fast?"

"That Kupf guy must pull alotta weight. I called him first thing yesterday mornin' and boom, today the State Liquor Authority terminates the investigation. We gotta deal with some little shit. The fire department hit us with a few code violations and the health department says you shouldn't eat offa our floors—"

"That's a shocker," I cut him off. "Well that's great news. I'm happy for you."

"Listen, Moe," his tone turned serious, "we know you didn't have to do this for us and—"

"Forget—"

"Will you shut up and let a man finish? We're havin' a party here on Friday night to celebrate and you and your girl—I forgot her name . . ."

"Katy."

"You and Katy are the guests of honor. Your boyfriend Jack's out right now buyin' your gifts, so don't even think about sayin' no."

"No."

"Fuck you, bud. Ten o'clock Friday. And thanks again."

He hung up. I wondered if he'd be so happy to include Katy if he knew she was Patrick's sister. I wasn't going to call him back to check.

DOWNSTAIRS ON MY way out, I spotted the mailman pushing his silly saddle-bagged cart toward my building. I hung back for a second and watched as the old men filtered into the lobby to watch the mailman fill up the hundreds of boxes lining the wall opposite the elevators. There was nothing sad or desperate in their eyes. It wasn't a Depression bread line and most of them had long ago given up the fantasy of the mailman as a messenger of their deliverance. No one was waiting for his million-dollar check. It was just a boyhood habit, revisited, perhaps, in the service during mail call, rediscovered in old age. Sometimes I liked staying with the old men, but not today. My million-dollar check would have to wait.

Rodriguez was at the desk of the Six-O precinct when I limped in. Although I'd been moved out of the Six-O for years before my forced retirement, my apartment building still fell within its patrol area.

"*¿Que pasa, viejo?*" I rapped my cane on the floor.

"Old man, pffff." He waved dismissively. "Who you calling old man? I bet your knee ain't the only thing on you that limps."

He asked someone I didn't recognize to take over for him for a few minutes while we got a cup of coffee. We spent some time catching up, bullshitting about the guys we'd worked with. I asked about his family. He asked about Rico and that cute sister of mine. Eventually we got down to business.

"You guessed right," he whispered. "The call about your car came directly here, to the desk, not through 911. Same thing next door." Rodriguez pointed to the firehouse which adjoined the precinct. "They got a call. Then the 911 calls came in through channels."

"Anonymous?"

"You know it, but I did like you asked and talked to the guys who handled the calls. Male voice, probably Caucasian, flat, unemotional—"

"—and unrecorded," I finished the thought. "Smart boy. Thanks, old man." I hugged him. "I owe you one."

"You owe me two. So what's the story here? You know who torched your car?"

"Maybe, but I hope I'm wrong."

I shook his hand and got out of there before he started asking questions I didn't want to answer.

THE BUFFALO ROADHOUSE was on 7th Avenue in the Village. In spite of the moniker, barbequed ribs and pecan pie was as country as the place got. The waitresses didn't wear Stetsons or lizard-skin boots and anyone who said shucks or howdy got the cold shoulder. Mike, the steady night bartender, was famous for knowing more trivia than any man alive.

"Second largest city in Upper Volta?" I asked as I came through the door.

"Bobo-Dioulasso. The capital's Ouagadougou," he rattled off. "Next time ask me a tough one, Prager."

"Okay, when are you going to get a life?"

"He said tough, not impossible, mister," the hostess winked, scolding me loudly enough for the barman to hear.

"Screw ya both," Mike shot back.

I spotted Katy at a corner table toward the rear and whispered an order for a bottle of Chianti Classico into the hostess's ear. Fruity, accessible, versatile and a good value, Aaron had tried to school me. No matter how old a man gets, it still makes him smile to think he's done something, even a very small thing, that would please his big brother. But by the time I got to Katy all the glow and good humor had run out of me.

Now all the awkwardness that had seemed so endearing during our first kiss just seemed awkward. She smiled. I didn't. I knelt down. She stood up. I went for her cheek. She offered me her lips. I said hello. She said nothing. Some of the thickness of the atmosphere was her fault. Some was mine. Still, as uncomfortable as it was, being near her made my heart race. That was a good thing, no matter what.

"About Sunday, Moe, I'm—" she started to say when the waitress came with the wine. I think both of us appreciated the interruption. Prepared speeches never quite work out the way you plan. After two glasses, Katy looked ready to start again.

"What, no notes?" I teased.

"Oh, God," she exhaled for what seemed a minute, "I was a real jerk."

"Sunday? Yeah, you were, but I forgive you."

"Fuck you." She smiled in spite of herself.

I stood up, walked around the table and kissed her hard on the mouth. Sitting back down, I asked her if what happened Sunday afternoon was, as I assumed, about guilt. Mostly, she said, but it was also about fear. There'd been men, too many, she thought, since her divorce. But there was an ocean of difference between being with and being close to a man.

We ordered dinner: salad and ribs. Eating ribs on a second date takes nerve. It's difficult to look suave gnawing on dead pig bones and licking red goo off your fingers. And scraping sinew out from between your teeth always drives 'em wild. I avoided dropping any bombshells while we ate, choosing instead to discuss Friday night at Pooty's. I repeated Pete's admonition about not attending and we speculated about what goodies Jack was out procuring. We agreed it wouldn't be a Springsteen album.

"Okay," she said, putting down her Irish coffee, "let's hear it."

I didn't play games. I told her about the threat, about how the arsonist had been careful not to leave a voice trail behind. She asked what I expected her to ask.

"Any enemies from the job?" I repeated the end of her question. "First thing I thought of, first thing any cop would think of. I swear, Katy, I sat at my kitchen table for hours going over every arrest I could remember. Did I ever really piss somebody off, you know, beyond the usual? I mean, deserving or not, nobody likes getting arrested. Hell, nobody likes getting a speeding ticket even when you catch 'em breaking the sound barrier."

"Well . . ."

"Sure I pissed people off," I admitted. "But in nearly ten years on the job, I never had a civilian complaint filed against me. I never took out my weapon in anger. For the life of me, I can't remember anybody threatening to get me. I mean, come on, this isn't an Agatha Christie novel where the cop, judge, prosecutor and jurors get it one by one. And yes, before you ask, there were some crazies. Did one just happen to take a special disliking to me? Maybe, but the guy on the phone didn't sound crazy."

Facetiously, she asked: "What do crazy people sound like?"

"Not like this guy," I said. "He sounded serious, not crazy."

We went round and round like that for a little while longer. Could it have been a jealous boyfriend or husband of an ex-girlfriend? No. A relative? No, I'd be more apt to blow up one of their cars. A practical joke gone wrong? No. Did somebody owe me or did I owe somebody money? No. An old grudge from another cop or someone else I might've worked with? Maybe, but unlikely. A vendetta from the old neighborhood? No. And with that line of questioning out of the way, the easy part of the evening's program had drawn to a close.

"Listen, Katy, I've gone over it until my head wants to explode, but the only thing I can think of is that someone doesn't want me out looking for your brother."

But instead of taking the next logical step, the only step I saw she could take, she fooled me. Smiling like she'd just stumbled over Judge Crater's body, Katy said: "You're right. You interviewed people, the people in Patrick's dorm, for instance. You spoke with Theresa Hickey the day you spoke to me. I'm sure there are lots of others. Maybe you said the wrong thing to one of them, stepped on the wrong toes or hit a nerve. It's not impossible that you came across some information that one of these people don't want you to have."

I hated admitting it to myself, but she had a point. Theresa Not-Hickey-No-More's cop husband couldn't have been thrilled with the nasty turn my interview with his hairdressing wife had taken. And Theresa had sent me to speak to Tina "Tits" Martell. If what Tina had told me about her sexual liaison with Theresa's husband and his buddy was true, I could see where he wouldn't want me nosing around in his business. As a cop, he'd have no trouble finding me. He'd know not to call the fire in through 911. I wouldn't recognize him, never mind his voice over the phone. Maybe Tina's biker friends didn't like my attitude. I didn't know many bikers in a meaningful way, but I didn't figure they all spent their afternoons watching soap operas.

As I was opening my mouth to give Katy my grudging respect for her conclusions, she went and strengthened her case.

"The other night," she said, "you mentioned Patrick having a new girlfriend. Moe, I'll be honest with you, Patrick and me, we didn't exactly swap love stories. We aren't close like that, so I don't know about the girls he's dated. But what . . ."

Katy's mouth kept moving, but her words no longer registered. Nancy Lustig's story was ringing in my ears. If Nancy'd broken down, confessing the truth of what had come between her and Patrick to her folks and told them that I too knew the facts, I could understand the Lustig's desire for me to keep my mouth shut. To what extent they would go to insure that goal, I couldn't say, but they had money, lots of money. And in some sense, that's all I needed to know. Unfortunately, Katy was not so easily satisfied.

". . . and my left breast speaks Mandarin Chinese," I thought I heard her say. Then she snapped her fingers. "Ground control to Major Tom. Earth to Moses. Hello, anybody home?"

"I'm sorry."

"You didn't hear a word I said. What were you thinking about?"

Katy wasn't the only one who could pull a rabbit out of a hat. It was my turn to surprise her. Instead of lying or making excuses, I answered her question. Like I said, I didn't lie, but I didn't tell the whole truth either. If Enzo Sica's sighting was just smoke and Patrick really was a lonely corpse somewhere, waiting for the winter thaw to wash up on a local beach, I couldn't risk the whole truth. To hear me tell it, Patrick and Nancy liked each other very much. At first, maybe, she more than him. Later on, that would change. Oh, he was still Beauty to her Beast, but they had discussed a future together. She got pregnant. She lost the baby. They were both devastated. There was a screaming fight and a messy breakup. Club Caligula? Never heard of it. The essentials were left intact if not unscathed.

"That's so sad. God . . ." is what Katy said before excusing herself from the table.

I'm not sure why I told her about Nancy. Did I hope the story would shake Katy up a little, elicit some response that would aim me in the right direction? Maybe. But it was just as likely out of frustration, because in a very real way it seemed to me I knew Patrick better than his own sister. I kept remembering how Francis Maloney had referred to his son as the boy. I wondered if the Maloneys had been so wounded and distant before Francis Jr. died.

"You okay?" I asked as Katy returned to the table.

"In the bathroom I was thinking . . ." she trailed off.

"About what?"

"About tonight, about our phone conversation today. And—" she stopped herself. "It's just . . . I don't know."

"Say it Katy," I urged, "I promise not to crumble."

"You thought it was my dad, didn't you? That's what the ominous warning was about when we talked on the phone."

"Yeah, I did think it was your dad, but now I don't know. And I'm not just saying that. I mean I was never sure. I couldn't help but think it was weird how right after Mr. Sica came forward, your dad cut me loose. I didn't know what to think. Maybe he's pissed off about the two of us. But now you got me thinking. There's a lot of other candidates I never even considered till now. Don't be mad, please."

"I'm not." She sounded like she meant it.

"But there's one thing if it's not your dad. You could be in danger."

"I'll take the risk," she said. "Take me home. I want to introduce you to my bed."

SHE HAD ONLY stopped laughing at me when we turned off West Broadway onto Prince Street. For some reason Katy found it hysterically funny I'd rented almost exactly the same car that had been torched. She was unmoved by my claim that renting another '76 Fury was my way of giving the arsonist the cosmic finger.

"Cut it out," I barked, brushing a loving hand across the dashboard. "It took me hours to find a place that rented these beauties. I nearly had to settle for a Pacer."

"Why don't I have trouble believing you?" she said, wiping tears out of the corners of her eyes. "Where'd you get it, Loan-a-Lemon?"

"What can I say? They were fresh out of Jaguars. You know, it's not like the insurance company gives you a big budget for a rental."

I parked up the block from her flat. She lived on Greene Street in a loft over an antiques shop that catered to the design trade. The shop pawned off art deco and art nouveau appliances as objects d'art. Only in New York could you make a mint selling old curvy toasters, broken radios and cigarette lighters. Somehow I didn't see it as a viable business venture in Baton Rouge or Ulan Bator.

"They sell some artwork, too," Katy argued in the shop's defense.

Now it was my turn to be unmoved.

As she removed the keys from her bag, someone shouted: "Katy! Katy Maloney. Over here!"

"Oh shit!" Katy whispered, as we turned to look across the street. "It's Kosta. He dates my roommate, Misty."

"Misty! What, you live with a topless dancer?"

"Actress."

"Come on, get over here," Kosta insisted. "Misty got the commercial. We're celebrating."

"Do you mind?" Katy asked.

"Maybe a little." I kissed her. "But I've always wanted to meet a Misty."

It turned out to be pretty much fun. Kosta was a darkly handsome guy from an unpronounceable town in western New York. He worked sound boards for rock bands and was between tours. Misty was young, about twenty-two, blond, smoked French cigarettes and would've weighed a hundred pounds in wet football gear. She was a lingerie model by trade, but an actress by passion. She had just landed her first paying part.

"I'm the whiny teenage daughter in a cereal ad," Misty announced, fluttering her eyelashes. "I get to say: 'Aw come on, dad, do I have to?' It ain't Shakespeare, but it's a start."

And with that, she proceeded to down the three shots of tequila lined up on the bar.

When the conversation turned to me, Katy answered: "He's a traveling tuna salesman."

Kosta and Misty took it in stride. This was New York; why not?

"How'd you hurt the leg?" Kosta was curious.

Following Katy's lead, I said: "Breaking up a fight between a yellow fin and an albacore. Nasty fish, tuna."

Leaving the bar after a few rounds of handshakes and kisses, I could feel myself falling more deeply for Katy. I was attracted to her looks from the second I saw her. After the first time we had a conversation, when I was up in Dutchess County, I knew I liked her. Having kissed her, and held her, having woken up with her flavor on my mouth, there was no question of physical chemistry. But her sly, unexpected sense of humor was incredibly alluring.

When we crossed back over the street to Katy's loft, a man stepped out of a doorway shadow. He asked: "Hey, Mac, you got the time?"

I don't know what it was exactly, his Harry Lime entrance or his tone of voice, but I got the distinct impression he couldn't've cared less about the time. My cop brain screamed: "He wants you to look down at your watch so you can't see what's coming."

Holstered beneath a blazer and overcoat, my short-barreled .38 was as much use to me as sharp edges on a bowling ball.

"Sorry," I shrugged, "no watch."

I sensed someone coming up behind me. I dropped my cane. Instinctively, I pushed Katy away and screamed for her to run. I leaned forward to try a shoulder roll. Anything, I thought, to buy time so I could get at my gun. Too slow. A pair of crushing hands pulled me back up straight. By chance, my right hand dropped into my coat pocket. My fingers latched onto the half roll of quarters that had gone unused the other night at Pooty's.

Now the hands that had pulled me upright were snaking around my arms, rendering my upper torso immobile. My right hand yanked so fiercely out of my pocket, I nearly dropped the half roll of quarters.

"You don't listen so good, do ya?" a voice I recognized from the phone whispered in my ear. "You were told the next time it wouldn't be your car."

And with that, Harry Lime buried a fist into my ribs. The wind went out of me so hard I nearly coughed up a lung. Even though Iron Hands hadn't relaxed his grip, the power of the other man's punch doubled me over. I'd lost sight of Katy. Where was she? Had they—

Something whooshed in the air behind me. A sharp crack, as if two pieces of oak had been slapped violently together, echoed through the SoHo streets. The arms bracing mine went utterly limp. Free, my right arm shot straight ahead, blindly, to where I hoped an unsuspecting jaw would be waiting. Whatever I hit made a sickening dull sound. Someone moaned. Something crumbled at my feet. I dropped to one knee, tossed the quarters and reached under my coat and jacket. But by the time I got my .38 unholstered, the man who had held me was holding a standard issue police special in his hand. His face was partially obscured by shadow. His gun hand, however, was perfectly visible.

"Even if you get the first shot off, I'll blow a hole in her before I go down," he warned through what sounded like clenched teeth.

Suddenly I was aware of Katy's hard breathing. She must have been standing fairly close by, over my left shoulder, toward the gutter.

"Pick your trash up off the street and get the fuck outta here," I snarled.

"First, back off, across the street, you and her."

Standing slowly, the pain in my ribs almost made me crash down, but I managed to step back and brace myself on Katy's shoulder. Anticipating my question, she whispered that she was all right.

"One thing:" I shouted in retreat, "tell your boss I know who he is and that I'll be paying him a call real soon."

On the opposite sidewalk, I tried to watch the gunman load his accomplice into a car parked almost directly in front of Katy's door. It was no good, pain was making a disinterested party of me. As they pulled off, Katy said she'd gotten most of the plate number.

"Good," I said, wincing as I spoke. "Write it down for me."

"Don't you want me to give it to the police?"

"We're not calling the cops," I insisted. "This is my business to take care of."

I could see in her expression she wasn't happy, but she was a bright woman. She knew I meant what I said.

"Okay," Katy relented. "Let's get you to the emergency room."

To show her how silly her idea was, I stood straight up. "I'm fine."

"Look at your hand," she screamed. "You're cut."

Only then did I notice my right fist was wet with blood. I didn't have much time to inspect the damage before the sidewalks of SoHo started spinning out from beneath my feet. I couldn't hold my footing and went down in a heap. When my side connected with the pavement, even my hair screamed in pain. I could feel Katy fishing around in my pockets for the car keys. She told me not to move. I didn't. I couldn't. I must have closed my eyes.

Katy, Kosta and Misty were mostly asleep when I walked from the treatment area into the waiting room. The news was all good. My ribs were bruised, not broken, and the blood on my hand hadn't been mine. Apparently, I'd broken the man's nose, not his jaw. Bruised ribs for a broken nose; I'd gotten the better of the deal. With every breath, my ribs begged to differ.

Checking my watch, I offered to treat them all to breakfast, but even I thought it was a stupid idea. We piled into my rented car and, stubborn fool that I am, I insisted on driving. The plan was for me to drop them off before heading home. I was two for two in stupid ideas. After the first time I turned the wheel, Katy drove.

At Katy's front door, Kosta took the wheel. He knew a cheap place to park the car until I was up and around. I wasn't in any position to argue. As Katy walked me from the car to the door, I first realized my cane was missing.

"Where's my cane?"

"In the trunk of the car in two pieces," she said. "I hit that guy over the back of the head with it."

"Like I said before, tough Catholic girls drive me crazy."

But by the time we made it up the steps, all I wanted to do was eat a handful of pain pills and go to sleep.

February 13th, 1978

I COULD ACTUALLY move without much pain, but I wasn't itching to practice my golf swing. I'd pretty much spent the previous day in bed. Katy couldn't join me. She had to go to work. Misty played nursemaid to me in spite of nursing her own hangover. Kosta went down to a medical supply store and bought me an adjustable metal cane. At first I was puzzled by the extent of their tender loving care, but when Katy got home she cleared up my confusion. In the ER, while I was getting my ribs tended to, Katy had fed them a line of bullshit about me saving her from two muggers. In her version, I broke one mugger's nose with a lightening right jab before dispatching the other with my cane. I was their hero for a day and in too much pain to set Misty and Kosta straight.

When Katy got home, she seemed pretty glum. Of course she was worn out by lack of sleep, but there was more to it than that. Yes, she said when we were alone, she was worried about me, about the attack, about when they'd try again. That wasn't it either. She had spoken to her father and things at home were deteriorating. Her mom, so encouraged by the sighting in Hoboken, was devastated by the lack of progress.

"It was like losing him all over again," Katy sighed. "And then it brings up all the heartache over losing Francis Jr. I don't know how much more of this she can take."

I told her to get her ass on home. Her mom needed her more than I did. Bruised ribs, I said, would heal in time. There was only one cure for what her mom was suffering from. I told her I'd be fine and that I didn't think whoever was behind the rough stuff would try again. My fingers were crossed the whole time.

"As long as you get back for the party tomorrow night, I want you to go back home," I half joked. It seemed to me the party would feel empty without her. Strangely, it was lovely to feel that way.

I treated for takeout pizza—Ray's Famous—beer and strawberry rhubarb pie for dessert. That was another thing you had to love about the city. You could get fresh fruit pie in the middle of February. Kosta and Misty went back to Kosta's apartment to spend the night, as much to give Katy and me some space as anything else. We used the time for gentle kisses, tears and sleep.

When I woke up in the loft, I had no one to tell about my vastly improved ribs. Kosta and Misty had not yet returned and Katy had already returned to Dutchess County. The shower felt great until I reached too quickly for the soap. Okay, so I wasn't quite ready to enter a twist marathon, but the pain was only short-lived. Katy left me a note with a partial license plate number, the location of my car and promising she'd meet me at Pooty's tomorrow night come hell or high water. On the flip side I wrote a note thanking Misty and Kosta for their help and inviting them to Pooty's Friday night.

THE LAST THING I wanted to do when I got back to my apartment was sprint to a ringing phone, but I did it anyway. Tossing my mail on the couch, I made it to the phone in record time.

"Yeah," I picked up.

A voice I wasn't sure I recognized wanted to know: "Where've you been, man? I been calling for two days." When I responded with silence, he said: "It's Nicky. You know, Nicky from Dirt—"

"Shit, I'm sorry, Nicky. I'm a little out of it. What's up?"

"I think I got a line on your boy."

"You know where he—"

"Easy, easy," Nicky tempered my enthusiasm. "One of my doormen got something to say to you. I think maybe you should listen."

"Put him on. Put him on!" I could feel my palms sweating.

"No, he wants to talk to you in person, in private. There's issues here besides Katy's brother. Okay?"

When I questioned Nicky about what those issues might be, he got stubbornly quiet. It wasn't up to him, he said. I complained about having just gotten back from the city. He was sympathetic, but unyielding.

"Look, Moe," said the little aristocrat, "it ain't up to me."

"You think this guy's leveling with you or trying to pick up some meal money?"

"I wouldn'ta called you if I thought he was full of shit," Nicky sounded hurt.

"No offense," I said. "It's just that at this stage of the game, false hope might be worse than no hope at all. If you catch my meaning."

"I understand, but to be on the safe side maybe you shouldn't let Katy in on the deal till you hear what's what."

I agreed that was a good idea. He told me to come to Dirt Lounge after 4:00 P.M. His man would be waiting. Though I figured he'd never be able to get a Friday night off, I invited Nicky to Pooty's as a gesture of thanks. I was right, but he seemed pleased I'd asked.

I switched ears and dialed Rico's office.

"Hey buddy, where ya been?"

"What's that, the question of the day?" I asked.

"I mean I been tryin' to get ya for days. Sully wantsa talk to ya. He tried to call and when he couldn't get ya, he asked me to try."

"What's he want?"

"A date. How the fuck should I know?" Rico bellowed in my ear. "Call him."

"Yeah," I said, "when I get a chance. Listen, I need you to run a partial tag number for me."

"This a lead on Patrick?" he perked up.

"You know I'm not working that case anymore, remember? You're the one who handed me my pink slip. You got a pencil?"

I'm not sure he believed me. I gave him the tag number as Katy remembered it and described the car as best I could—though, given the amount of pain I was in at the time—I wasn't sure my best was very good. He was pessimistic about getting me a quick answer and once again reminded me to call Sully. I began to invite him to Pooty's, but the words stuck in my throat. I thought his presence might be an unwelcome reminder to Katy about how this whole mess got started in the first place. That's what I told myself, anyway.

I looked at the mail sitting on the couch and decided my million-dollar check could wait a little while longer. My ribs were insisting that I find the closest bed and make good use of it.

The phone was ringing in my dream before it rang next to my bed. It was Nicky wondering where I was. Not in the dream; I forgot that the second I opened my eyes. I looked at the clock next to my bed. It was nearly 5:00. I was late. I apologized and promised to get to Dirt Lounge before 6:00.

I kept my word with twenty minutes to spare. Other than 1:00 A.M., rush hour's about the only good time to drive into Manhattan from Brooklyn. The bulk of traffic is headed in the opposite direction.

Nicky greeted me at the door and ushered me upstairs to the office. I immediately recognized the big guy seated at the desk as the doorman Nicky had referred to as Bear the night Katy and I had first visited Dirt Lounge. Bear was sucking furiously on an unfiltered Camel, drawing the smoke in so hard I didn't see how the tobacco stayed in its wrapper. The ashtray in front of him was littered with cigarette butts he'd apparently handled in the same rough fashion. Between puffs, he'd rinse his mouth with Budweiser.

"You want a beer?" Nicky asked me, as he gestured for me to sit behind the desk.

"Beck's, if you—"

"This is Dirt lounge, Moe. You want Beck's, go to Bavaria."

"Bud it is."

Bear nodded that he'd like one, too.

When Nicky left, Bear stood, reached across the desk and offered me a huge hand. It would be a lie to say I took it. His hand sort of swallowed mine, munched on it some and spit it back.

"Nicky says he talked to his cousin Tony about you and that I can trust you," Bear fairly whispered. "That's important, that I can trust you."

"And Nicky says I should trust you. So now that we've got that out of the way, maybe we can get down to business."

Bear looked hurt. "This isn't business. Nicky explained about how this kid's family is going crazy. That was his sister here with you the other night, right?"

"Yeah. Look, Bear, why don't you give me what you got and we can sort out our feelings later. So, do you know where Patrick is?"

Nicky picked that moment to walk in with the beers. Bear lit up another Camel and said: "No."

I slapped the desk. "So what the—"

"Hear the man out, Moe," Nicky pleaded. "This ain't easy for him."

"I work at another club," Bear said, clearing his throat nervously. "It's a different kinda club." He looked at me as if he expected me to catch his drift, so he wouldn't have to explain further. But I didn't catch on.

"It's on the West Side, Moe," Nicky interpreted for me, "the West Village."

"Holy shit!" I slapped my thick head instead of the desk. "A gay club."

And in a dizzying rush, the puzzle with mismatching pieces nearly put itself together. I had the right uniform—short hair, earrings, tattoos—but the wrong team.

"SBNF's on West Street, north of the Ramrod," Bear said.

"SBNF?" I puzzled.

"Seafood, But No Fish," the big man explained. "Sailors, but no women."

"Cute," I said, tipping my beer to him. "So you've seen Patrick there?"

"Two or three times, a few months ago."

"How many months? What month?"

"October, I think. November. Maybe both."

"But definitely not December?" I asked, hoping he was wrong.

"Not December."

I stood to leave. "Thanks, Bear. You cleared some stuff up for me. Maybe now I can understand why he split in the first place. But if you haven't seen him since November, it doesn't really—"

"My cousin Tony was right about you, Moe," Nicky chided. "You are an impatient fuck."

I sat back down. "Sorry. There's more?"

"He, Patrick wasn't alone when I saw him," Bear continued. "He was with the same guy every time. They weren't buddies out trawling, if you know what I mean. They were a couple, I think. The thing about it is, I saw that guy, the guy he was with, in here Sunday night."

"This last Sunday?"

"This one just past, yeah," Bear said.

"Alone? Was he by himself?" I wondered.

"Without Patrick, you mean? Yeah, he was alone." Bear frowned. "But I was thinking that if you could track down this other guy, maybe he could lead you back to Patrick."

"That's good thinking, Bear," I complimented. "I'm sorry I was such a schmuck before."

Bear gave me a detailed description of the man he had seen at both clubs: white, five foot seven or eight, honey brown eyes, short brown hair, mid-twenties to thirty, thin, maybe one hundred and sixty pounds, thin brows, full lips, crooked mouth, angular nose, sharp chin, strong jaw line.

"Sexy more than handsome," Bear thought, "if you liked that type. A little edgy, I mean. But he's no New Yorker by birth. He thanked me here and at SBNF when I let him through the door. He had kinda a white-bread voice."

If only the cops could get descriptions like this on a regular basis, I laughed to myself, the crime rate would plummet. Manhunts are tough in a city of four million men, but we wouldn't have to weed through all four million. Blacks were out, the Spanish and Orientals, too. And though not all gay men lived in the West Village or in Manhattan, for that matter, I thought it was a safe bet to focus on the Village. I told Bear I might try to have him work with a sketch artist. Before he could balk at the idea, I swore he wouldn't have to repeat any of what he just told me.

"Just the description," I vowed.

He agreed. I thanked him for his help and tried, as diplomatically as I could, to offer him some compensation for his trouble.

"Don't ask me that again!" He screwed his face up into a raging mask. Then, just as quickly, unmasked himself, winking at me before heading downstairs.

"That's why he works the door," Nicky said. "Would you fuck with him if he made that face at you?"

"He did and I wouldn't."

Once again Nicky asked that I keep Bear's part in this just between the three of us. "He's in a motorcycle gang and he doesn't think some of his brother members would appreciate—"

"I understand."

But did I? Sure I understood about not betraying Bear's trust. But I don't think I understood anything about men like Bear or Jack, if what Pete Parson said about him was true, or Patrick. What could I know about the men who sought comfort at SBNF? Unlike some of my brother cops, I never saw homosexuals as the enemy. I never saw any group as the enemy. Maybe I never saw them as anything at all. No, that's not right. I guess I viewed them like some people view the Amish, except you didn't have to go to Pennsylvania. All you had to do was cross west over 6th Avenue to eavesdrop on their "quaint" customs and "odd" manner of dress. And how was I supposed to reconcile what Patrick had done with Tina Martell and to Nancy Lustig?

I asked Nicky if I could use the phone. He nodded that I could, apologized again about not being able to come to Pooty's and left.

"What you got for me?" I asked Rico when he got on the phone.

"Good afternoon to you, too. Did ya call Sully?"

"Yeah," I lied again, "but he was out. So . . ."

"You got a pen and a long sheet a paper?"

"You can throw out any tags registered to persons with addresses north of Orange, Putnam and Dutchess Counties, okay?"

"Ya'll still need a long sheet," he cautioned.

We were on the phone a good ten minutes. Though Rico recited the names and addresses I wanted to hear within the first two minutes after he began the list, I copied down all twenty-six names and addresses. I couldn't afford to tip my hand—not to Rico, not to anyone. I rushed Rico off the phone and looked at the digital clock on Nicky's desk. I don't know why I bothered. It was already too late when I arrived at Dirt Lounge to do the cross-checking I now needed to do. Tomorrow couldn't come soon enough.

I got Miriam on the phone and invited her to tomorrow's party. It happened that Ronnie would be off from work, but she was iffy about their attendance: "I don't know, Moses. Ronnie's always so drained when he gets home from the hospital."

"Come on, you guys love dancing. And there's . . ." I drifted off purposefully.

"There's what?"

"There's someone I want you to meet."

She tried prying the details out of me, but I steadfastly refused. I wasn't the only pathologically curious member of the Prager family.

"We'll be there," she promised, "even if I have to give him intravenous caffeine."

The nature of my call to Aaron was less innocent. Sure he'd help me buy a few bottles of wine as gifts. He didn't ask why or for whom. I was just to come on over. Not overtly inquisitive or overly analytical to begin with, marriage and fatherhood had further blunted his curiosity. Aaron's talent was single-mindedness. He could focus his attention so fiercely, so intently, on something—the wine shop, for example—that distractions were never an issue.

I've admired him for that since we were kids. There's no doubt in my mind that if Aaron and I had flip-flopped careers, he would have made detective first grade in spite of the obstacles. And instead of being area manager for a major pharmaceutical company, I'd still be going from doctor's office to doctor's office doling out samples and promotional golf balls.

When I got downstairs at Dirt Lounge, neither Nicky nor Bear were anywhere to be found. I guess I was glad for that.

AS I WALKED through the front door, Aaron handed me a glass of red wine. Having been thoroughly schooled by my big brother, I swirled the wine in the glass, checked its legs, its nose, admired its bouquet and sucked air into my mouth as I swished the fermented grape juice around my cheeks and over my tongue. I felt a pop quiz coming on.

"Well?" he demanded.

"Peppery with hints of black and raspberries. A zinfandel?"

"Bravo," Aaron bowed slightly, kissed me on the cheek.

"We'll make a sommelier out of you yet."

"Watch your language around the kids."

But the kids were out with Cindy buying shoes for impending spring. I drove halfway across Brooklyn to Cobble Hill, where, Aaron claimed, the only decent wine store in the borough did business. During the trip, Aaron caught me up on family matters. I invited Cindy and Aaron to Pooty's. Even when I mentioned my desire for him to meet my date, Aaron's response was to the point: "No babysitter."

I wanted one good bottle of red, two good bottles of champagne and one top shelf champagne. Aaron thought I was nuts. It was going to cost me a small fortune. Of course he wasn't exactly a disinterested party. Every dollar I spent at this shop was less money toward the down payment on a shop of our own. When he saw he wasn't going to talk me out of it, he went about his task with his usual fervor.

"So," he said as I pulled on the Brooklyn-Queens Expressway, "what is it you wanna talk to me about?"

He knew me, my big brother Aaron.

"Let's say I found out something really bad about Daddy. Would you wanna know?"

"Daddy's dead. Why would I wanna know?"

"What if he wasn't?" I kept on. "What if you found out he was a bank robber or a con man?"

"It wouldn't matter if he was a murderer," Aaron said calmly. "I wouldn't wanna know. He would still be my Dad. I don't think you can deconstruct love, little brother. And if I knew, I think it would hurt me more than him. The conflict would be mine, not his."

That was the most intuitive thing I think I ever heard my brother say. It took me a moment to catch my breath.

"What if it was Miriam?" I wondered. "What if I found out she was using heroin or cheating on Ronnie? Would you want me to tell you?"

"That's different," he said. "I'd kick your ass if you didn't tell me."

"Why?"

"Because I'd wanna know," he barked. "It's just different with brothers and sisters than with parents."

"Why?"

"Because it is." So much for intuitive answers.

"Thanks," I said.

"For what?"

"For confusing the shit out of me."

I dropped him off and headed home.

For once, the phone wasn't ringing when I got in. I placed the box with the wine on the table and tossed today's mail atop yesterday's pile. Looking down at my metal cane, I resolved to replace it before the party. You had to love my brother Aaron, he hadn't even noticed. Like I said, his attentions were focused elsewhere.

February 14th, 1978

ONLY WHEN I sat opening my mail over morning coffee did I realize it was Valentine's Day. There were all sorts of discount coupons from florists, restaurants and candy stores mixed in amongst the bills and notices. I hadn't gotten halfway through the pile when the phone rang.

"Sully, geez, I meant to get back to you," I yawned, "but you know how things get."

"I'm surprised I haven't heard from ya," he said like it was a coded message, "if ya know what I mean."

"I don't," I said plainly enough. "Should I?"

"That's okay," he assured me. "Better to play it this way."

"If you say so."

"Just wanted to let ya know, there's a reporter gonna call ya in the next few days. He's doin' a big piece on the Maloney kid's disappearance. Feel free to give him anything ya got, anything at all."

I repeated my favorite phrase: "If you say so."

"Okay then. Take it light."

I didn't bother asking why, of all the investigators searching for Patrick Maloney, a case only Katy and I knew I was still working, I had been selected to talk to the reporter. It was clearer now than ever I was being played, that I was to be a conduit through which certain information was supposed to flow. What that information was, I still hadn't a clue. Frankly, I was a little too preoccupied to care. After I made sense of what was really going on with Patrick, maybe then I'd care. Maybe then I'd stop to feel the hurt of being used by the man I considered my closest friend. Sully? What did I care about Sully? He was a bigger stooge than me, a stranger. Betrayal isn't something a stranger can do, but Rico was almost blood.

Thinking I needed some professional help to sort through what I'd learned in the past twenty-four hours, I put in a call to Dr. Friar at Hofstra.

"She's unavailable at the moment," the receptionist informed me as I ran a finger under the tab of a large brown envelope with no return address. "If you leave your name and number I can have her get back to you."

"Moe Prager, that's P-r-a-g-e-r. Just tell the doctor I'm Nancy Lustig's friend. My phone number is (212) 332-85 . . ." I grew silent studying the contents of the brown envelope. It appeared to be a photocopy of Francis Maloney's NYPD personnel file and a redacted copy of an old Internal Affairs report. That's what it appeared to be. What, in fact, it was, was the answer to another part of the puzzle. All at once I understood my bruised ribs and Sully's cryptic banter. I understood my role as a conduit and the lines I had been set up to parrot to the reporter. I might've understood it all a lot sooner had I been more conscientious about opening my mail.

"Mr. Prager," the receptionist lost patience, "can you please repeat your—"

Without apology, I finished giving her my number.

I could taste the coffee turning sour in my mouth. No, it was me that was turning sour, not the coffee. I went into the shower and stayed there until I felt like cream would no longer curdle in my hand.

ARMED WITH MY spiffy new cane, I limped heavily into the offices of the Patrolmen's Benevolent Association. I made nice with Sondra, the woman who greeted me there, flirting, showing her my union card and purposely complaining about my wounded knee. It was a horribly manipulative way to act and maybe I didn't have to lie to her about the ricochet my kneecap had taken when I threw my body over the little girl's, but it put Sondra in the frame of mind to help me and help is what I needed. I had neither the time nor patience for the usual bureaucratic bullshit.

She demanded I take a seat. And when, with great empathy, she uttered the phrase: "What can I do to help you?" I knew no red tape would stick to me today.

"When I got on the job there was an old-timer who taught me the ropes. Now that I'm retired I wanted to return the favor and throw him a big party, you know?"

"Oh that's so sweet."

"Anyway," I feigned embarrassment, "I've gotten most of the names and addresses of the guys who were on the job with him. But these three guys . . ." I handed her a paper with the names and addresses. "These three guys, I'm having trouble confirming their addresses. Now I don't wanna cause you any trouble, but—"

"No trouble at all," Sondra assured me. "I'll be right back."

I'd see soon enough whether Katy's memory and Rico's information were any good. I didn't like the frown on Sondra's face when she returned.

"I'm so sorry, but we have no record of these two," she said, pointing at two of the names. "Maybe there's been a mistake. I can always double-check. But the address you have for Philip Roscoe is correct; 1287 Clay Pitts Road, Janus, NY 1—"

"Thank you so much, Sondra. Phil is really the man I was looking for. The other two weren't as important."

Standing too quickly, I winced in genuine pain. I didn't see what it would accomplish to tell Sondra it was actually my ribs that hurt. My twisted expression simply lent an air of authenticity to my half-truths.

DR. FRIAR RETURNED my call while I was back home resting up for the party. She expressed pleasure at receiving my message and seemed eager to help. She admitted to being somewhat haunted by our previous conversation. Had I any luck in locating the hypothetical construct who walked the perfect square? Her question made for a seamless segue. I explained I was very confused, and added the latest details.

"Your confusion is perfectly understandable," Dr. Friar laughed at the internal contradiction of her words. "This is 1978, Mr. Prager. Modern psychology is less than a hundred years old. Many of my colleagues will tell you it's half as old as that. In either case, it's in its infancy. And though we've made monumental strides in some areas, fully comprehending the scope of human sexuality is a daunting task. Human sexuality by its very nature is confusing and because of the complex balance between its genetic and environmental components, I'm not certain how far we will come in deciphering its code.

"You are confused because a man who is apparently homosexual has, in the recent past, at least, successfully consummated heterosexual intercourse. This is not as unusual as you might think, Mr. Prager. Though a vast majority of homosexual men and, to a lesser but not insignificant degree, lesbians, claim to have known from an early age that they had a same-sex orientation, society frequently forces them to experiment with heterosexuality. We must never underestimate the power of societal forces brought to bear when considering human sexuality.

"Maybe someday there will be a more gender-neutral orientation in our society, but as it stands today, almost every societal institution positively reinforces the heterosexual model while either ignoring altogether or actively condemning the homosexual one. Everyone from your mom and dad to your clergyman to your teacher to your friends work, either consciously or unconsciously, to protect and reinforce societal norms. There's nothing sinister or overtly conspiratorial about it. It's how societies function. Has anyone in your family married outside of his or her race or religion?"

I said: "My cousin Arty wound up marrying a Puerto Rican woman from the Bronx who refused to convert."

"And what was your family's reaction, Mr. Prager?"

"My aunt and uncle sat *shiva*. They treated his marriage like a death in the family. He was dead to them."

"Can you imagine what their reaction would have been if your cousin had brought a man home?"

"I don't know," I joked. "If he was Jewish . . ."

"Jewish or not," Dr. Friar pointed out, "no grandchildren. Although there is a lot of ignorance and mean-spiritedness wrapped up in the enforcement of taboos, there is an underlying, if often distasteful or irrational, logic to it. It is uncomfortable enough for people when they feel different in purely innocent ways: their hair is red when the other kids have brown or black hair. Their hair is curly. They have freckled skin. Can you possibly imagine the torment a young boy or girl must suffer when he or she has a same-sex orientation?"

"I guess I can."

"Then is it really any wonder to you why this man was pushed to try on heterosexuality for size? Can you understand why he wanted the girls to keep the babies and marry him?"

"To get the world off his back," I said, "and maybe try to convince himself he really was straight."

"Very good, Mr. Prager. While some homosexuals have the tools and wherewithal to simply come out and present themselves to the world as they know inside they are, some live secretive, closeted lives. Others still, fight a desperate battle, trying to live, quote unquote, conventional lives. You might be surprised at how many homosexual men have wives, children, two cats, a dog and a house in the suburbs."

As Dr. Friar uttered those words, Nancy Lustig's voice rang in my ears. Patrick, she had said, seemed to have a script, a blueprint that included a wife, children and a split ranch.

"Of course," the psychologist continued, "there are always hints and signs that all is not as it seems on the surface. Often, the charade cannot last. The internal pressures cause cracks and—"

"Doc, if I recall our first conversation correctly, you said obsessive-compulsive neurosis is basically a reaction to profound anxiety and that sometimes sexuality and issues of self-esteem are the root causes of the—"

"If only my students paid such careful attention," she interrupted. "Now I must warn you I am loath to make diagnoses over the phone and without careful considerations of the individual dynamics, but it would not be inconsistent for someone facing the conflicts you've described to exhibit obsessive-compulsive symptoms."

"Thanks, Doc."

"You're welcome, Mr. Prager. I've got to caution you, the coming out process can be a very delicate period in a person's life. Issues of sexuality are volatile and the pressures great. If you should cross this man's path, remember what the labels read on shipping cartons containing antique china."

"Fragile," I said. "Handle with care."

She wished me luck. And in spite of being sorely tempted, she regretted having to take a pass on my invitation to Pooty's.

PETE PARSON HID Katy's roses in his office along with the gift-wrapped bottles of wine I'd purchased with my brother the day before. Pete's partners, the ex-hippies from his old neighborhood, cleaned up real good. One guy, the one that looked like a baked potato with hair, wore enough gold jewelry to finance a small revolution. The other, clearly the numbers man, looked like a mortician. Both, however, were genuinely thankful for my help. They had a lot of cash sunk into the place and were only too glad to throw this little party in my honor. But every time I looked over at the undertaker I could almost hear him thinking: "We shoulda given the guy a fucking watch and been done with it. We're losing a fortune!"

Believe me, I was tempted to tell him Katy was Patrick Maloney's sister. Somehow I don't think he would have appreciated the irony, Katy having introduced her younger brother to the charms of Pooty's in the first place. But since Katy and I had carefully neglected to share that information with anyone at Pooty's to this point, I resisted the impulse. Why spoil everybody's fun? Someday, when this whole mess was behind us, we might be able to laugh about it over a drink.

When I first arrived I found myself strangely disappointed at not seeing Jack behind the bar. In his stead was some burly bearded guy who looked like an escapee from Henry's Hog. I asked after Jack and Pete Parson assured me: "Don't worry, your boyfriend'll be here later. He's home putting cute pink ribbons on all your gifts." Pete also asked if it was all right that he had had Jack invite some of the regulars. I didn't mind and since it was a moot question to begin with, I was magnanimous as hell.

Miriam and Ronnie got there at ten on the nose. That was Dr. Ronnie's doing. He was a good guy. He was a sweet, caring man who loved the air my sister breathed, but he was so earnest it could make you nauseous. If the party was scheduled for ten, ten is when he got there. The concept of tasteful lateness was lost on my brother-in-law. Miriam, with her long sable hair and fierce green eyes, looked stunning but tired. So I could have Miriam to myself for a few minutes, I made sure to introduce Ronnie as Dr. Stern to the assembled crowd. Within thirty seconds, Pete Parson's wife was chewing Ronnie's ear off about her painful ulna nerve.

"That was cruel," Miriam admonished, smiling and punching my arm.

"Don't worry, I'll rescue him in a few minutes."

Over a glass of champagne we discussed the usual things brothers and sisters talk about. Yes, she was tired. Yes, she was looking forward to the end of Ronnie's internship. Yes, she was sick of his hours and of being poor. Yes, our niece and nephews were the prettiest, most handsome, smartest, most gifted children God had ever created. Yes, Aaron's wife Cindy still made her crazy. Yes, she remembered Daddy's memorial candle. Omitting certain details, I talked about how I'd gotten involved with Patrick Maloney and how this party came to be.

"How is Rico, that foxy old friend of yours?" Miriam's bad girl persona came out of hiding.

"Very married." Her attraction to Rico had always made me uncomfortable. Now it was up a few notches from just uncomfortable.

Miriam moved on, "So where's this person you—"

"Coming through the door," I said. "Listen, Mir, her name is Katy. Go over and introduce yourself. I've got to get something from downstairs."

Bringing the bouquet of roses back upstairs, I wondered if springing my sister on Katy like that had been a good idea. Miriam could be a little overprotective and jealous where her big brothers were involved. After ten years in the family, Cindy had yet to gain Miriam's full blessing.

Visions of Katy and Miriam involved in a bloody saloon brawl gave me pause. But listening at the top of the stairs, I heard only music, chatter and laughter, no bar stools breaking. Someone had pumped quarters into the jukebox.

With "Mony Mony" blasting, Ronnie was dancing the Pony with Pete's wife. Apparently her ulna nerve wasn't terminal. At the bar Katy and Miriam were giggling like little girls. When they saw me, they tried very hard but unsuccessfully to stop themselves. I think maybe I would have preferred a brawl.

"Marry this woman," Miriam suggested, pushing Katy forward. "She thinks my stories are funny." I didn't want to know what embarrassing childhood story Miriam had shared and was careful not to ask.

I handed Katy the roses: "These are for you. Happy Valen—"

She covered my mouth with hers, swallowing my words. "I missed you, Moe."

"Uh oh!" Miriam wagged her finger. "He's got it bad, Katy. I've never seen him look at a woman like he looks at you. I think I'm going to steal my husband back and see if he still looks at me that way."

Before Miriam could get away, Pete Parson bunched us together for a picture. I think both Katy and Miriam made donkey ears behind my head.

"Never mind my sister," I said, swatting Miriam on the behind as she walked toward Ronnie. "She's a pain."

"I like her," Katy said. "She's devoted to you, you know."

The burly barman poured us two champagnes. We toasted the day and found a booth so we could talk. Her mom was better, if you considered numb preferable to distraught. Her father, however, was starting to show signs of wear. He was quick-tempered, impatient and loud. He was never a screamer, Katy said, but we always knew he meant business.

"He even yelled at my mother. He never yells at my mother."

I kept my mouth shut, though I knew exactly why Katy's old man was beginning to lose it. I wasn't going to ruin our first Valentine's Day together. Without any specifics, I told her I thought I might finally be making some progress on locating Patrick.

"I don't know what it is exactly," I said. "Optimism isn't usually my forte. I think you might have something to do with that."

Pete manned the door, taking snapshots of everyone who entered. Some of the regulars shuffled in. Next came Misty and Kosta. Ronnie was a little drunk by then. He kept telling me he thought Misty was awfully cute. If my sister hadn't said the same thing about Kosta, I might've gotten pissed off at my brother-in-law. The introductions seemed endless and by the time Jack strolled in, we all just gave up.

Neither Katy nor I could believe our eyes when we saw our new buddy Jack. He had eschewed his loose black turtleneck, painter's pants and earth shoes for an impeccably tailored, blue, pin-striped business suit, white shirt, red silk tie and black wingtips. But before we could comment, my brother Aaron walked through the door. Something was wrong. I could see Ronnie and Miriam had the same reaction.

"Will you guys calm down?" he whispered sternly. "Everything's fine. Cindy told me I should come. She said I should be here for you."

"But it's Valentine's Day," Miriam scolded.

"You'll see," Aaron predicted. "After ten years of marriage and two kids, Valentine's Day loses a little of its ambiance. Besides, Cindy already got her roses. We had dinner and the kids are asleep."

To ease the tension or maybe because he was drunk, Ronnie asked what wine they had shared for dinner.

"We didn't have wine."

"You didn't have wine?" Miriam was incredulous. "You always have wine with—"

"What's going on here?" I too was suspicious. "Are you and Cindy fighting?"

Aaron couldn't hold it in: "Ronnie, wasn't it you who told me pregnant women shouldn't—"

Miriam started: "You son of a—"

"*Mazel tov!*" I shouted. "I'm gonna be an uncle again."

Now it was a party. I don't know what it is exactly, but news of a coming birth elicits this sort of joyous tribal response. Despite our big brains and layers of denial, humans are not so far removed from timber wolves or lions or ring-tailed lemurs. Complete strangers were hugging Aaron, shaking his hand, trying to give cash donations towards baby furniture. Even the undertaker smiled. Pete Parson's wife began listing boys' and girls' names she thought Aaron should consider. I didn't have the heart to tell her it was traditional for Jews to name their children after the respected dead.

Miriam, struck by the emotion of the moment, confessed to me she had always resented Cindy for taking Aaron away from home.

I hugged her and whispered: "Listen, Mir, it says on her death certificate that cancer killed Mom. But it wasn't cancer, it was resentment. It'll eat you up. Don't let it."

"It was pretty generous of Cindy to make Aaron come tonight," Miriam said as much to herself as to me. "I'll try, Moses."

After a round or two of toasts, someone pulled the jukebox plug. Pete handed the camera over to the bartender. There were a few speeches by the partners: Pete, Mr. Potato Head and the money man. I had saved them from financial ruin and I was the best thing to come down the pike since the rotary engine. I kept watching Katy's face. I think it was killing her not to confess her heritage and unwitting role in all of this, but mainly she rolled her eyes and looked contrite.

Next, Jack took center stage. For the uninitiated, he recounted the night of the Bruce Springsteen marathon and how, after Katy and I had already left, he threatened to shoot anyone in the bar who was either from New Jersey or even considered playing Springsteen or Southside Johnny. After the laughter died down, the presentation of gifts began. Jack went to the front door and made a sign to someone waiting outside. A man walked in carrying what appeared to be a round, gift-wrapped tabletop. Placing that against the bar, he went out and returned with several smaller, but no less beautifully wrapped, gift boxes. Jack tipped him a five-dollar bill.

When the front door was relocked, Jack called Katy and me up to where he was standing.

He pointed to the tabletop and asked that we both undo the wrapping. I don't know where he got it, but it was a giant vinyl facsimile of Bruce Springsteen's *Born to Run.* Pete Parson nearly keeled over with laughter. The other boxes contained his and hers Rutgers sweatshirts, I Love New Jersey key chains and Garden State vanity license plates. One of the plates read: "THE BOSS." The other read: "IS GOD." Funny, I thought Eric Clapton was. The final package contained a complete set of ABBA albums. The barman posed Jack and me as bookends around Katy, the three of us displaying the gag gifts.

The laughter having died down some, Pete Parson wheeled in a strawberry shortcake covered in red jelly hearts. He made Katy and me go through the cake-cutting thing.

Miriam shouted out: "Just do it. It's good practice."

Someone plugged the juke back in and we were serenaded by Frank Sinatra singing "The Summer Wind" while we ate our cake. Pete Parson called me and Katy over behind the bar.

"I just wanted to say thanks again. My partners could afford to lose this place, but not me. To get my stake, I borrowed from relatives against my pension. When the shit hit the fan, I thought I'd end up as one a those guys that cleans the seats for ya at Shea Stadium. Here," he said, shoving a big gift-wrapped box into my hands, "take this and open it up later when ya get home, okay?"

I agreed.

By 2:00 most everyone was gone. Miriam, Ronnie and I had sent Aaron packing at midnight. How dare he, we kidded, abandon his pregnant wife at home on Valentine's Day? Before leaving, Aaron pulled me aside to tell me how much he liked Katy and how well we seemed to fit together.

"Katy, huh?" He raised his brow. "Not too many Jewish girls named Katy. Listen, I just want you to know that if she makes you happy, being with her is the right thing."

Unless you know my brother, I don't think you can appreciate how difficult it was for him to utter those words. In his awkward way, he was actually trying to play matchmaker. When I hugged him a little too long for his comfort, Aaron pointed at Katy. "Her, putz, not me!"

Miriam and Ronnie left around 1:00. Misty and Kosta nearly followed them out the door, but I asked Katy to stall them until I could retrieve their gift from Pete's office. The champagne, I told them, was a token of my appreciation for their help.

"If it was up to me, I wouldn't've gotten you a thing," I winked, "but my sore ribs insisted."

"Champagne!" Kosta feigned surprise. "Tuna salesmen must make a nice living."

Pete's partners and their escorts had long since headed home, taking Pete's wife with them. At 1:45, Pete gave last call to the inevitable stragglers. Katy, having hours ago changed into her Rutgers sweatshirt, was half drunk and mostly asleep at one of the booths. After Pete and Jack carried the last "guest" out the front door, Pete handed the bartender $75 cash and bid him a good night.

I went back downstairs and returned with two more gift bottles. Pete's was a bottle of champagne much like the one I'd given to Misty and Kosta. We did the usual It's-not-necessary-but-I-insist cha-cha. It was a stupid dance because we both knew he was going to keep the damn champagne. But rituals are like that, I guess. Pete excused himself. He had to change clothes. Sneering at Jack, he said: "Somebody's gotta clean this place up."

When Pete turned his back, Jack gave him the finger. Jack loosened his tie, peeled off his suit jacket and ducked down behind the bar. When his resurfaced, he showed me a bottle of what looked like scotch.

"You like good scotch?" he asked knowingly and poured a dram for the both of us. "It's a single malt, Cragganmore. Very unusual flavor."

"Cheers!" We clinked glasses.

Jack knew his stuff. The scotch was smooth as polished ice and smelled of heather and highland peat. We shared one more Cragganmore before doing taste comparisons with every other scotch in the joint.

In my pre-hangover haze, I asked: "What was with the suit tonight?"

"I felt like dressing down," he joked. "No, I just get tired of the playwright uniform, the angry young man thing. Besides, I just got this shirt as a gift," he said, tugging at the gold cufflinks, "and wanted to let the world see it."

"It's a great shirt, classic. Here, this is for you," I handed Jack his bottle of '68 French cabernet.

"This is awfully generous of you," Jack's voice cracked slightly. "Why?"

"Pete told me you were in charge of buying the gifts, so I figured it was only right to get you something. Also, I think it's a way of apologizing. The first two times we met, I pretty much thought you were an asshole. You know, just too cool. But now Katy and I agree, you're a good man. And even if you're not, you're pretty fucking funny."

Shaking my hand and nodding at Katy, Jack wondered: "How's she holding up?"

"Holding up?" I puzzled, the alcohol starting to take its toll.

"With her brother missing and all. How's she—"

"Oh, sorry, sorry. I'm sorta out of it. Katy's all right, I think. She's pretty tough. But her family's losing it."

"Thanks for the passes you left me," he quickly changed subjects, as Katy shifted in the booth. "Visiting Dirt Lounge is like visiting Disneyland or Auschwitz; everybody should do it at least once."

I recounted for him Katy's experiences in the Dirt Lounge bathroom. Jack offered a final toast in her honor. In spite of what he'd said about only darkening its door once, I assured Jack I could probably get him as many passes to Dirt Lounge as he wanted. I took his long-winded response to mean: Thanks, but no thanks.

Katy was stirring to consciousness. I thanked Jack again, excused myself and headed down to the office to bid Pete Parson farewell. He was dead asleep in his chair. Rather than trying to rouse him, I wrote him a note.

"Pete's sleeping," I informed Jack as I reemerged from the basement.

Jack told me he'd take care of it. There was a cot and bedding downstairs. Given Pete's alcohol intake, Jack and I agreed it was probably best he not drive back to Long Island tonight. I took my own advice, packing the semiconscious Katy and our gifts into a cab.

I left her to sleep in the cab while I hauled everything upstairs to her loft. When I shook her shoulder that it was time to come with me, she whispered "Happy Valentine's Day" and kissed me softly. "I love you, Moe."

At that, my heart should have soared. Drunk or not, she had mouthed the words I'd secretly hoped to someday hear her say. Yet in spite of her proclamation of love, in spite of Aaron's joyous news, in spite of the party, the gifts, in spite of it all, my heart was anchored to the street. What it was exactly that robbed me of my pleasure, I could not say. The swirl of the alcohol left me unsure of my footing.

February 15th, 1978

I HAD DONE it. I found him. He was somewhere just beyond this door, sitting at the kitchen table with a cup of coffee in his hand or maybe still in bed, his lover's arms wrapped protectively around him. Brought into the case not to find Patrick, but to play the fool, I'd accomplished what all the Sullys in the world stacked end to end and all the high-priced talent had failed to do. Today I could hold my head up high, for though the city bureaucracy and a misplaced piece of carbon paper had reduced me to a lame ex-patrolman, I felt I'd earned the gold shield I would never have the opportunity to carry. Why then, after my finger touched the bell, did my heart fill with regret? Why did I want to run and not look back, ever?

I can't point to the moment it hit me. There was no bolt of lightning, no epiphany. Somewhere in my fitful drunken sleep, the random lines and incomplete trails had woven themselves into a road map. I simply woke up knowing all I needed to do was take a last few steps.

Katy was still heavy with sleep when I crept out of her bed. My head ached, my breath and sweat stank of scotch. I hesitated at the foot of the bed, listening for ambient sounds that might let me know whether Misty and Kosta were also still asleep, if in the loft at all. I did not want to explain myself to anyone until I had proof of what I believed to be the truth. In Manhattan it's impossible to hear nothing unless you're stone deaf. Even then, I'm not so sure. But after a minute or so, I decided either Misty and Kosta were still out of it or over at Kosta's place. I showered as quietly as I could. Figuring she had an emergency set, I borrowed Katy's house keys before I left.

From a pay phone on Hudson Street I dialed Pooty's number. I let it ring ten times before hanging up. I repeated the process, hoping I'd dialed the wrong number on my first try. On the eighth ring, someone picked up. Well, they didn't really pick up, they sort of dropped the phone on the floor. I waited.

"Christ, Louise, I'll be home in a few hours." Pete Parson's voice was thick with sleep and alcohol.

"It's not Louise, Pete," I said. "It's me, Moe Prager. I'm down the block from you at a pay phone. Do me a favor, go upstairs and let me in. I'll explain when I get there."

I hung up and walked half a block to the bar. I had maybe a minute to whip up a bowl of bullshit Pete would swallow like blueberries and cream.

"Hey, I'm really sorry about this," I begged his pardon, "but it couldn't wait."

"It's 7:30 in the freakin' A.M. What couldn't wait?"

"Can I have the film from your camera?" I asked, handing him a cup of black coffee.

"Thanks, I need this. My head feels like lead. So," he said, going around the bar to get some milk and sugar, "why's the film so important ya hadda interrupt my hangover?"

"There's this picture you took last night of Katy that I thought maybe I could get a rush job on . . ."

"Yeah, yeah, yeah, whatever. Just lemme finish this coffee and I'll go downstairs and—"

"I'll do it," I said. "I'll be right back up."

"Suit yourself."

After a quick peek around and with film in hand, I was back up in the bar within two minutes. I thanked Pete again for the party and for being so understanding about the film. I vowed to make a set of copies for him.

"Ya know," he called to me as I headed out the door, "I ain't been off the job so long that I can't smell bullshit when I step in it. Whatever ya want with that film is okay with me, but I just want ya to know I'm not fooled."

I didn't bother trying to defend my lie: "Sorry, Pete. You're right, I should've just asked."

Calling from the same phone on Hudson Street, it took me almost half an hour to find a photographer willing to develop the film. Desperation and the Yellow Pages came through in the end. Along with actors, dancers, writers, painters and musicians, there are plenty of starving photographers living in Manhattan. The problem was finding one desperate enough to do darkroom duty at 8:00 A.M. Saturday.

His studio/apartment was on Hester Street on the Lower East Side. Getting up to his rooms was an adventure in urine and broken syringes. Julio greeted me at the door with a joint in his hand. I politely turned down his offer to share. There was a pale skeleton of a girl passed out on his living room floor. With a pair of striped pajamas and a yellow star, she would have cast well in any concentration camp role.

Julio put his hand out for the film. I delivered it to him wrapped in two twenties and a ten.

"That's two sets," I reminded him, "and a proof sheet."

For another ten bucks, he let me have unlimited use of his phone. I wonder if Julio would have upped the ante if he knew I was going to call Florida? Tony the Pony Palone was just as surprised, but less grumpy, about my call than Pete Parson had earlier been. We talked old times, my retirement and discussed his bourgeoning construction business there in Fort Lauderdale. He offered me a job.

"You can't trust these Bible-bangin' yahoos down here. They quote scripture to you and rob you blind. I need to import a New York Jew. There's plenty of 'em here already, but they're all like a hundred and fifty years old. You know what I mean? Forget about it."

I told him I'd think about it—which I did for a second—and mentioned that his cousin Nicky and I were becoming friendly. He knew that, he said, Nicky had called him about me. Unfortunately, I said, I only had Nicky's number at work. This was no good because I got a sudden request for passes to his place tonight and couldn't reach him. Tony came through with Nicky's home number. Tony took my number down and promised to call. I hung up thinking I'd probably never hear from him or him from me again.

I didn't wake Nicky up because Nicky hadn't yet been to sleep. He was happy to hear from me, but turned sour when he found out it was really Bear I was looking for. He loosened back up when I told him I'd just spoken to his big cousin Tony. We talked about the party at Pooty's for a bit and he begged me to come in again soon. Like Tony, Nicky didn't trust the people he had chosen to surround himself with. He too wanted an old neighborhood type around.

"You can work security. I'll pay you cash."

Frankly, it was a more tempting offer than Tony's and when I told him I'd consider it, I meant it. But in the meantime I needed Bear's address and/or phone number. He gave me both. I promised to see him soon and to kiss Katy for him. The whole time I was on the phone, skeleton girl hadn't moved. I was about to check her pulse when Julio reappeared.

Handing me the pictures, he seemed surprised, almost wary. Apparently he was taken aback by their rather innocuous subject matter. I suppose he was more accustomed to bare breasts and rubber lingerie. Private porn and divorce work was more than likely his bread and butter. When I surveyed the photos, I understood his desperate conditions. He did shitty work, but the pictures I needed were clear enough and he gave me back the negatives. I thanked him out of habit.

"Anytime," he said hopefully.

Somehow I didn't think so.

I decided against calling Bear. The motorcycle club where he crashed wasn't too far from my final destination. I dropped the negatives off at a real photo lab on the way.

"I'm coming," he shouted through the door, his heavy footfalls registering as he approached.

"Hey Bear," I greeted him warmly.

Panic looked almost comical on his big brooding face. "What do you want? What are you doing—"

I shoved two pictures at him: "Is this the man you saw with Patrick at SBNF and stag at Dirt Lounge?"

"That's him. Look, you gotta get outta—"

"Can you remember whether he paid his way in," I continued, "or if he used a guest—"

"Guest pass," Bear answered distractedly. "He definitely used a pass. Is that all?"

"I think so, yeah."

He slammed the door shut before I could thank him.

It had taken less than ten minutes for me to walk from Bear's clubhouse door to where I now stood. I didn't have to ring a second time.

"I've been waiting for you all night," Jack said, pulling back the door. "I suppose you had better come on in."

He directed me toward a small kitchen table and poured me a cup of coffee.

I demanded to know: "Is Patrick here?"

Jack nodded at a closed bedroom door. "In there."

"Come on, open up and let me speak to him. Let's get this over with."

"He asked me to speak to you for him. What will it cost you to hear me out?"

"How do I know you're not stalling for him? He could be headed down the fire escape or already be halfway to God-knows-where by now. How do I know he's even in there?"

"Because I give you my word." He extended his right hand. "Do I have yours?"

I shook his hand that he did indeed have my word. He sat down across from me and poured coffee for himself. He lit a Marlboro.

"Oh, how rude," he said. "Do you mind?"

"Go ahead."

"What was it? How'd you know?" he wondered. "It was that I asked how Katy was holding up, wasn't it? God, I knew it the second I asked."

"No, not necessarily. I was pretty drunk when you asked after Katy. I'll admit to being confused by your question because Katy and I had been real careful to not mention her last name or connection to Patrick. But it had been a long night. Everybody was tired and drunk. I couldn't be sure one of us hadn't let something slip. I figured maybe one of the regulars knew Katy."

"What was it then?"

"A lot of things," I said. "The shirt, for one."

Jack was confused. "The shirt? I don't under—"

"When Patrick was spotted in Hoboken, there was a second witness."

"But the papers didn't say anything about a second witness."

"It never made the papers," I explained. "They dismissed it as unreliable info. I guess no one figured he'd be out buying dress shirts."

Jack smiled sadly. "It is a beautiful shirt."

It was more than the shirt. Without referring to Bear by name or description, I detailed how I had hit upon a source who'd spotted Patrick with a companion at SBNF. The source had also spotted Patrick's companion at Dirt Lounge. I reminded Jack that he was the one who'd brought up his visit to Dirt Lounge.

"It was right after I asked about Katy," he remembered. "I was trying to change subjects so you wouldn't dwell on my faux pas. I didn't know I was just digging myself in deeper."

I tried letting him off the hook: "Like with the shirt, you couldn't have known. It wasn't one thing, Jack. It was a lot of little coincidences that added up in my sleep. And even though I woke up knowing, all the *ifs* broke my way and against you."

If Pete hadn't taken pictures last night . . . If Pete had gone home instead of sleeping it off at Pooty's . . . If I'd failed to get a rush job on the developing . . . If my source wasn't home or was out of town and couldn't identify Jack as the man he saw with Patrick and again at Dirt Lounge . . .

Had any of the *ifs* gone against me, I offered, it could have been days or even weeks before I could confirm Jack's connection to Patrick.

He laughed, "I suppose that should make me feel better."

"That's up to you, I guess."

"I guess."

I downed my coffee in one swallow. "So now you know how I got here, but . . ."

"You want to know about Patrick and me."

"You could say I'm a little curious, yeah."

He tamped his cigarette out in a crowded ashtray, lit himself a new one and braced himself with coffee. But caffeine and nicotine weren't doing the trick. Jack's yellowed fingers still shook terribly. "I don't know where to start."

I suggested he begin with Tina Martell.

Jack looked surprised and impressed all at once. None of the other investigators had even mentioned her name. But when he hesitated, what Jack saw on my face was impatience. "A lot of us have our first sexual experiences with women," he said, confirming Dr. Friar's information. "For me the experience was so antithetical to my being that it allowed me to finally confront my gayness and accept it eventually. But we all grow up in different worlds, Mr.— What should I call you?"

"Moe is good."

"While in our bones, Moe, people like Patrick and me and the man who saw us together at SBNF might have a very similar sense of ourselves sexually: we are unique, as distinctive from each other as, let's say, you and me."

"Individual dynamics. Yeah, Jack, I've already heard this lecture," the impatience crept from my face into my voice. "I want details, not paperback psychology, okay? Because, if you don't give them to me, so help me God, I'll march into that room and drive him up to Dutchess County at gunpoint."

"Patrick," Jack continued, "has been struggling since he was a kid to deny his sexuality. I did the same thing. But high school makes it almost impossible. Dances, class trips, proms, everything about high school forces you to deal with who you are, especially the stuff you hate about yourself. In his senior year, Patrick found himself profoundly attracted to another man, his art instructor. That was difficult enough to handle, but when the teacher made advances toward Patrick, Patrick freaked out."

"So what's this got to do with Tina Martell?"

"Patrick wasn't stupid," Jack explained. "He knew he was good-looking and he knew about Tina's appetite for co—for boys. For Patrick, she was the path of least resistance."

"She was easy."

But unlike Jack's dreadful encounter with the opposite sex, Patrick's didn't force him to deal honestly with his sexuality. Instead of seeing Tina as a tramp, Patrick saw her as vulnerable, someone he could manipulate. Naively, Patrick believed he could trade on his looks and respectability to exorcize his demons. Tina Martell would become his girlfriend and marry him eventually. Though he was a little vague on the mechanics of it, Patrick convinced himself he would transform her while she was transforming him. And when she got pregnant, he thought his plan was working out better than expected.

"Silly notion, but it just shows you how desperately inexperienced he was," Jack said, staring mournfully at the bedroom door. "I guess you know that Tina wasn't interested in playing house and had—"

"—an abortion. Yeah, I know."

"You see, unlike Patrick, she knew what she wanted and what she wanted didn't include Patrick and a baby and a mortgage. She probably didn't even like him very much."

"I don't think she likes anybody very much," I said, "including herself."

Jack agreed about Tina. Most gay men, he thought, having gone through that experience with Tina, might have just chucked the whole transformation fantasy and gotten on with their real lives.

"You know, it's like the denial our parents go through. When I told my father I was gay, he was eerily calm about it: 'You just haven't met the right girl,' he said. 'That's all. Come on, we'll go into Cincinnati and catch a Reds game.' My mom was the same way."

His attempt at transformation having failed, yet still unwilling to accept himself, Patrick was in a bad place. That's when, according to Jack, the obsessive-compulsive behaviors started. The disease progressed just the way Dr. Friar had described it to me. When I asked Jack about walking the perfect square, he was again surprised and impressed.

"Patrick says his symptoms abated somewhat his freshman year at college. He immersed himself in schoolwork and student government. He tried to be social, woefully unprepared as he was. But even the best camouflage breaks down under prolonged scrutiny. He couldn't suppress his attraction to other men forever. The strain of his attractions started getting to him and by his sophomore year, the symptoms were worse. He began to withdraw. I guess he panicked."

"That's panic, spelled N-a-n-c-y-L-u-s-t-i-g."

Jack shook his head in resignation. "It was Tina Martell all over again. But there were cracks in his fantasy this time, even early on. He started seeing a therapist at school, a Dr. Blum."

"I didn't know that," I confessed.

"You mean there's something you didn't know?" Jack feigned shock. "Anyway, it was while Patrick was seeing Nancy that we met. Katy brought him in a few times. Of course, I didn't know who Katy was then. I can't say what it was exactly, but I was drawn to him. He's god-awful handsome, but that wasn't it. Maybe I'm just a sucker for wounded men. I don't know."

"He talked about his . . . um, his—"

"God, no," Jack laughed. "But one knows. Blacks can spot a light-skinned brother or sister trying to pass as white. I spotted him. That's all."

Jack said he cultivated a grudging friendship with Patrick, being careful never to discuss his own gayness. Soon, Patrick began to frequent Pooty's without Katy. And when he did, Jack would play the patient bartender, listening to Patrick's complaints about his unfriendly roommates and his relationship with Nancy. Then at the end of March or in early April, something changed.

"He started coming in a lot, a few times a week," Jack said. "I didn't think it was the beer or the jukebox. It's quite a haul from Hofstra to the city and back again. He cut his hair short and flirted with me a bit."

Just as Bear's revelation about SBNF had hit me, I was floored again: "Holy shit! Caligula's! There was a couple that—Nancy ran. He stayed. You mean he . . . he let—"

Jack confirmed what I hadn't finished saying. "For Patrick it was the perfect setting to finally take the—to experiment. Being there with Nancy was like work for Patrick, a chore. When she ran home, it was like being given a day off. He was free of her. Have you ever been to a sex club?"

"Like Caligula's? No."

"I don't prefer them myself," Jack was quick to say, "but the atmosphere inside them can be quite intoxicating."

"That's weird," I said.

"What is?"

"Nancy Lustig said something like that to me. She said it was amazing inside Caligula's; raw and sweet and dangerous."

"So after years of trying to hold himself back, Patrick finally let go. I think the fact that there was an approving female presence made it easier for Patrick. And the anonymity of it helped. No one knew who he was. No one cared about how much political clout his old man had or felt sorry about Francis Jr. getting shot down. With no audience to play to, he . . . well . . ."

"I think I can understand."

"One night with an anonymous man at a club didn't transform him any more than humping Tina in the back seat or forcing himself on Nancy in her dorm room had. It was the beginning of an arduous journey. Patrick being Patrick, though, he retreated into his old fantasy. Now, as symbols go, Nancy took on mythic importance. The part of Patrick that stubbornly refused to acknowledge his gayness invested everything it had into poor Nancy. And if she hadn't become pregnant," Jack supposed, "the entire charade would have collapsed under its own weight."

I pointed to the bedroom. "Did your boyfriend tell you what he did when she turned down his marriage proposal? How he dislocated her—"

"Can't you understand what he was going through?" Jack pleaded defensively. "Years of denial and self-recrimination and false hopes came crashing down all at once. You can't believe he meant to hurt her."

"I don't know Patrick," I said. "I know of him. Even now with him ten feet away from me on the other side of a door, he exists to me only in other people's words. He's a handsome face on ten thousand posters. That's it. He's as much a myth to me as Nancy was to him. If he wants forgiveness, tell him to go to confession."

"I'm sorry," Jack apologized. "I love him. He's very real to me."

"Fair enough."

"After she had the abortion," Jack went on, "Patrick turned to me for help. But it wasn't magic. He wasn't ready to come out to his family and his symptoms had almost taken on a life of their own. Even as he became more comfortable with himself, he couldn't seem to get past the tics."

Just then I noticed a small, framed illustration of what looked to be a Chinese character with a red rose running through it. The long stem of the rose was skillfully woven through the black strokes which conspired to create the character. I recognized the PMM in one corner.

"Do you like it?" Jack, happy to break the tension, was eager to know.

"Very much. I think I recognize it, but I'm not sure where from."

He rolled up the right sleeve on his now very wrinkled white shirt to reveal a replica of the illustration tattooed on his forearm. Patrick, he said, had one just like it. He didn't know what the character translated into in English, but they liked to think it meant forever.

"The rose was Patrick's doing. It's woven in there like that to show that love is part of the fabric of eternity. That's what I like to think it means. Patrick says it's just a rose."

"You were telling me about his symptoms."

According to Jack, Patrick had stopped seeing Dr. Blum months before his crisis with Nancy. Even during the time he saw the shrink, Patrick made little progress. And, as far as the obsessive-compulsive problems, talking therapy alone didn't really seem to be of much use. Jack did some research and found a psychologist at Mount Sinai who had had some success treating obsessive-compulsive neurosis using an integrated program of behavior modification, drugs and traditional therapy.

Patrick took a few summer school classes at the New School to justify his being in the city. He scheduled his therapy sessions around his classes.

"Sounds expensive," I commented.

"I had some savings and the tips at Pooty's are good."

"Is the treatment helping?"

Jack lit another Marlboro. "Not miraculously. It's like peeling the skin off an onion one thin layer at a time. Don't misunderstand, there's been a lot of improvement and some of the intensity of the behaviors has quieted down. But it's not as if

Patrick's conquered it. It's more like he's made a working agreement with the disease."

"Then I'm confused. I guess I can understand everything up to a point. But if what you're saying is true, then why the disappearing act? He must know what he's putting his family through. Does he know how many people from his home town bus into the city every goddamned day chasing his ghost around?"

"He knows, Moe."

"Then why all this?"

Jack said: "You're asking the wrong man."

"But you won't let me talk to—"

"Not Patrick."

"Who then?"

"His father. Go talk to his father," Jack sneered venomously. "Maybe he can clear up your confusion."

I explained to Jack that I knew a little bit more about Francis Maloney Sr. than he might've expected and that I had my own reasons to want to rip his head off. "But so far, Jack, you haven't given me reason enough to not pass Go and collect my two hundred dollars. Over the years, I put cuffs on a lot of people I had sympathy for."

Jack clamped his hand over my wrist. "Do this one thing for me. Go see that bastard and if you can't understand what drove Patrick to this, come and get him. He won't run. I swear on my life, he won't."

"I'd like to help you, but—"

"Friday." Jack let go of my wrist, shot out of his chair and leaned his head against the bedroom door. "Give us till Friday."

"What happens on Friday?"

"We've talked about it for weeks. Even if you hadn't found us out, we couldn't go on like this much longer. Even in a community that treasures it privacy, you can't keep a secret in perpetuity. It's time to end this madness. Come Friday evening, Patrick'll walk right down the front steps and take a cab to wherever you wish."

I was skeptical. "To Missing Persons?"

Jack did not hesitate: "If that's what you want, I'll deliver him personally."

"What I want is for him to come with me now and get this over with."

"Please, Moe, give us a few more days to get ready. Coming out under the best of circumstances is difficult enough, but he'll have a lot more baggage to deal with than even you're aware of. Please, we've come this far. What's another few days?"

Fragile. Handle with care. Dr. Friar's metaphor about antique china popped into my head. "I must be out of my fucking mind."

Jack embraced me, tears welling in the corners of his eyes. He kissed my cheek.

"Easy, easy!" I panicked slightly, pushing him away. But seeming to understand my discomfort, he smiled at me sympathetically. "I didn't agree to anything yet. I need to know this is what Patrick wants," I said, pointing at the door.

"Oh, he does. He—"

"Not good enough. Patrick," I talked loudly at the raised panel door, ignoring Jack completely, "I need to hear you say you agree to this. Regardless of what happens between now and Friday, I want you to give me your word you'll show up at Katy's loft by 8:00 A.M. Saturday. No bullshit. No excuses. No nothing. Do I have your word?"

His answer came quickly: "Yes."

"Okay," I turned back to Jack. "Gimme his coat."

Jack looked confused. "What do you want his coat for?"

"Insurance. Anyway, from this point on, you don't get to ask questions. I'll keep my part of the bargain. Your secrets are safe until 8:00 Saturday morning. Now just get me the blue parka."

Dutifully, Jack collected Patrick's coat from another room and handed it to me.

"Have you got a pen and paper?" I asked.

"Have I got a pen and paper? I'm a writer, what do you think?"

I wrote down my name, address and phone number twice and ripped two business card-sized pieces off the sheet of lined paper Jack had supplied. "You take one and make sure he gets one. I don't want any surprises. Anything, anything at all comes up before he gets to Katy's, I wanna know about it first. Understand?"

"Understood."

To cover all bases, I asked: "Do you have Katy's number, just in case?"

"I have it."

"All right then," I said, wadding Patrick's blue parka into a ball. "Saturday, not a second late."

Jack walked me down to the street, promising again and again they'd keep their part of the deal. He confessed to being happy this would all soon be over. The pressure was getting to him and he hadn't been able to write a shopping list, let alone dialogue, since

December. I told him if he thanked me again, I'd shoot him on the spot and haul his boyfriend out by his ears.

I walked back past Bear's place to where I'd parked my rented Fury. The clubhouse was the garage area and loading dock of an old Westside warehouse. Motorcycles were lined up outside, parked in token defiance within a loading zone. But there were no signs of life among the big Harleys. I stopped to listen closely. No sounds came to me from behind the corrugated steel garage doors or the black steel door Bear had stood at so nervously an hour before. Clubhouse, I thought, was a stupid description of this place. Clubhouses are for little boys, playing games in secret. . . . Then again, maybe clubhouse was a perfect description.

February 15th, 1978 (after Jack's)

KATY WAS STILL battling her hangover with sleep when I got back to the loft. Now along with my single malt sweat, I smelled of Jack's nervous cigarettes. I showered again. As the soapy water washed the stale scent of smoke, sour highland heather and peat, into the sewers of the city, I prayed for Katy to wake up. I wanted the simple pleasure of her pale, lightly downed skin against mine. But I wanted more than anything to tell Katy her brother was alive. The promises I'd given to Patrick and Jack were already weighing me down. All Katy needed do was kiss me softly and whisper the words, "Where have you been?" and I would have given Patrick up on the spot.

"Come on, Katy, please wake up," I mouthed.

I guess God couldn't hear my prayers for the running water. Katy was stone asleep when I crawled in next to her.

I woke up to the opening music and narration of *Wide World of Sports*: "The thrill of victory. The agony of defeat . . ."

"There's nothing wrong with de feet," I shouted back to the TV. "It's my head that hurts."

"What?" Katy called from the common area of the loft. "You want something to eat?"

Following the sound of the TV, I found Kosta, Misty and Katy sharing the bottle of Veuve Cliquot champagne I'd bought them as a gift.

"Shit, you guys don't waste any time, do you?"

"It's an old Greek tradition," Kosta said, pouring me a glass. "Champagne and *Wide World of Sports*. It's the Olympics thing, it's in our blood."

"Champagne, huh?" I was suspicious. "Not ouzo or retsina?"

Actually, it was the only alcohol in the house and they were trying the hair of the dog remedy. I drank my glassful and joined them around the TV. Katy came and sat close to me on the sofa.

"You okay?" she whispered.

"About the same as everybody else, I guess."

Of course that was a lie. Maybe the biggest one I ever told. Here I was watching the tube, pretending the world was the same as it was yesterday and would be tomorrow, while at the same time withholding information that could rescue Katy and her family from months of anguish. And at what expense, really? Jack and Patrick's anger! I could live with that. I'd lived with worse. But they'd been shrewd. This was about honor now, my honor. It didn't used to mean so much to me. I wondered what had changed to make it so.

We settled in to watch an odd sport from Ireland, hurling or curling or some such thing. It was played on what looked like an American football field, goal posts included, by men carrying broken hockey sticks hitting a rock. It seemed to require blind courage and a hard skull. There were plenty of collisions, a lot of blood and several fights.

"Gotta love the Irish," I laughed, suddenly missing the job very much. "Gotta love 'em."

No one was very hungry, so we skipped dinner. For lack of a better idea, Katy and I opened the box of gifts Pete Parson had given us. The first thing we pulled out of the box was a bottle of Calvados, that inglorious butane substitute from France. Katy and I rolled our eyes. Why had we told him we liked the stuff? It's always the polite lies that come back to haunt you. Next, Katy opened an envelope which contained two tickets for *A Chorus Line* on Broadway.

"Orchestra," Katy exclaimed, clapping her hands with joy, "first row, center."

Misty jumped gracefully onto the coffee table: "Tits and ass," she sang, featuring both.

You didn't have to be drunk as my brother-in-law had been to notice Misty's good looks. There was a second envelope. "From the Partners" was printed neatly across the front.

Inside was a note of thanks. The partners had also arranged for a pre-theater dinner at 21 and post-theater entertainment at the Rainbow Room.

"That's awfully generous," Kosta noted. "You'd think you'd raised them from the dead." The smile ran away from Katy's face.

Kosta had struck a little too close to home. "God, Katy, I'm sorry," he was quick to apologize.

But the damage had been done; Katy was on the verge of tears. I could have killed Kosta. Not because he had hurt Katy's feelings; you can't walk on eggshells too long without having one crack, but because he had unknowingly brought my dilemma to the fore. One sentence and I could wipe all of Katy's tears away.

She recovered quickly enough, gave Kosta a big hug and suggested we get out. We walked up to a coffee house on Bleecker Street and had espressos all around. Afterwards we strolled through Washington Square. The smell of marijuana was intense and not unwelcome. I'd smoked my share in college, baked hash brownies, the usual stuff. And there'd been an occasional party over the years at which I'd taken a hit or two, but I missed the aroma more than the smoke itself. The thing I liked most about grass was its effect on the people around me. I couldn't remember a party where people were getting high that a fight broke out. On the other hand, I could scarcely recall a party at which alcohol was featured that a fight didn't break out. Still, I wondered how many brain cells a kid like Doobie would have left if and when he graduated.

"Man," Kosta made exaggerated sniffing sounds, "you wanna cop a nickel bag?"

Misty said nothing. I thought Katy was going to faint. She stared at me with a puzzled look in her eyes. I kept my mouth shut and excused myself. Katy followed.

"We'll meet you over there." I pointed at an empty spot on the ledge of a fountain. Kosta waved his agreement. Katy wrapped my arm around her. We sat quietly enjoying the tenderness and proximity. But our private time lasted only thirty seconds. When Misty and Kosta found us, Kosta was looking pretty flustered.

"I'm really sorry, Moe," he begged my forgiveness. "I didn't know. You're a cop!"

"I was a cop," I clarified. "There's a big difference."

Alas, the truth was out, I was not a traveling tuna fish salesman. Apparently Katy had previously shared this insight with Misty. Misty, however, had only just relayed this information to her boyfriend. As we walked back to the loft through the park, I used my new cane to point out several people smoking joints within thirty feet of uniformed officers.

"It's just not a big priority, pot smoking. Who knows when, but the cycle will change," I said with great confidence. "In five, ten years maybe, they'll probably arrest you for smoking cigarettes on the street."

Back in the loft we broke down and opened the Calvados. Kosta liked it okay. The rest of us experimented by mixing it with any non-toxic liquid we could find. Nothing helped, but we all got pretty giddy. Misty broke out her script from the cereal commercial and assigned us roles. Kosta was the father. Misty, the mom. Katy was the whiny teenage daughter—the part Misty was to play in the actual ad. Me? I was the obnoxious little brother. We ran through it a couple of times, then switched parts. In the end we gave out our own Oscars for who was best at which part. I won for my role as the little brother. A part, Misty averred, God put me on earth to play.

Noting that almost anything tasted good in coffee, we brewed some up and finished off the apple brandy. It was true, *almost* anything tastes good in coffee. Calvados just happens to be one of the four things on the planet besides motor oil, Passover wine and sauerkraut juice that coffee can't save.

Pulling the bedding onto the floor of the loft, we shut the lights out and watched a movie only Katy had seen before. *Touch of Evil* was a '50s black-and-white flick about a corrupt cop and a Mexican drug prosecutor set in a small Texas border town. Orson Welles directed it and played the drunken, candy bar-eating cop. You had to love Orson Welles. Either there was no budget for makeup or he simply willed himself to be more obese and sloppy than an unshaven whale. I take that back, there was a budget for makeup, but they spent it all trying to make Charleton Heston look Mexican. To me, Heston was an unconvincing Jew, but as a Jew he looked more like the chief rabbi of Israel than a Mexican. Instead he looked like a white basketball player who'd fallen into a vat of sunless tanning lotion. You know, the shit that turns your skin orange.

Janet Leigh, looking a hundred times sexier than she did in *Psycho*, played Heston's wife. She wasn't supposed to be Mexican. Maybe in the original script she was, but they ran out of tanning butter. And in a casting decision almost as bizarre as Heston's, Marlene Dietrich played a raven-haired, chili-cooking prostitute who had once been in love with Welles's cop. Unlike Heston, Dietrich pulled it off. But I'd always been a little in love with Marlene Dietrich.

Somewhere in the middle of the night, Katy pulled herself close to me and we made silent, hungry love. The need for silence made it terribly intense. We were like a runaway engine unable to exhaust its fumes, finally exploding from the buildup of unvented heat. A few minutes later I noticed our silence had inspired Misty and Kosta.

February 16th, 1978

THE COUPLES TOOK turns in the shower. Breakfast, however, was a completely communal affair. I made pancakes. Kosta fried up peppers and eggs. Misty ran out to the bakery for fresh rolls and Katy, covering both halves of her immigrant heritage, cooked a potato frittata. It was wonderful, but I didn't linger. Explaining the week ahead of me would have been difficult even if full disclosure was an option. Given the restrictions I was operating under, it would have been as laughable as the studio head explaining to Welles why Charleton Heston was going to be the best damned six-foot-four Mexican he ever saw. In the end I lied, telling Katy that Aaron and I had to scout possible locations for the wine shop.

Before heading home, I told Misty to break a leg. Her shoot was tomorrow. I made sure Kosta knew I wasn't going to sic the narcs on him and I promised Katy I'd call her every day. "Dinner Wednesday night okay with you?" I asked between kisses.

"Tuesday?"

"Maybe Tuesday," I relented. "Listen, everything's going to be fine. I feel it."

Walking to the car, I absentmindedly fished the pictures from Pooty's out of my coat pocket. A picture of Jack playing emcee was on top of the pile. Without Katy around I felt less guilty about the deal I'd made with Jack and Patrick. In a way, they'd done me a great service by asking for more time. With Patrick's reappearance set for Saturday morning, I could handle the rest of my agenda and not have to look over my shoulder.

JUST AS SULLY had predicted, a reporter called. He asked if we could meet. I told him to come on over. Neatly, but casually dressed, Conrad Beaman was a dark-skinned black man of slender build. He was in his late twenties or early thirties and wore his hair in a mid-sized Afro. I recognized him from his frequent appearances on local Sunday talk shows.

He laughed when I said I knew him from TV. "The token *schwartze*," he said with a perfect accent, using the less-than-flattering Yiddish word for black. "The producers figure I'm a safe bet, like easy-to-chew food for people with dentures. Have you read my stuff in *Gotham* magazine?"

I lied about not having read his work. Every city cop knew Conrad Beaman's writings. A bulldog and fierce defender of New York's minority communities, only a fool would think of him as easy to chew. I was a little offended he thought me such a dope, but I had long-term goals that required I not challenge Beaman for underestimating me. Maybe he was just trying to bait me.

In any case, many of Beaman's investigations had led to significant and long overdue changes in the way the city was governed. He had, for instance, uncovered the shocking conditions at many publicly funded nursing homes. He had exposed building inspectors for approving substandard steel to be used in major skyscrapers. But Conrad Beaman was best known and roundly hated for his relentless attacks on the NYPD. His blistering indictments of the post-Knapp Commission department were legendary. Cops tend to take that sort of thing personally. Beaman's "good deeds be damned" was the company line, even if some of what he wrote about was true.

"Just think of me as your favorite easy-to-chew food," he tried to reassure me as we sat down at the kitchen table.

Beaman buzzed through cigarettes at a rate which made Bear and Jack look like rookie smokers. He tried to lull me into a sense of false security by first talking about me: Where had I grown up? How long was I on the job? How had I hurt my knee? How had I come to be involved in the case? He even pretended to take copious notes during my retelling of Marina Conseco's nightmare. But it was all crap, a reporter's trick. He knew all of this stuff before he ever walked in. Then we talked a little Mets baseball, some Knicks basketball. Then, when he was satisfied that I was half asleep, he started asking about Patrick.

They were routine questions any high school reporter might have asked and I answered them as I'd been taught to answer questions in court. I didn't expound or offer information that wasn't asked for. I didn't speculate or theorize. I gave ambiguous answers about things that hurt my position and was detailed about things that strengthened it. No, I said, I didn't have any reason to believe Patrick was dead. At the same time, other than the alleged sighting in Hoboken, there was nothing to be very hopeful about.

"If he's alive," I concluded, "I'm confident we'll find him."

Only when there was a subtle shift away from Patrick himself and toward his upbringing, did the questions become more pointed: Did I think Patrick might simply have run away of his own volition? Had I heard any speculation from my police sources about that possibility? Was there anything about Patrick's upbringing which might indicate Patrick was the type of person to drop out of sight? What did I know about the effect his brother's death had had on Patrick? What did I know about Patrick's mom? His sister? Wasn't his father politically connected? Wasn't his father a former member of the NYPD? Did I know why his father had left the job?

That was my cue to regurgitate the information about Francis Maloney Sr. I had so conveniently received in the mail. Unfortunately, I had to disappoint Mr. Beaman and the men who had guided him to me. He tried prompting me several times, but I claimed ignorance. Poor Mr. Beaman was going to have to find another horse's ass. I wasn't playing.

He thanked me politely and wondered if I'd be available to have a staff photographer take my picture later in the week. I said that would be fine. If nothing else, I figured he'd use the Marina Conseco story—without mentioning her by name, of course. Even I could see it would make good copy. But I hadn't given him what he had hoped for. My sense was he didn't know the specifics before he walked through my door. More likely, Beaman had been tipped off about me having dirt on a corrupt politico who was once a very naughty boy during his career as a New York cop. Throw in the aspect of the missing son and you've got a triple play, a Conrad Beaman kind of story. He must've been licking his chops on the ride over. Instead he'd be licking his wounds on the way home.

"You're a smart man, Mr. Prager," Beaman shook my hand.

"Oh, and why is that?"

"Because you figured out you were being used before I figured out I was. I'd still like to hear what you've got," he said, trying one more time to massage the story out of me.

"No, Mr. Beaman. I'm not smart. I just have a conscience."

February 17th, 1978

CARS DRIFTED SLOWLY into the fenced parking lot outside the Sanitation and Highway Department garage. Stories-high piles of asphalt crumbles, road salt and sand peeked over the ledge of the garage's flat roof like distant mountaintops. The air smelled of hot tar, though I could see from where I sat that none of the paving trucks had fired up their rolling furnaces. It was similar to how airports stink of spent kerosene even late at night, when runways go unused for hours at a time. I suppose it's a scientific impossibility, but sometimes it just seems that, like a rug or silk tie, the atmosphere can be permanently stained.

I'd left Brooklyn hours ago under cover of darkness. Now as the sun was rising over the false asphalt mountaintops, the parking lot was nearly full. Both cars I'd been watching for were here. Somehow, I couldn't bring myself to get out of my car and do what I needed to do. I tried several times, never getting more than my leg out the door. But when the coffee truck pulled into the lot and I recognized the faces of two men in the crowd who gathered around it, I knew I would finish what other men had started. "It's not who throws the first punch that counts," my old partner, Danny Breen, liked to say. "But who's standing after the last one."

When the coffee truck had gone and all the men in their green thermal jackets and gloves had retreated back into the garage, I got moving. Starting toward the main entrance, I left my cane on the front seat. A man with a cane could not sell the lies I would have to sell. As I took the first few unsteady steps, my knee hurt like hell. I wasn't sure if the pain was the result of walking unsupported for the first time in months or from the makeshift brace I'd rigged out of old Ace bandages and a wooden ruler.

"Bill Tate, State Insurance Investigation Bureau," I introduced myself to the man at the assignment desk. His back was to me as he busily marked up a wall-sized road map of Dutchess County.

"Who? From where?" he said, turning around.

I let him catch a glimpse of my badge as I quickly closed the credentials case: "Tate, Bill Tate. State Insurance Investigation Bureau."

"Yeah and so what?"

That was one lie out of the way. He wasn't impressed, but he wasn't questioning me either. I didn't even know if there was such a thing as the State Insurance Investigation Bureau.

"You've got two gentlemen employed here who were recently involved in an accident," I stated authoritatively, being purposefully vague, "a Mr. Philip Roscoe and a Mr. . . ."

I didn't know the other man's name, but I'd spotted him earlier at the coffee truck. His face covered in white tape and bandages, he was hard to miss. I scanned a sheet of paper I pulled from my jacket pocket, hoping I'd get his name momentarily.

"Pete Klack?" the desk man wondered.

"Broken nose?" I said, my eyes still focused on the paper.

"That's him."

"Good," I looked up. "Have Roscoe and Klack meet me in Mr. Maloney's office in about fifteen minutes. And do me a favor, don't warn anybody off. Because if you do, your ass is gonna fry in hotter oil than either one of theirs. *Capisce*?"

"Yeah."

"Okay, point me towards a bathroom and to Maloney's office."

In the bathroom, I pulled a neatly folded garbage bag out of my pocket and stuffed the coat I'd been carrying inside. I didn't want to show Maloney all my cards early in the game. In front of his office door, I showed Maloney more courtesy than he'd shown or was likely to ever show me. I knocked.

"Come."

His expression didn't change when he saw who it was. I hadn't expected it would.

"I told you to contact me through Rico."

"I don't give a fuck what you told me," I said in a strangely removed voice. "You're in no position to tell me what to do and I don't know what made you think you ever were."

"Nice speech," Maloney sneered, then looked back down at the paperwork on his desk. "Now get out of here. Next time make an appointment."

I didn't answer nor did I leave. I threw a plain brown envelope with no return address onto his desk. The force with which I tossed it scattered his papers everywhere.

"What's this?" he asked in spite of himself.

"Take a look."

He seemed to know what it was even before he got it out of the envelope. There was almost a wistful look in his eyes as he scanned his NYPD personnel file and the Internal Affairs report.

"So," Francis Maloney Sr. said, as he held his bald head up to face me, "is it blackmail money you've come for?"

I ignored the question. "You know I shouldn't've been able to get ahold of those files. It'd probably take a court order or special dispensation from the pope for me to look at my own files let alone yours. Somebody wanted me to have those."

"How much?"

"How much what?" I asked, annoyed that Maloney didn't seem to be on the same page.

"Oh, don't play me for a stupid donkey, kike. People don't get far underestimating me. It shows a proper lack of respect. I don't like that much."

"I don't want your money, you cold-hearted son of a bitch bastard. For all I care, you can stick those files up your ass and light a bonfire. And I'll tell you what I don't like much. You. From the second I saw you there, sitting at Molly's with that cup of coffee in your hands, I didn't like you. And the more I know about you, the less I like."

"Well, that just makes me want to kill myself," he said sarcastically. "How much?"

"That again. For the last time, I don't want your money."

"Then tell me what you're doing here and get out of my office. I'm a busy man."

"What I want," I said, "is for you to answer some questions. Then maybe I'll go."

"Maybe, he says! Okay, let's have your questions."

"How long before Rico told your wife about me finding the Conseco girl did he ask you to put me on the case?"

A light of recognition clicked on behind Maloney's cold blue eyes. He now understood, as I did, that Rico had been working both sides of the fence. Rico, he explained, had been pestering him to use me for weeks. I was a good cop, Rico said, and recently retired. I could use the cash and I was bored to distraction. But Maloney didn't see the point. Between volunteers and hires, he had hundreds of people working the case within the first few days, most of them with more experience than me. I'd just be an extra wheel. Besides, he had no use for Jewish cops.

"We're not reinvesting our retirement funds here, I told Rico," Maloney delighted in recounting. "I haven't met a Jew cop who was good for anything but filling out a neat complaint report. But then Rico, the stupid wop, had to go tell Angela about you and that girl. After my wife heard that, I had no choice."

I asked: "When did you get the call?"

"What call would that be?" he played dumb.

"Come on, you know what call. The anonymous one that gave you a heads up I was nosing around about your time on the job and that Conrad Beaman was doing a story on Patrick."

Dropping the pretense, Maloney said he'd received the call about a week after we met at Molly's.

"When'd you decide to sic your boys on me?"

"I don't know what you're talking about, sheeny," Maloney feigned innocence and goaded me for distraction. "Have you been drinking? I thought Jews didn't drink."

I didn't take the bait. My proof would come walking through the door in a minute or two. In the meantime, I rambled on about my confusion.

"I couldn't figure out what was going on, exactly. Finally there's some progress in the case and the next day you fire me. But Rico brings a thousand in cash and the name of the guy at the liquor authority. I guess you thought that was pretty smart. You didn't want to piss me off, but you didn't want to give me too much money. Too much money might make me suspicious. Then boom, you have my car torched. You have your boys rough me up. Was it that I was fucking your daughter?" It was my turn to goad him. "Nah, I said to myself, Maloney's an anti-Semitic prick, but he couldn't risk Katy finding out. That would drive her right into my arms. He couldn't afford to lose her too.

"What then? Was it some of the things I was finding out about Patrick? So what if he knocked up two girls and they didn't want the babies?" I walked past Maloney and stared out his office window at the parking lot. "That couldn't be it, though, because I'm pretty sure no one else knew. Besides, you're just the charming old-world type to take pride in your boy for getting girls pregnant, but managing to clean up the mess. So what was—"

"Look, sonny boy," Maloney growled, "I don't know what you're going on about, but I think you've wasted enough of my—"

There was a knock on the door. I remained at the window, forcing myself not to turn around. Before Maloney could respond, the door pushed in. Having only the back of my head to work with, they didn't recognize me. I couldn't see his face, but I imagined Maloney's eyes got as wide as saucers.

"Joey at the desk says there's a guy from the State Insurance Bureau here to talk to us," a monotone voice I'd heard twice before addressed his boss.

When I did turn around, there was a .38 in my hand. "Hello, gentlemen. Remember me?"

Philip Roscoe, the voice on the phone and the man over whose head Katy had broken my cane, was unexcited. Guns didn't frighten him. The other man, Pete Klack, was more agitated and fidgeted nervously, staring back and forth from my gun hand to my face. My lucky punch hadn't done a lot for his looks. Deep purple bruises crept out well beyond the edges of the bandages protecting his broken nose.

"You were saying something about me wasting your time," I reminded Maloney.

Cool as could be, he said: "You're in need of help, Prager. These men were involved in a one-truck accident along the Bainbridge Service Road last week. Would you like to see a copy of the hospital report?" He reached to open his desk drawer.

"No thanks. Keep your hands on top of the desk. Get behind the desk with your boss," I ordered, motioning to Roscoe as I circled in the opposite direction. "Not you, Klack. You stay. So, is your boss right? You two were in a truck accident on the Bainbridge Service Road?"

"Yeah," they harmonized, better than the Beach Boys.

I hit Klack square on the nose with the butt of my revolver. Just as on Greene Street, he collapsed into a pile of himself. The gauze covering his face turned a wet, angry shade of red. I repeated the question about the truck accident. Roscoe stuck to his lie. Understandably, Klack was too preoccupied to answer.

"You broke it again," he moaned.

"Last chance," I said, bending over Klack. "Were you two in an accident or what?"

Roscoe put his left hand on an imaginary Bible, raised his right hand and lied. I stuck the .38 against Klack's temple, pulled back the hammer and ran my finger flirtatiously along the trigger. Klack got stiff with fear. His moaning came to an abrupt halt. I looked Roscoe straight in the eyes. He kept mum. I pulled the trigger. Click.

"That was just for practice," I joked. "But the next chamber's live. There's a hollow point on deck with your name on it. Hey, Klack, how fucking stupid are you? Didn't you notice your two friends over there were willing to let me put a cap in your brain? You gonna keep protecting them?"

"Fuck them and fuck you!" he yelped.

I pulled the hammer back again and moved the barrel of the gun. "Tough shit. Maybe I'll save you the trouble of having it reset and just shoot it off."

"Okay, okay," Klack pleaded, "enough already."

"Shut your mouth!" Maloney seethed.

"It was him, Maloney. He gave us both an extra week's paid vacation and three grand to split."

I wasn't sure who should have been more insulted: me for costing so little or Roscoe and Klack for coming so cheaply.

"Whose idea was it to torch my car?"

"Phil worked the Bomb Squad when he was a cop," Klack volunteered as I pulled the gun away from his bloodied nose. "He said fire makes more of a statement than slashed tires or a broken windshield."

"All right, get up. Roscoe, help your buddy and get the fuck outta here."

Roscoe had a suspicious nature: "That's all?"

"Just watch your back," I said. "You don't have to work the Bomb Squad to know how to make things go boom. And your protector over here, Mr. Maloney, he's got enemies with more juice than him. I wouldn't be counting on him in the future to cover your asses. Now go!"

When they'd gone, I holstered my gun and sat down across from Maloney.

"How'd you find them?" he wanted to know.

"You'll love this," I laughed sardonically. "Katy got a partial tag number the night they worked me over in the city and I got Rico to run the plate. Did Roscoe tell you it was Katy that cracked him over the melon with my cane?"

He let that slide. "But how did you connect Roscoe's car to me? There must have been hundreds of cars with similar tag numbers."

"I figured it was you to begin with, so I knew where to look. And the way Roscoe operated, I thought he might be an ex-cop. When he torched my car, he called it in straight to the precinct and the firehouse, not 911. He knew if he called 911, there would've been a record of his voice. And when he pulled his gun on me—"

"He pulled his piece on you?"

"Yeah, with your daughter a foot or two away," I educated him. "Oh, I guess he left out the part where he threatened to blow a hole in her, huh?"

Maloney turned redder than Klack's bandages. "That stupid son of a—"

"You get what you pay for. So anyway, his gun was a .38 Special. He just smelled like a cop to me. I took a list of names to the PBA office and got a hit on Roscoe. It was a little too much of a coincidence for me that he happened to live three blocks away from you. I didn't know Klack's name until this morning."

"It's the second time you impressed me."

The first time, I knew, was the night I'd gotten to the Gowanus Canal and had a look at the floater before him. That wasn't my doing, though: I'd been tipped off about the floater.

"The people who were using me to take you down wanted me there," I admitted, "just like they wanted me to get a hold of your personnel files. I was like a dog thinking I was taking my master out for a walk. And I was such an obedient dog, they didn't even have to use a leash. I got curious and asked for your files on my own."

"Instead of finding me out, don't you suppose you should have used your energies to find the boy? That's what you were to be paid for, wasn't it?"

"Speaking of that . . ." I leaned down, retrieved the plastic garbage bag that had sat on the floor unnoticed and tossed it on his desk.

"What's this?"

"A gift. Open it up."

As he pulled Patrick's blue parka out of the bag, Maloney's face was torn in half by a startling display of fear and relief. Joy was nowhere to be found, not even in the folds around his eyes nor in the creases at the corners of his mouth. When I blinked my eyes, the emotionality was gone. His face again was cold and blank.

"They sell these by the truckload." He thrust the coat at me.

"Who you trying to convince? You know that's his."

"Bullshit!" he blustered. "How do I know you've not been a part of the scheme to take me down from the get-go? This is just meant to shake me, get me off my game."

Wrong though he was, he had a point.

"I was told you were the reason Patrick split," I paraphrased Jack's words to me. "What could have happened between the two of you? What could you have said?"

"You don't know what you're talking about," he responded. "Take your prop and get the fuck outta my office."

I closed my eyes so I could see. I shut my ears so I could listen.

"When you pulled his coat out of the bag, you seemed scared and relieved, but not happy. That confused me for a second," I explained. "I can understand the relief. What father wouldn't feel relief? But why scared and why not happy?"

"Get out!"

"Patrick told you, didn't he?"

"Told me," he scoffed. "Told me what?"

I ignored him. "Almost everything makes sense then: Why you refer to him as the boy. Why you used a dated picture on the poster. The son you loved, the boy you really wanted to find, didn't exist anymore."

"For the last time, get—"

"You thought he was dead, didn't you? Or was that wishful thinking? Would have been neater that way. Better a dead son than a breathing queer, huh?"

For a man his age, Maloney jumped over the desk with great agility. Good thing for me I expected it and slid, if somewhat clumsily, out of the way. Using my good leg, I kicked him a shot in the kidney. That took the starch out of him. He curled up, choking in pain and gasping for breath.

"So he told you," I shouted at Maloney. "Do you have any idea the balls it took for him to come to you first? I like your son only slightly more than I like you. But it took courage to go to you. What I wanna know is, what did you say to him? What spooked him?"

In a surreal transformation, Francis Maloney's gasps turned to laughter. I don't mean giggles or cynical, sneering stage laughter. I mean belly-holding, side-splitting, choking laughter. When the laughter died down, he sat up.

"The Internal Affairs report," he said, rubbing his left kidney. "What horrible crime did it say I perpetrated on the good people of New York City?"

"That you assaulted several patrons outside a night club without provocation," I summarized.

"I thought Jews were supposed to be smart."

"We're supposed to be rich, too. That's why I drive a Plymouth Fury."

"Do you suppose in the year 1964," he wondered, "before anyone had heard of the Knapp Commission or installed a civilian review board, that roughing up a few drunks would have been enough to get a man thrown off the job?"

"Not really," I said. "Even now, a cop'd probably only get suspended for a while, lose some time."

"Okay then. Even if I were to admit, which I do, that all charges alleged in the IA report are true, do you think I'd fight so hard to not have the report leaked? What harm could it do me? Conversely, if it was the report itself that was so damning, do you suppose my detractors would have gone through the hijinks they did to have it leaked through a man like yourself? Is that not right?"

"Good questions."

"And did you take notice, Mr. Rocket J. Scientist, that none of these allegedly assaulted patrons chose to press formal charges against me nor did any of them file a civil suit?"

"I did."

"Why do you suppose that is?"

"I don't know, but what's this got to do with—"

"Think, man. Think!"

"Okay," I threw up my hands. "Let's say they were black or Puerto Ricans, back then—"

"That's better, but wrong. In '64 they passed that godforsaken Civil Rights Act. Word was passed down that we had to tap-dance around the niggers and learn a word or two of Spanish for the spics. Come on, boyo, you're on the right track."

"Oh my God!"

"Well," Maloney shrugged, "it was you who mentioned fags in the first place, wasn't it?"

"Why didn't the IA report say—"

"The IA report didn't say a lot of things. Did it not seem strange to you that all the men giving statements were referred to by number, not by name and that the location of the incident was never specified? It was 1964, Prager! A cop could bash queers all he liked. What were they gonna do, report it to the papers? In those days, a homo would lose his job if his cock-sucking became public knowledge. For the most part, they took all we could give 'em."

"If all that's true, then why'd you lose your badge?"

"I was a few years on the job and just off duty. I'm in a bar having a few to unwind when a husky-throated broad comes and takes the stool next to mine." His icy eyes sparkled as his spoke. "She was fine-looking in her print dress and smelled like a million bucks. We get to talking about the job and she says she's a fool for cops and would I like to go outside with her for a few minutes. Around back of the bar, she started working on me before I could count to three. When she's had her fill, she stands up and tells me it's my turn. But when I reach for her box, there's a—"

"She was a transvestite."

"Indeed, you do get the picture."

"You roughed him up, huh?"

"Oh, I did more than rough him up. Since my little boyfriend was so fond of policemen, I introduced him to the tools of the trade." Maloney smiled cruelly. "You should've heard him scream when I rammed the barrel of my .38 up his ass. A few of the patrons did. I think the fairy thought I was gonna pull the trigger. He cried with relief when I yanked it out. That was a mistake. You see, my .38 was dirty now. Someone had to clean it."

I felt queasy. "You didn't . . ."

"But I did, keeping my finger on the trigger just to make sure he did a good job. It's not as if he wasn't familiar with the flavor, was it?"

"The report said there were—"

"—others involved," he spoke over me. "There were. Like I said, people inside the bar had heard the screaming. Poor Kitty Genovese screamed her fucking head off and they ignored her. But this little cocksucker screams and they come running. Some took objection to the gun in his mouth. Two of 'em even had the . . . what's the word you people use? Chu . . . Chu something."

"*Chutzpah*."

"That's it! Two of them had the *chutzpah* to try and stop me. I used to carry a leather blackjack in those days. It was a little thing, but it hurt like a son of a bitch. Just ask the two queer-lovers who got in my way. I broke the one's cheekbone and three fingers on the other one's hand.

"I almost got away with it, too. I claimed I was forced to defend myself against citizens who were interfering with the arrest of a male prostitute. The citizens were understandably confused, I said, as I was out of uniform and the prostitute was made up as a woman. Had one of the patrons—the one with the smashed cheekbone, as I recall—not been the half-brother of a city councilman, the whole thing would have been swept under the rug. As it turned out, the councilman's brother liked sausage as well. Had he not, I could have lost more than my job."

"I can see," I said, "why you wouldn't want a reporter like Conrad Beaman getting a hold of the IA report. He would have smelled coverup and started digging. He'd have buried you."

"I fear he would have, yes. And do you know what the shame of it is?"

There was plenty of shame, I thought, to go around, but said: "You go ahead and tell me."

"It was the best damn blow job I ever had."

"You're a sick bastard, Maloney."

"That was the boy's sentiments exactly when I told him what his father had done. Only for him, I didn't gloss over any of the details. I offered him my gun to see if he wanted to try it on for size."

"Your son comes to you in distress and you offer him your gun to . . . do what, to kill himself?" At that moment I was so filled with loathing and disgust I wanted to explode. How could Katy be this twisted man's daughter?

"You know, he took the gun," Maloney said, almost proudly. "But, alas, he was a faggot through and through. He started crying like a little girl."

"Then this whole thing—the search parties, the posters—it was all an elaborate sham."

"No," he protested, "I was hoping we'd find a body for his mother's sake. So, where is he and how much do you want?"

"You're nuts! I wouldn't tell you where he was for all the—"

"Well, how much then? I'm a man of my word."

"You're not any kind of man. You're a cancer."

"Don't be so naive, Prager. The only kind of man worth knocking down is one who's sitting higher than the rest. Name your price."

"You want my price, okay." I put my face right up to his. "Quit! Quit today, tonight. Walk away from your job and the party activities gracefully before it gets really ugly. You're smart enough to know that your enemies won't stop because they misread me. You were lucky this time. They didn't know about Patrick being gay. They were just using his disappearance as an opening, hoping Beaman could dig up your skeletons. Next time they won't be so clumsy and your son won't be conveniently absent. They'll take you down and everyone around you."

"See, I knew you were a clever Jew. But why would you want to protect me?"

"Not you, asshole, your family. I don't want Katy to know what's happened here today, none of it! For some reason I will never understand, she loves you. I don't think she needs the burden of knowing who and what you really are. I don't want her to hurt anymore. As far as Patrick goes, he can speak for himself when he turns back up. He can tell who he wants what he wants. But nothing out of your mouth."

"And you, will you not tell my daughter what you know?"

"I just said—"

"I'll meet your price," he cut me off, the disdain heavy in his voice. "You're a fool to sell yourself so cheaply and to believe in secrets. When more than one person knows anything, secrets can't exist."

"But you're a man of your word," I spit his vow back at him.

"Do Jews believe in ghosts, Prager?"

"What?"

"Never mind. I'll keep my word. Now get out!"

He didn't have to ask me again. I would have run if I could have.

Not wanting to be stained by the black-hearted man in the corner office, the sun no longer lingered at the garage's flat rooftop. In my car, I cut the brace off my throbbing knee. That done, I sat for what seemed hours watching as road trucks fat with asphalt rumbled by. The stink of hot tar was no longer just from the furnace of my imagination.

I should have been happy, I thought, calculating the sum of the parts. I'd found Patrick in spite of the all doubts and roadblocks. I'd found his sister, a woman I could love and one who could love me. I'd rediscovered ambition and self-confidence and my right jab. I'd even begun to form friendships outside the job for the first time in a decade. By all accounts, I'd won. But my life wasn't simple math and never did victory taste so bitter as it did just then. I was changed.

Finally driving away, I caught a glimpse of my eyes in the rearview mirror. They were vaguely foreign to me and I thought I could see the faint outline of a ghost. Accelerating onto the entrance ramp for the expressway, I forced myself not to look back.

February 18th, 1978

AS DIFFICULT AS it had been to confront Francis Maloney, I knew today had the potential to be worse. Maloney hadn't meant anything to me. He was just an awful little man who turned out to be smaller and more cruel once you scratched the surface. And maybe I would never feel completely clean again for having made a deal with him, but Rico was something else altogether. I had loved and trusted Rico. Now I would have to undo with my head what my heart still fiercely wanted to feel.

I'd kept the phone off the hook all night, trying to work out how to approach my old friend. So I got no calls and no sleep and failed to come up with a blessed thing. Ironically, like so many times before, Rico bailed me out. Almost the second I put the phone back in its cradle, it started ringing.

"Hey buddy, how ya doin'?" Rico asked with a big grin in his voice.

"Tired. Couldn't sleep. What's going on?"

"You up for lunch today?"

"Sure, why not?"

"Geez, Moe, your enthusiasm's killin' me."

"Sorry. I'm beat."

"Well, go back to bed," he advised. "Let's say we meet at Villa Conte's at one. And screw Karl Malden, leave your American Express card at home. Lunch is on me."

Located on 4th Avenue near the Verrazano Bridge, Villa Conte's was atypical of Italian restaurants in Brooklyn. The menu featured recipes from the north of Italy: no meatballs, red sauce or lasagna here. Conte's was renowned for its veal dishes and wine sauces. It was equally famous for its high prices and snooty waitstaff.

Rico was all smiles and hugs when we met. Everything was roses in Rico Tripoli's world today. Even when the waiter sneered condescendingly at Rico for his crude Sicilian dialect, Rico let it roll off his shoulders.

"I ordered for us," he said, holding onto the waiter's arm. "First we're gonna have a green salad with champagne vinaigrette. After that there's grilled portobello mushrooms. Then we're havin' an appetizer portion of tortellini in cream sauce. The main course is a double-stuffed veal chop with asparagus in white wine and lemon. That okay with you?"

When I nodded my approval, he let go of the waiter's arm. The waiter looked at his forearm as if he wanted it amputated.

"That's a lot of food," I commented. "What are we celebrating?"

Just then, a man in a beautifully tailored silk suit—the owner, I assumed—arrived at the table with drinks. He bowed, placing a glass before each of us: "*Due* Campari."

"Campari tastes like Vick's Formula 44," I protested, "only it doesn't help your cough."

"It's good for your digestion," Rico countered. "Just drink it. The wine's comin' with the food."

We ate the salad, mushrooms and tortellini in relative silence. As advertised, the food was incredibly good. But I was already stuffed. Having anticipated this, Rico told the waiter not to start cooking the veal until he gave the word. I asked again about what we were celebrating.

"The word came down last night," he said, puffing out his chest, "I'm gettin' my gold shield."

I congratulated him, raised my wine glass and signaled to the waiter.

"Champagne," I ordered, explaining that I was to be billed for it. The waiter liked that.

I think he liked even better that I didn't ask how much. Rico blushed, pleading that it wasn't necessary. I disagreed. He let me win.

The sparkling wine poured, I toasted my old friend and clinked his glass. "So you broke this big case you've been working on, huh?"

"Not exactly," Rico squirmed a little. "We're close there . . . anytime now."

I claimed not to understand. How could he make detective without making a big case? Gold shields were hard to come by in the best of times and now with the city always on the verge of fiscal meltdown, they were nearly impossible to get. He squirmed some more, giving the waiter the sign to start cooking the veal. Rico suddenly decided he'd rather not talk about his making detective.

"This wouldn't have anything to do with Francis Maloney's unexpected retirement," I asked innocently between sips of champagne, "would it?"

Rico didn't spit out his wine in mock surprise. He didn't stand, throw his napkin down and storm out in a cloud of indignation. He'd been found out and he knew it.

"I told 'em you was too smart for your own damn good," he said. "I warned 'em you'd catch on sooner or later. Which one was it, sooner or later?"

"Sooner, but it wasn't you. I didn't connect the dots to you until late in the game. Sully, on the other hand, was about as subtle as a blind elephant. He should've let me stumble into things instead of serving 'em up on silver platters. My good fortune made me suspicious."

"I warned 'em. I warned 'em," he repeated. "But they were worried that the kid would turn up before they could get the shit on Maloney out to the public. If the kid turned up too soon, they were afraid *Gotham* magazine would kill the story."

"They, who's they?" I wondered.

Fidgeting with his fork, he said: "Powerful people."

"Powerful enough to buy you off with a shield."

"Powerful enough to get ya back on the job, if that's what ya want, with a shield a your own," he offered like a mother's kiss to make the hurt go away. "They were impressed that ya got Maloney to quit without givin' up . . . you know, the stuff about the fags. How'd you do that, anyways?"

I'd like to say I wasn't tempted by his offer of a return to the job, that a shield gotten with a nod and a wink wasn't worth having, but I was tempted. There's no doubt in my mind people had sold more than their self-respect for a gold shield. Having gotten a taste of detective work and realizing how much I missed the job made the offer all that more appealing. But I was weary of making deals. It had to stop somewhere. I just didn't tell Rico. As long as he thought I was interested in the bait, he'd keep his line in the water. There was more I wanted to know.

"Don't you worry about what music I played to make Maloney do a jig," I snapped. "Why'd they want to get rid of the bastard in the first place? You did say he was a big-time fund raiser, right?

So why get rid of him at all and why go through all of the shenanigans to do it?"

Looking a little shaken, Rico excused himself and made for the bathroom. That was all right. I needed some time to myself, to organize my thoughts. When he returned, Rico seemed steadier, calmer. I reminded him that he'd left some questions hanging. Unfortunately for me, they were going to have to stay that way.

"To tell you the truth, old buddy, I'm in no position to answer much about Francis Maloney," he regretted to say. "That's all political crap that I got nothin' to do with."

I didn't quite believe him and guessed he must have used his time away to make a phone call to his handlers. But I couldn't afford to antagonize him if I wanted my answers, so I tried a different line of questioning. These were questions he couldn't sluff off on somebody else. They were questions about us.

"Okay, Rico, I understand, that's not your territory. But what about us? Why'd you do it to me? Couldn't you find somebody else's chain to yank?"

"I didn't so much do it *to* you as I did it *for* me. I don't see where you come out so bad in this deal."

"You don't, huh?"

"No," he raised his voice defensively. "You got at least a grand and the contact at the State Liquor Authority. For what, a few weeks of playin' detective? Where's the downside to that?"

"You used me. There's a big downside to that."

"Grow up, Moe. People use people all the time."

"Even if that's so," I said, "why me? I thought we were close."

"Not close enough for me to partner up with you and your brother in the liquor store. My money isn't good enough for you two."

"I explained that twenty times already, Rico. It has nothing to do with you. It has to do with my dad going bankrupt and Aaron's plans. So you used me because you wanted to hurt me somehow, is that it?"

"Maybe that's part of it," he admitted. "But there was other things. There wasn't alotta time, so it wasn't like I could go research the perfect candidate. I knew you were gettin' antsy and would wanna get outta the house after sittin' on your ass. And I knew if I could get you curious, you'd go for it. You've always been a nosy bastard."

"There's more you aren't saying."

He slapped the table: "See what I mean? You always wanna know every fuckin' thing. No answer's ever good enough for you, is it? All right, I'll tell you. I figured you was smart enough to follow where we led you and not experienced enough at detective work to fuck things up."

"You figured wrong."

"No, it was Sully, that fat moron. I told him not to be so obvious, that you'd get curious about the wrong stuff, but . . . Hey, it worked out better than I coulda hoped for. The little shanty prick is out and no one got dragged through the mud."

"What about finding Patrick?" I asked disapprovingly. "Or don't you give a shit about him? What the fuck was he, just a convenient excuse? You gonna think everything turned out better than you could have hoped if he washes up on Manhattan Beach?"

"That's not what I meant. You know me better than that."

"No I don't. I don't know you at all anymore. Can you really want the shield that bad?"

"You bet your ass I want it," he hissed. "And I need the pay."

I was incredulous. "What happened to all the bread you inherited? You know, the money you were going to use to come in with me and Aaron? You told me you could've walked away from the job, moved down to Florida and—"

"My divorce settlement happened to it. I got to keep the house, two pair of underwear and my fly swatter. She even got my Rangers season ticket. She cleaned me out. I guess I deserved it. And Rose, she's great, but she pushes me. She was never married before, so she don't understand things. She coulda married any uniformed jerk, she tells me. A cop's nothing without a shield. I know it's her old man talkin'. And every week the house needs a new this and a bigger that. What the fuck could I do?"

The veal was served before I could answer. It might as well have been a live calf for all the interest I took in it. At least Rico tried to eat his. The waiter panicked over our lack of appetite. People had sent veal back for being under or overcooked, but no one, apparently, had rejected it on purely aesthetic grounds. I enjoyed his temporary despair. Before he ran screaming to the chef, I called the waiter over and asked him to wrap mine up. I wasn't feeling well. Report of my illness cheered him right up. As the waiter removed my plate, I noticed Rico's eyes widening and focusing on something over my left shoulder. Rico made to stand up.

"That's all right, don't get up," a relaxed male voice called from behind me. Then a strong hand clapped me on the shoulder. "This must be Moe Prager."

I turned, looking up at a handsome man in his mid-fifties. His silver hair was swept back and perfectly coifed. He had sparkly blue eyes, a pleasantly crooked mouth full of capped, white teeth and pointed jaw. He was dressed in a charcoal grey wool suit, a maroon silk, square-knotted tie with matching pocket hanky and light pink shirt. The hand on my shoulder had once lived a rough life but was now manicured. Its cuticle-less fingernails were clipped in perfect symmetry and reflected the candlelight like a freshly waxed car. On the ring finger was a gold Claddagh ring atop a plain wedding band.

The spiffy Irishman held his right hand out to me: "Joe Donohue. Perhaps you've heard the name."

Joe Donohue was a legend. A highly decorated cop who'd been wounded twice in the line of duty, he'd risen through the ranks of the NYPD faster than any man before or since. After retirement, he made a small fortune in the private sector and had recently reappeared on the public stage as the mayor's chief consultant on police affairs. Rumor was Donohue was angling for a run at the office itself. But most recently, I'd heard his name coming out of Rico's mouth. Joe Donohue was supposed to be Francis Maloney's hook in City Hall. I shook the legend's hand.

"*Prego, Alphonso, tre espressos*," Donohue addressed the waiter by his first name, holding out a crisp twenty-dollar bill. "Then you give us some privacy, okay?"

Alphonso made a show of trying to refuse the money, but took it in the end. Donohue's little passion play with the tip money wasn't lost on me. Pay attention, Prager, it was meant to say. They always take the easy money in the end.

"So," he said after the espressos and bottle of anisette were served, "it seems we underestimated you. It's rare that I underestimate a man."

"Is this where I'm supposed to kiss the ring?" I wondered.

"A smart man with a smart mouth. Rico didn't tell me you had balls on you, too."

"He didn't know. I just grew 'em. It's like that stuff on TV. You rub it on, add water and there they are! Chia Balls, I think it's called."

Rico was too nervous to laugh. Donohue laughed a little, then got stony-faced.

"Now that you've showed me what a tough guy you are, can we get down to business?" It wasn't really a question. "You're pissed off because you were used. You'll get over it. What impressed me was that you caught on and instead of whining about it, turned the situation to your advantage. Poor old Francis is out of it, but without the bloodshed. I've been trying to get Francis to retire from his fund-raising duties for a year. How'd you get that stubborn—"

"First you answer some questions, okay?"

Rico looked about ready to chew through his bottom lip. God, Donohue must have had Rico by the short hairs. I felt like reminding him this wasn't the pope I was talking to, just an ambitious ex-cop.

"You've already earned the answers," Donohue said.

"I thought you and Francis Maloney were tight. Why muddy him up?"

"We were tight," Donohue did not hesitate. "Friends since grade school. A loyal man, Francis, and a hell of a money machine. I think every soul who's gotten a job in Dutchess County since Francis arrived has generously tithed a portion of his or her salary to the party. Those nickels and dimes add up. And he's surprisingly shrewd for an unsubtle fellow. He knows how to do and use favors. You don't think all those volunteers who've come looking for Patrick did it out of warm, gooey affection, do you?"

"But . . ."

Donohue frowned: "Thing is, he's become a political liability."

"Just because he hates blacks, Jews, Puerto Ricans, Orientals and—"

"Yes, Mr. Prager, I see you've been on the receiving end of Francis's charms. I guess he was always a bit of a bastard," Donohue admitted, "but after Francis Jr.'s tragic death, he got worse. Up until recently, Francis's indelicacies wouldn't have mattered. The money he raised was everything. It's the lifeblood of a political party. Times, however, have changed and a candidate needs the support of all the people. You can't afford to alienate whole groups of people because you don't like the way they dress or the god they pray to."

I applauded lightly. "Nice speech, it'll wow 'em at the convention."

"Thank you. I like the sound of it myself. Anyway, Francis doesn't see things that way. When I asked him to step aside, let's say he didn't much like the idea. In fact, he was looking to be rewarded with a commissioner's appointment for his years of loyal service."

"Imagine that," I said with all the sarcasm I could muster. "The nerve of him."

"Don't be too harsh on me," Donohue pleaded. "It's not as if I handed him a gold watch and showed him the door. Francis was offered several incentives to leave gracefully, but you can ask only so many times. He forced my hand."

"Lucky thing for you Patrick disappeared. He gave you a good opportunity to shove a stake through the heart of your old friend's career. How do you treat your enemies, I wonder?"

"Don't be naive, Mr. Prager. Politics is politics. It's like hockey with bigger sticks, more blood and no referees. You use the opportunities when they come wherever they come from. Francis knows the rules. He knew there was always a chance that unfortunate incident might resurface."

I clapped my hands together: "Now I understand your dilemma. You had to get rid of Maloney before he could damage you politically. He wouldn't go gracefully, so you were going to drop a bomb on his career using his past indiscretions. But how could you set off the chain reaction without getting your own career incinerated in the blast? The answer's simple: use an errand boy, someone who could never be traced back to you.

"Normally reporters are fine conduits for leaking information as long as they get a story out of it. They protect their anonymous sources and you get whatever it is you want into the public's consciousness. But you couldn't risk regular channels this time, because all it would take would be one ambitious reporter willing to break his word and your political career'd be dead in the water. A hero cop, millionaire, political fair-haired boy is a bigger catch than some corrupt party toad doling out the patronage jobs upstate. So what if he sodomized a homosexual with his gun barrel twenty-something years ago? The fact that you knew about it and turned a blind eye to it as long as he filled the party coffers would be more newsworthy. Maloney would be a footnote, but you'd be the story."

"So when Patrick fortuitously disappears, you jump on the opportunity. You reach out to Rico and he starts working on Maloney to bring me on board. Then you have someone else, probably another ignorant errand boy like myself who could never be connected to you, whisper in Conrad Beaman's ear that there's more to this missing college guy's story than meets the eye. I get curious about Maloney's NYPD career. His personnel files magically appear in my lap. Beaman finds me. I hand the files to Beaman. Beaman digs some more and Maloney's a dead duck. The party brass claims ignorance and express their disgust. And even if Maloney screams his head off that you knew about him all along, he has no way to prove it. Your hands seem perfectly clean."

"In a nutshell, yes, that's about it," he yawned.

"It's a lot to go through to get rid of one potential problem. Shooting the guy or planting drugs on him would have been easier. There's fifty places your cockamamie plan could have gone wrong. It did go wrong! I figured out I was being played."

"In retrospect, I suppose you're right. Working on the fly with limited talent can cause trouble, but you handled it so no one had to hang publicly. And that's what I wanted to speak to you about. Frankly, I realize I don't want the details of how or what you did to pull it off. Sometimes it is better not to know."

"I wasn't going to tell you anyway. What's between Maloney and me is my business. You were saying you wanted to speak to me . . ."

"Yes," he cleared his throat and nodded for Rico to leave.

I grabbed Rico's arm. "He stays. I want him to hear this."

"Fine. I'm sure Rico made it clear what I could do for you. You want back on the job with a shield in your pocket, I can do that for you."

"Sorry, Mr. Donohue. I may buy wholesale, but I sell retail. I won't come as cheaply as my old buddy, Rico."

Donohue flashed his fancy dental work at me. "I would have been disappointed had you been that easy. The easy ones are trouble. I need a man like you who knows how to think on his feet and knows when to keep his mouth shut." Staring directly at Rico, he said: "I already have Moe and Larry in my pocket. I think my career would be better served without adding Curly, don't you?"

"What if my price was a little payback?" I asked. "What if, to have me on board, I wanted you to make sure Rico not only doesn't get his shield but loses his job and pension benefits? Could you do that?"

Anger, panic and humiliation flashed across Rico's face.

"Of course I could," Donohue seemed insulted. "But would I?"

"Come on, Mr. Donohue, you were prepared to drag your childhood friend and political ally through the mud while his son might be lying dead in a ditch somewhere. Of course you would, if you thought I was important enough."

Joe Donohue did not speak immediately, taking a moment to process our conversation. Rico just sat there looking defeated.

"You know, Mr. Prager, Rico did warn me about you. Now I understand why. You have no intention of coming to work for me, do you? This last part of our conversation was meant to be—"

"—instructional," I completed the phrase. "Yeah, I thought Rico might find it interesting. When you sell yourself cheap, chances are you'll get sold out even cheaper."

Donohue was not a man to waste time. He stood up and offered me his hand. I shook it just to move things along. "This has been enlightening," he said. "I hope I can count on your vote."

I was noncommittal. "What's to stop me from going to the press myself?"

"You mean beside the fact that you have no proof?" He winked. "In any case, I was never here today. Just ask Rico or Alphonso. And perhaps the most compelling reason is, you'd have to smear Maloney, even if indirectly, in order to damage me. Isn't that what you found so offensive about this in the first place? Have a good day, Mr. Prager."

Rico was shaken to the core. Sweating and pale, he kept shaping words in his mouth that wouldn't come out. It was better that way. I didn't feel like talking anymore. When I left, I made it a point not to take the doggy bag. Table scraps are table scraps no matter how you dress them up. I had a sneaking suspicion Rico now understood that all too well.

PART OF ME really wanted to keep my promise to have dinner with Katy, but the last few days had taken a lot out of me. I went home and rested, hoping to recharge my batteries a little. It didn't work out that way. It would still be several days, I realized, before I was likely to relax. So I called Katy at her office to beg off. She was disappointed, but not mortified. She had a project to work on and just recently she was having a difficult time focusing on work.

"My concentration's been a bit suspect lately," she said.

"Why's that?" I asked.

"I've met someone. I can't seem to get him off my mind."

"Good-looking?"

"He's all right, if you like that type."

"What type is that?"

"Oh, I don't know," she purred. "You standing near a mirror?"

"That handsome, huh? I don't think I should let you out of my sight."

"I'd like that."

After we stroked each other's egos a bit longer, she asked if I'd taken care of the business that was supposed to be occupying my time. I said I had. I lied and told her that her father hadn't been behind my car getting torched or the beating on Greene Street. When Patrick showed up on her doorstep, there'd be enough fireworks to deal with. What was the point in complicating matters?

"It was Theresa Hickey's husband. Don't worry," I assured her, "I handled it in my own way."

Katy didn't pursue the issue. If I said it was handled, it was handled. That was my business.

"Speaking of my dad," she said, "he's put in his papers. He's stepping down from his job and from his fund-raising position. Did you know about his fund-raising? Anyway, he says he's tired of the grind. Yesterday he just up and quit. It's the first impulsive thing I think he's ever done. Mom's really happy about it."

"Me too. I'll call you tomor—"

"Oh," she interrupted, "before I forget. Misty called a few hours ago and said that Jack from Pooty's called for you at the loft, but didn't leave a message. What do you suppose that's about?"

"I don't know," I swallowed hard. "Maybe there's a gift he forgot to give us."

HE PICKED UP at the first ring: "Patrick! Patrick?"

"It's me, Jack, Moe."

"Get over here, please! Something's wrong. I just know it."

He didn't give me a chance to discuss the matter and I got the sense that ringing him up a second time wouldn't have helped.

The apartment stank of cigarettes and bourbon. Jack looked like shit: disheveled, unshaven, red-eyed. His hands shook terribly as he offered me a seat and a drink. I took both. If I had some bourbon, there'd be less for him. From all appearances, less for him was a very good idea.

"He didn't come home last night," Jack ranted as he paced.

"Fuck!" I slammed my fist into the table. "He split? I knew I shouldn't—"

"He didn't run!" Jack was adamant. "He was better than he'd been in weeks and needed to get out. All he wanted to do was walk over to the pier for some air."

"Jack, you promised."

"He didn't run! We were both gearing up for Saturday morning. Everything was fine."

"Jesus fucking Christ! You just let him walk out the door?"

"I walked him downstairs and kissed him. He said he'd be right back. Moe, he had five dollars in his wallet. He didn't run. He was finally ready."

"Yeah, like with his dad," I sneered. "That was such a positive experience he just couldn't wait to tell everybody else, huh?"

We went round and round like that for about an hour before I walked out. If Jack was right, Patrick hadn't run. But I needed to.

August 6th, 1998 (late evening)

THE RUSH BACK from the pizzeria was to no avail. Tyrone Bryson had slipped back into a coma. Fearing the worst, Sister Margaret let me have a look at the man who had reached across two decades to bring me here. What was the harm? she thought; if Bryson couldn't see me, I could, at the very least, see him. To Sister's way of thinking, a look from me may have been all God required of us. Who was I to argue?

Funny, when I set my eyes on this stranger, all I saw was my father, lying silently in bed waiting for death to take away the pain. When the memory washed out of my eyes, I saw the nearly inert, cancer-decimated body of a small black man. I tried imagining him as a younger, fuller man, but couldn't. I was exhausted and confused and could work only with the information my eyes were supplying me.

"Here," Sister Margaret said, placing something in my palm, "I can't imagine Mr. Bryson would mind. Come with me into the lounge and have a look under better light."

"Will you stay with me, Sister?"

She checked her watch. "My shift is over. I'd love to."

"I wrote this twenty years ago," I said, unfolding the business card-sized piece of lined paper I'd torn off Jack's sheet. "See here, that's my old number in Brooklyn before they changed all the area codes." I unfolded a very old copy of Conrad Beaman's article from *Gotham* magazine. "Nice picture, huh? Did I ever look like that?"

"You're not so very different now." Sister was kind.

"I was interviewed on a Sunday afternoon. I lied through my teeth, Sister Margaret. I thought I knew better."

"You did? How's that?"

We sat there for hours as I explained. She seemed genuinely fascinated by the most insignificant detail. It was good for me. I hadn't ever told anyone before. There were parts I hadn't even admitted to myself. Oh, various people knew various aspects of my involvement with Patrick Michael Maloney, but I'd always had a good reason for protecting people from the whole truth. It was odd how those reasons no longer seemed to make any sense.

"So," Sister Margaret said, "he never did turn up on Saturday morning."

"No. No one ever saw or heard from him again. When I left Jack's apartment that night, I really believed he'd gotten scared again and run. But over the years . . . I'm just not so sure anymore."

Sister kissed my cheek: "Don't give up on Mr. Bryson just yet."

My cell phone rang and the nun excused herself, promising to return after checking on Mr. Bryson's condition.

"Hello."

"Daddy?"

"Sarah? Hey, happy birthday, kiddo! Sorry, I know you hate when I call you that."

"That's okay, Dad. You all right? You sound tired and kinda far away."

"I'm in New Haven. Hamden, really. Don't ask, it's a long story. Where've you been? I've been trying to get you all day."

"I had things to do. Listen, Mommy says it's okay with her if it's okay with you."

"What is?"

"I wanna go to school."

"Are you crazy? Of course it's all right with me."

"But I've got to like be there in two we—"

"We'll work it out, honey. Don't worry. I'll call your mother about it tomorrow."

"I love you, Dad. You're the bomb."

"The what?"

"The bomb. The best."

"You're the best thing that ever happened to me and your mom. Did I ever tell you that I only pretend to be happy for you on your birthday? It's really me I celebrate for."

"You're so weird. Aunt Miriam was right about you. You're a big mush."

"So does this mean you and—"

"No, Dad, we're not breaking up. He's the one who thought I should go to school."

"Then kiss him for me. Happy birthday, again. I love you, kiddo."

I folded the little phone away, burying it in my pocket. Suddenly, my vision wasn't very clear.

"Are you feeling well, Mr. Prager?" Sister Margaret came up behind me.

"That was my daughter on the phone. Today is her eighteenth birthday. Did I tell you that? She wants to go to school," I said, wiping my eyes with my sleeve.

"That's wonderful. I think you'd better come with me. There's someone else who wants to talk to you."

Bryson stared me right in the eyes the way Joe Donohue had stared into Rico Tripoli's eyes twenty years ago. I will never get over how he looked at me. I think he saw his salvation in my face. I shook his hand and, weak as he must have been, he would not let go.

"When I was a boy I used to push bags of weed for Elephant Eddie Barker," Bryson whispered. "Eddie used kids cause wasn't no chance we was gonna get prosecuted. He'd drive us into the Village from East New York. That's in Brooklyn, you know."

"I'm from Brooklyn."

Bryson smiled weakly. "So one night, Dee, he one of our crew, was working a schoolyard over on the Westside by 8th Avenue and a fag—'scuse me, Sister—Dee says this guy touched him where he shouldn'ta and took his product, if you know what I'm sayin'. Well, the Elephant goes crazy, man. He packs us all back into his ride and we goes cruisin' for the fag—the man that done what Dee said he done. 'Fags got to respect a man's property,' the Elephant kept on. 'Got to teach somebody a lesson.'

"We drivin' and Dee don't see nobody looks like the man who done what he said. But Elephant, he gotta teach somebody a lesson, right? So we goin' down this one street and the Elephant spies these two men be kissin' on the stoop of a buildin'. One goes back inside, but the other one he come down the steps. We follow him a little ways till he get to the corner, then, let's jus' say Elephant offered him a ride. You know like in *The Godfather*, it was like an offer he couldn't refuse. You hear what I'm sayin'?"

"Where'd you take him?" Sister Margaret asked.

"Back to Brooklyn, a place on Livonia Avenue where nobody be botherin' us."

"You killed him," I guessed.

His eyes got wide and he gasped for breath: "Not me! I never killed nobody. Elephant, he done it. First he cut him up pretty bad, you understand?" Bryson could see by the horror in my eyes that I understood all too well. "Elephant made us wrap him up in a shower curtain and we took the body over to a empty lot by Cypress Hills Cemetery." A smile flashed across his face. "All sorts a old famous people buried in Cypress Hills. What's the name of that escape guy?"

"Yeah," I confirmed, smiling myself, "Harry Houdini's buried there."

"That's him." Then the smile ran away from Bryson's face. "First, Elephant was gonna jus' leave him there, you know. Then he got scared somebody mighta seen us, so we buried him. Don't know what kinda lesson that was gonna be to anyone, buryin' him like that. Elephant jus' kill the man cause he was mad, that's all."

"You took his wallet."

"There was a few dollars and that slip a paper with your name on it. I shoved them into my pocket cause I didn't want nobody else to see. Later that night when Elephant drop us off, Dee tol' me ain't no man be touchin' him. He was jus' mad at Elephant for makin' him work that schoolyard. He threw his take and the weed down a sewer hole. That man died for nothin'. That's why I kept the paper with your name on it, to remind me. I didn't know who you was then. Then when I was livin' on the streets, I was sellin' old books and magazines for nickels and shit. I read the magazines sometimes. I can read, you know." He was becoming agitated. "I'm a good reader."

Sister Margaret came around me and began stroking Tyrone Bryson's face, but he would not be consoled. "I never killed nobody. I want you to know that. I never killed nobody. You got to tell that man's family there wasn't nothin' I could do 'bout it. I was jus' a boy."

"I am that man's family, Tyrone. I married his sister," I said, fumbling for my wallet. "Look, this is his sister, Katy. And this is our girl, Sarah. She looks a little like Patrick."

Bryson calmed down. "She's a pretty girl."

"Thank you, Tyrone. It's her birthday today. And thank you for telling me about Patrick. There's a lot of people, including me, that will rest easier now."

His whole body seemed to untense and, looking away, he finally let go of my hand. I asked if he could remember where

Elephant had buried Patrick. He said he did and gave me the location. Sensing our business was done, Sister Margaret nudged my shoulder to leave. She came out to the lounge a few minutes later. I asked if Mr. Bryson had passed on.

"No, Mr. Prager, nothing so dramatic. I think getting that weight of his chest has given him a last rush of energy. But I don't think he'll last till morning. Cancer can be considerably less forgiving than God's children."

"I'd like to pay for the funeral, if that's okay with the diocese, Sister."

"I'm sure we can work that out. It's very kind of you."

"Not really," I confessed. "You see, the weight he's been carrying around all these years, I've been carrying, too. He saved me as much as he saved himself. It's the least I can do."

"It's still a very charitable gesture," she said, taking my hand.

"I better go, Sister Margaret. There's a lot I have to do now. Will you call me about the arrangements?"

"Of course."

"Thank you, Sister." I kissed her hand. "Thank you for getting me here."

"I suspect I had very little to do with that. You were meant to be here."

I began to walk out of the lounge. Then, turning back, I called to Sister Margaret: "If Patrick is where Mr. Bryson says he is, will you please come to the funeral? I want you to meet my family."

"You just try to keep me away."

Looking up at the stars outside the hospice, I remembered what my high school physics teacher used to say: "Time travel is possible, no matter what anyone tells you. When you look at the stars, it's the past you see." When I got to my car door, I felt as if I'd forgotten something. My cane, I thought. But no, I hadn't used a cane in nearly twenty years. I guess I was just time-traveling.

Epilogue

Twenty Years Gone

I DID NOT tell Katy. What was I going to say? "Your brother wasn't really missing, but now he really is? Oh, and by the way, he was gay and the father that you love is a homophobic sodomist who asked Patrick if he'd like to kill himself."

There were moments when I felt as Rico must have that day at Villa Conte: words of explanation, sentence fragments, pleas for forgiveness formed in the back of my throat but were never given voice. The guilt of my complicity gnawed at me constantly. Then, after several months, at about the same time the doctors told me to ditch the cane, I convinced myself that I had shed Patrick's ghost forever.

I fooled myself about many things, but never about my love for Katy. On the night we went to see *A Chorus Line*, I asked her to marry me. Miriam and Cindy, fat with baby, had helped me pick out the ring a few weeks before. I had everything arranged with the bartender at the Rainbow Room. When I gave him the sign, he screamed in pain.

"What's the matter?" I wondered, innocent as a lamb.

"Nothing, I'm okay." He chewed the scenery. "I seem to have cut myself on something here in the ice. Geez!" he bellowed, "will you look at that."

"Let me see," Katy asked, as if on cue.

The bartender handed her the ring.

"It's yours," I said, "if you want it."

Without any encouragement from me, Katy decided to convert to Judaism. I told her she was out of her mind, that it was like volunteering for being hated. She said that God had failed her as a Catholic. It wasn't God who failed her, but she insisted. For the sake of my parents' memory, I was happy.

"You know," I warned her, "they don't give out big prizes when you're done. In some places all you get is a yellow felt star and a number tattoo."

She did it anyway, but there wasn't enough time to complete the process before the wedding. We got married at the United Nations Chapel in late July of '78. A sort of generic minister performed the service: I mean, if the UN can't handle a Jew marrying a Catholic converting to Judaism, who can? Like my grandfather used to say, that should only be their worst headache. Aaron was the best man and Katy's old best friend, Sue, was the matron of honor. My brother-in-law Ronnie got to live out his dream as he was paired with Misty walking down the aisle. Miriam and Kosta were the yin to their yang. Cindy's pregnancy wasn't going smoothly, so she just sat with her kids cheering from the first pew. We held the reception at a neighborhood Italian restaurant in Brooklyn. Lots of red sauce, lots of lasagna and lots of cheap red wine.

We kept the crowd pretty small. Nicky and Pete Parson were there, a few of my friends from the job and a couple of relatives. Same for Katy. Her parents came without a word of protest or fuss. Though her mom wasn't thrilled with the idea of Katy's conversion, I think tragedy had schooled Angela Maloney to cling tightly to what she had left. She was good to me and my family until the day she died. Francis Maloney was categorically civil to me in front of his daughter, but he'd always smile at me in a way that made me uncomfortable. Even during those times when circumstance made cellmates of us, he never brought up the ugliness between us, nor did he once ask why Patrick had failed to reappear. Over the years, however, he did occasionally ask me if I believed in ghosts. It would be years before I would understand his unnerving smile or his affinity for the spirit world.

At the restaurant, only Miriam asked where Rico was. "Not here," was what I said. There were many absent faces and neither Katy nor I felt compelled to explain. Of course many of the absent faces needed no explanation at all. I invited Dr. Friar, but she politely refused. "It would be like eavesdropping," she said. I never heard from her again. Jack came to the party and left after a few drinks. We'd kept in touch, but the conversation inevitably degenerated into an argument over whether Patrick had run or not. That was the last time we saw him. Pete Parson told me Jack moved back to Ohio in late August to run a drama program at a high school for troubled teens.

In October of 1986 I received a package in the mail from a Mrs. Mary White of Dayton, Ohio. Mary White was Jack's older sister. Jack, she was sad to inform me, had died of AIDS in early September. She had taken it hard and was only now able to bring herself to disburse Jack's things according to his wishes. She wrote:

> "Jack was very clear that you were to have this. He told me about Patrick and what happened back there in New York. He understood your anger, Mr. Prager, but to his dying day insisted you had not misplaced your trust. He was sure Patrick had not run. If you ever do find out what happened, please let me know. Jack told me he was happy to have known you and your wife. I'm glad there were people he liked back then . . ."

The package contained Patrick's illustration of the Chinese character with the red rose running through it. I was touched that Jack should have wanted me to have it, but since I couldn't share it with Katy, I was forced to keep it in storage for too many years.

In March, when all my holiday time, sick time and disability ran out, I borrowed against my pension. The loan put Aaron and me over the top and we purchased the wine shop on Columbus Avenue. Needless to say, our license was approved in record time. In tribute to our father, the corporation name was Irving Prager and Sons, Inc. I think Aaron finally buried Dad that day. Since then we've opened up five other stores in the New York metropolitan area. We also do a thriving internet business. I'd still rather be a cop.

To keep me from going completely out of my mind, I filed for and received my private investigator's license from New York State in 1979. I work cases now and again, missing persons mostly.

On October 9th, 1978 at 10:50 P.M., a seven-pound, six-ounce girl was born to Cindy and Aaron. With Katy's blessing and eternal thanks, they named their daughter Laurel Patricia Prager. We were asked to be her godparents. I think it took us less than a second to take on the responsibility.

Sarah F. J. Prager was born to us on August 6th, 1980. She used to hate the F. J. part of her name until Grandma Angela showed her all of Francis Jr.'s shiny medals and pretty ribbons. Katy's mom gave Sarah Francis Jr.'s wings. To this day, she displays them proudly in her room. When she first got them, she used to tell everyone she was going to be a pilot like her Uncle Francis in heaven.

"Yeah," Katy joked, "Sarah Flying Jew Prager."

Unfortunately, Sarah hates flying. She loves painting. Her cousin Laurel, much to the dismay of Cindy and Aaron, is in the Air Force Academy in Colorado. Names, I guess, are nice tributes, but what do they mean, really?

Miriam and Ronnie now live in Albuquerque, New Mexico. He teaches at the medical school and oversees the trauma center. His time at Kings County in the emergency room turned out to be a godsend. Ronnie came to appreciate that the people who show up in the ER are the neediest, poorest, most neglected among us. He always wanted his medical training to have some significance beyond a Mercedes and a big house in Sands Point. He sleeps well at night.

Miriam got her degree in occupational therapy and works with developmentally handicapped children. She and Ronnie have a girl of their own, Hope. She's having her bat mitzvah this year. Everyone says she kind of looks like me. I guess she does, but I always claim not to see it. They've also adopted a boy, Jimmy, of Apache heritage. And now they're thinking of adopting a girl from China.

"It's your fault," Miriam tells Katy and me. "If you hadn't gotten married at the UN, we would have had a very conventional family."

We proudly take the blame.

Rico got his shield and actually made that big case he was working. The guys running the stolen car ring had also taken on work as the latest embodiment of Murder, Incorporated. They became the hired enforcers for the New York mob. That arrangement didn't last very long as too many internal conflicts of interest arose and the crew developed a taste for blood even when none was called for. They started killing people just to stay in shape. The crew liked to grind up its victims in industrial meat-processing machines. Several books were written about the case: *Chop Shop* by Van Mason and *Bump Off and Grind* by Steve Horner were the two best. Rico's picture is in both books.

But after that case, Rico hit a wall. He started drinking heavily and was caught by Internal Affairs running protection for a

Columbian cocaine ring. If Joe Donohue hadn't been killed in a small plane crash in upstate New York during a fund-raising swing, he might have been able to intercede on Rico's behalf. As it was, Rico only had to serve five of a possible fifteen-year sentence in Batavia. Five years, for an ex-cop, however, is a very long and lonely sentence. They isolate ex-cops to protect them from the rest of the prison population. His wife left him, of course. About five years ago, he came to me begging for a loan. I gave him the two thousand bucks he asked for, though I knew I would never see a dime of it paid back. I would have given him more, but he still hadn't learned about undervaluation. He died last year while on a waiting list for a liver transplant.

Let me warn you. In case you were going to take what happened to Rico and Joe Donohue as a sign of cosmic justice, don't bother. Good old Sully, the biggest stooge of us all, retired as Chief of Detectives. So much for balance and karma, huh?

Conrad Beaman underwent a religious conversion of sorts. He went from being a card-carrying liberal firebrand to a leading black conservative. He's the darling of the religious right and supports just about every fringe policy he would have scoffed at in his former incarnation. He hosts a weekly talk radio show and is rumored to want to run for office. One thing hasn't changed: he's still a fixture on Sunday morning shows.

Pooty's was sold and closed its doors in 1991. The space it once occupied is now an art gallery and the apartments above it are currently a steal at $1.5 million per. It's just as well Pooty's closed. I could not bring myself to go there very frequently. Eventually, Katy and I stopped going altogether. Pete Parson moved down to Florida and works for the Coral Gables PD as an administrator. For some time, he tried to get Aaron and me to open up a store down there. Now I get a holiday card from him every year.

When punk turned into New Wave and the impending nuclear holocaust fizzled, Dirt Lounge went the way of Studio 54. I'd lost track of Nicky years ago. Then one day I was watching a special on VH1 about New York's early punk scene and there's Nicky being interviewed. He was still skinny, but he sported a rich tan and his hair was short and gray. He owns a few golf courses in South Carolina. I wonder if the clubhouses only have one bathroom.

Misty and Kosta got married, but to other people. After her cereal commercial, Misty moved out to L.A. She did a few more commercials, starred in sitcom pilots that failed to get picked up and worked in several cheesy movies. I've seen her twice on

Mystery Science Theater 3000. She married a producer, divorced him and moved up to Napa Valley where she owns a gourmet shop. Kosta moved out from behind the sound board to manage New Wave bands. One of his bands, The Christheads, actually got a record deal. When they couldn't come up with a name for their first album, Kosta dubbed it *Traveling Tuna Fish Salesmen.* I think they sold about seventeen copies and I've got two of them. It wasn't all bad though: Kosta married the bass player. After his less-than-stellar foray into the world of music management, Kosta came to work for Aaron and me. He's a sharp wine buyer. And though he's never come out and said anything about it, I think he especially enjoys his buying trips to Napa Valley.

I don't know nor do I care what happened to Philip Roscoe and Pete Klack. I don't know what happened to Nancy Lustig, Maria, Doobie, Bear, Theresa She-ain't-Hickey-no-more, Enzo Sica or Bobby Klingman's mother, though I find myself wondering about them occasionally as I get older. The only one I'm sure about is Doobie. I just know he designs supercomputers. Henry's Hog is still there in Dutchess and so is Tina Martell.

TYRONE BRYSON DIED on August 7th just before dawn. He was buried in a Connecticut cemetery, compliments of the Catholic Church. It turned out to be too complicated for me to reimburse the diocese directly or to take responsibility for the burial and services. Sister Margaret found out what the costs were and I donated an equal amount to the hospice. I was allowed to purchase the headstone.

TYRONE BRYSON
Born—? Died—Aug 7, 1998
A man who wanted to do
right in the end and did.
May he and those like him
rest eternally in peace.

FRANCIS MALONEY SR. died in his sleep on September 12th, 1997. Katy and Sarah suffered terribly. Although I didn't exactly click my heels in celebration, I was glad the charade was finally done with. Over the years, the forced civility between us had begun to take its toll. My relief was short lived.

Included in Katy's inheritance were the contents of a safe-deposit box. In amongst the bonds and jewelry was an envelope addressed to Katy and me. In the envelope was a note, and a receipt for a package kept in cold storage. The note, in Maloney's own hand, asked that we retrieve the package as soon as possible. "Probably my mom's wedding dress," Katy supposed. That sounded about right to me. Only it wasn't.

Patrick's blue parka, looking much like it did the day I rubbed it in Maloney's face, was what was in the box. At first, it didn't register with Katy. Her eyes seemed to say: "What's this? There must be some mistake. Are you sure this is the right box?" Then the light of recognition snapped on. "Oh my God!"

She brushed her hand along the front of the coat and caressed it as if it was Patrick she found and not his coat. I said nothing. I was practiced at it. This time, however, my long silence would hang, not save, me. In the left pocket was another note, again in Francis Maloney's hand:

"Your boyfriend gave this to me on February 17th, 1978. Ask him where he got it and why he swore me to secrecy. Did he never tell you he found Patrick?"

Just as Tyrone Bryson would later reach across time for me, Francis Maloney reached out from beyond the grave. Now in a dizzying rush, I understood his unnerving smile and questions about ghosts. He would have his revenge, a revenge in the making since the morning of February 17th, 1978. That day, the day I confronted him about Patrick, was the first time he asked me about ghosts. In the end, I'd underestimated my father-in-law's cruelty and capacity to inflict pain.

For when Katy did as the note said and asked me those questions, what could I say? I could keep up the pretense and claim I didn't know what her father was talking about. In short, deny, deny, deny. But that approach would wither under any sort of scrutiny. In the note, he'd called me Katy's boyfriend. That meant he'd put the coat in storage even before the wedding. Checking the date would be simple enough. How could I convince Katy her father hated me so much that he'd planned to ruin me twenty years ago? To do that I'd have to tar the man she was still grieving for and it would fly in the face of the civility with which he'd treated me over the past two decades. Even if I thought there was a chance to successfully deny it, I wouldn't have. Like I said, I was weary of the charade, of lying to Katy.

Yet telling Katy the truth would in many ways be worse, because the truth was much uglier and more complex. I would still have to tar the man she was grieving, only now the tar would consist of more than some vague accusations about her father's anti-Semitism. She would have to be told about Maloney's vicious assault on the transvestite. She'd have to hear about Patrick's homosexuality, about how her father'd offered Patrick his gun. There was no way around the fact that her father was behind my bruised ribs and burned-out car, nor was there any way of getting around my lying about it. But the two most damning things were that I had in fact found Patrick, cavalierly letting him slip away forever, and my silence.

And ultimately, what proof did I have of any of it? The IA report, which I'd discarded years ago, was a distorted pack of half-truths. Rico and Donohue were dead and somehow I didn't think retired Chief of Detectives "Sully" Sullivan would come riding to my rescue. Either way I was fucked. That was Francis Maloney's evil genius.

As I knew it would, my long silences is what did me in. I think Katy accepted as fact the rest of what I told her. She wasn't blind. She understood her father had a capacity for cruelty beyond what he displayed to his family. Though she was surprised that Patrick was gay, she was willing to admit he was always good at disguising himself to the world. But what she found unforgivable were my lies. No one, not now, not ever, needed to protect her from anything. And how dare I have let her and her family continue to suffer when I knew where Patrick was? Who was I to play God with her family? Who indeed? Our marriage, she insisted, was a shell game, all sleight-of-hand and diversion. All I could say in my own defense was that nothing about Sarah was sleight-of-hand.

I moved into an apartment near the Columbus Avenue store a few weeks later.

THEY FOUND PATRICK'S body within fifteen minutes. It was right where Tyrone Bryson had remembered. During the exhumation, I studied the fancy tombstones in the nearby cemetery. Which one, I wondered, was Houdini's? The medical examiner made positive identification through dental records. Elephant Eddie Barker was no longer available to be punished. He had died of AIDS in Attica in 1989.

Katy and I declared a cease fire for the funeral. Sister Margaret drove down from Connecticut and I paid for Jack's sister to come in from Dayton. Aaron and Cindy were there. Ronnie, Miriam, Hope and Jimmy flew in from Albuquerque. Sarah, who was leaving for Ann Arbor the next day, seemed angry, as if she blamed Patrick for what had happened to her parent's marriage. Though Katy and I kept the details of the separation to ourselves, Sarah knew it had something to do with the circumstances surrounding Patrick's disappearance. Someday, but not today, I remembered thinking, I'd have to remind her it was her Uncle Patrick's disappearance which had brought her parents together in the first place.

After the cemetery, we held a little get-together for everyone at Aaron's house in Dix Hills. Jack's sister couldn't stop thanking me for arranging her attendance. I explained it was the least I could do. "Let's just say," I told her, "it's my way of apologizing to Jack for doubting his faith in Patrick." She said she knew he would have forgiven me.

Sister Margaret was a hit with everyone but Katy. I think the nun's presence made her very uncomfortable. I think the church, the graveside rites, all of it, reawakened in her things she assumed were gone forever. Just because she had long ago converted to Judaism didn't mean it wiped away her upbringing. Back in church, I noticed her lips moving almost involuntarily in response to the priest's prayers. Katy must have felt terribly conflicted, disoriented.

Before heading back to Hamden, Sister Margaret asked me to walk her to her car.

"Your daughter is beautiful," she said.

"Come on, Sister," I was skeptical, "you already told me that three times. What's the real reason you lured me out here? I don't think we have enough time to run into the city for some Ray's pizza."

"I can see," she said, sadly, "that you and your wife are still apart."

"Yeah."

"Is that what you want?"

I shook my head no. "It's what Katy wants."

"I don't think so."

"You've got to stop reading those tea leaves, Sister." I wagged my finger. "I don't think the Holy Father would approve."

"Don't carry such regret to your grave with you, Moe," she counseled, resting her hand on my forearm. "Unlike Mr. Bryson, you can do something about what's happened."

"Like what?"

"Make a gesture," she said, removing her hand. "Think about it. You'll know when it's right."

Even after her car pulled out of Aaron's driveway, I watched until she disappeared around a corner.

BOTH KATY AND I took Sarah up to school. Ann Arbor's a lovely city and Sarah seemed to fall under its spell almost immediately. I arranged to come back up for the Wolverine's home game against Indiana. Sarah and I loved watching football together. When I was sure she was set, I headed home. Katy stayed on just to make doubly sure.

I let a few weeks pass before asking Katy to dinner. Walking through the front door of what used to be my house, I handed my wife a package.

"What's this?" she asked suspiciously.

"A gesture."

"No, Moe, what's in the box?"

"A poem," I said, "that you asked to read a very long time ago. I was always too embarrassed to show you."

"Andrea . . . Andrea Cotter."

When I applauded, Katy shaped her thin lips into a smile I hadn't seen since . . . well, for a very long time. She opened the package and began to read the poem, but her eyes were drawn to what remained in the box. It was the Chinese character with the red rose running through it.

"Patrick did that for Jack. They both had it tattooed on their forearms."

She started to cry, but held herself together well enough to ask: "What does it mean?"

"The character means forever. The red rose is a symbol that love is part of the fabric of eternity."

I prayed very hard at that moment for it to be true.

AFTERWORD

By Reed Farrel Coleman

Even while I was teaching myself to write detective fiction with my Dylan Klein series—*Life Goes Sleeping, Little Easter,* and *They Don't Play Stickball in Milwaukee*—I was working on two other novels featuring NYPD Detective Moe Einstein. Neither was published and neither has seen the light of day for many many years. The first was my obligatory serial killer novel. The other featured many plot and thematic aspects that would later re-emerge in *Redemption Street.* I mention these two unpublished works because they help to make the point that some novels—*The James Deans*, for instance—are born whole, while others are the product of evolution and confluence. *Walking the Perfect Square* was most definitely a product of the latter.

Although I hadn't looked at or thought much about these two unpublished works for years, I could never quite get the Moe Einstein character out of my head. He was, in his original incarnation, a little too clever and proficient at his job, and he was too much of a loner, too much a derivation of Phil Marlowe. And that last name! It was way too obvious and smart-alecky. But Moe Einstein had an essential goodness, a loyalty to family and friends and, most especially, to the truth, that made him vulnerable to all kinds of hurt and opened him up to all sorts of possibilities. It was this aspect of Moe's personality that stuck with me. Something else stuck.

Whereas Einstein had to go, Moe seemed just right. It summed up the kind of character that appealed to me as both writer and reader. It was a comfortable, friendly, working class name that harkened back to my parents' generation. But Moe, as short for Moses, was quite different. Moses was anything but unthreatening—Let my people go or else—and had all sorts of useful implications for an author interested in exploring the meaning of what it was to be a Jew in the United States during the last two decades of the twentieth century. It is no accident that his siblings are named Aaron and Miriam. The old fashioned nature of the name Moe actually helped shape the character, especially his obsession with the past. I'm afraid I chose Prager for less romantic reasons. I liked the sound and rhythm of it and thought its sharpness cut well against the softness of Moe.

The proper first vehicle for the character of Moe Prager also developed over the course of many years. I've always been a newspaper reader and would occasionally run across a story about a college student, usually male, who had come into Manhattan for a night of partying or clubbing only to disappear and never to be seen or heard from again. Even before I turned to a life of crime fiction, I would find myself creating myriad scenarios for these lost young men; the lives they had led before coming to Manhattan and what had actually happened to them. Some, I imagined, had met terribly violent ends. But a very few, I just knew in my bones, had used their alleged disappearances as a means of escape.

As early as 1995, I had a pretty firm notion of who Moe Prager might be and I had the basic idea for a plot, but what I didn't have was the chops. I hadn't developed my craft to a point where I was confident that I could pull off a book like *Walking The Perfect Square.* And this is where my failure to get those two earlier, overly ambitious novels published served me well. I had been trying to shed the Dylan Klein books and move up to a bigger house almost from the day *Life Goes Sleeping* was published in 1991. In fact, the two unpublished novels bracketed my second Dylan Klein novel *Little Easter.* What my failures taught me was that ambition unmatched by skill is a recipe, if not for disaster, then trouble. So instead of fighting against the current, I wrote the third installment of the Dylan Klein series, *They Don't Play Stickball in Milwaukee.* Although unconscious of it at the time, I was using *Stickball* as a testbed for things, both in terms of the writing itself and the emotional gravity of the story, that would later reappear in the Moe books. It should be no surprise then that central plot of *Stickball* revolves around a missing college student and it is no coincidence that the missing student is related to Dylan Klein.

What ultimately led to my writing *Walking the Perfect Square*, however, was an odd confluence of factors. Yes, there was another one of those stories in the papers of a college student gone missing in Manhattan. Prominent among the other factors were my two children, Kaitlin and Dylan, each for different reasons. My daughter was eight, nearly halfway between her birth and leaving for college. I often found myself reliving her birth and imagining her at eighteen going off to school. You will note that Moe is pondering this same thing about his daughter Sarah very early on in the novel. And it is this timeline, the echo and sway between future and past, that sets not only the tone of *Walking*, but its format as well. At around this time, my son was entering kindergarten and I became friendly with Jim, a dad of one of

Dylan's classmates. Jim was a retired NYPD sergeant who had been, as fate would have it, forced to leave the job because of a knee injury. He had slipped on a piece of paper left on the squad room floor. Once I heard how Jim had been injured, Moe took fuller form.

I realized one of the problems I had with the bulk of detective fiction was that too many of the protagonists tended to follow the fifty-plus-year-old template way too closely for my taste. Marlowe, Spade, Scudder, and Spenser didn't need any freshening up at my hands. So I made a conscious choice to move away from the haunted, Christian, white guy, alcoholic, gun-crazed, fist-happy loner, with or without sidekick. Moe, I decided, would be a faithful family man, a stable man with stable people in his life. He'd have a wife and a kid, a car payment and a mortgage. He'd have a steady source of income, own a successful business that had nothing to do with police work. He'd have been a cop, but not a detective. He'd have been hurt on the job, but not in the line of duty. He would be haunted, but not by something he did on the job. No dead innocents, no stray bullets, no dirty deals in his past. The thing that would haunt Moe, that would threaten all he held dear would be not an act of commission, but of omission. I also wanted Moe to grow, to change, to age with the series. I have never much cared for the conceit of the static, ageless detective whose new case comes right on the heels of his last.

As I wrote Moe on the pages of *Walking the Perfect Square*, I realized that his voice was very intimate, certainly more intimate than I had anticipated. It was almost as if you could hear his internal voice. On the page, Moe Prager *né* Einstein, for all the years he evolved in my head, was more than I had dared hope for. For Moe, it seemed, simply having the reader understand what he was going through wasn't good enough. He wanted you to feel what he was feeling when he was feeling it. He wanted to live beyond the page. Believe me, I was very surprised by how strongly he asserted himself, but that is the magic of writing. Writers are surprised by their own creations quite a bit more often than you might expect. Somehow, Moe has managed to survive five books in the series. Now it is up to you to determine whether or not his life is worth pursuing beyond the pages of *Walking the Perfect Square.*

Reed Farrel Coleman
January 2008

ABOUT THE AUTHOR

Reed Farrel Coleman was Brooklyn born and raised. He is the former Executive Vice President of Mystery Writers of America. His third Moe Prager novel, *The James Deans*, won the Shamus, Barry and Anthony Awards for Best Paperback Original. The book was further nominated for the Edgar, Macavity, and Gumshoe Awards. The fourth Moe book, *Soul Patch*, was nominated for the 2008 Edgar Award for Best Novel. He was the editor of the short story anthology *Hardboiled Brooklyn* and his short stories and essays appear in *Wall Street Noir*, *Damn Near Dead* and several other publications. Reed lives with his family on New York's Long Island. Visit him online at www.reedcoleman.com.

Read the entire Moe Prager series!

WALKING THE PERFECT SQUARE (#1)

New foreword by Megan Abbott.
New afterword by Reed Farrel Coleman.
Busted Flush Press; paperback; $13; 978-0-9792709-5-6
"Reed Farrel Coleman is one of the more original voices to emerge from the crime fiction field in the last ten years. For the uninitiated, *Walking the Perfect Square* is the place to start."—George Pelecanos

REDEMPTION STREET (#2)

New foreword by Peter Spiegelman.
New afterword by Reed Farrel Coleman.
Busted Flush Press; paperback; $13; 978-0-9792709-0-1
"Reed Farrel Coleman makes claim to a unique corner of the private detective genre with *Redemption Street*. With great poignancy and passion he constructs a tale that fittingly underlines how we are all captives of the past."
—Michael Connelly

THE JAMES DEANS (#3)

New foreword by Michael Connelly.
New afterword by Reed Farrel Coleman.
Busted Flush Press; paperback; $13; 978-0-9792709-8-7
Winner of the Shamus / Barry / Anthony Awards.
Nominated for the Edgar / Gumshoe / Macavity Awards.

SOUL PATCH (#4)

Bleak House Books. (www.bleakhousebooks.com)
Winner of the Shamus Award.
Nominated for the Edgar / Barry / Macavity Awards.

EMPTY EVER AFTER (#5)

Bleak House Books. (www.bleakhousebooks.com)

A Fifth of Bruen:

Early Fiction of Ken Bruen

By two-time Edgar Award nominee Ken Bruen.
Introduction by Edgar Award nominee Allan Guthrie.
Trade paperback, $18, ISBN: 0-9767157-2-4

"[A] beautiful book... [T]his is a must have for all [Bruen's] fans."
–Jon Jordan, *Crimespree Magazine*

"If you love complex, thought-provoking work, then you'll find something in this collection to intrigue you. If you love Bruen, there's no doubt, you'll already have cracked the spine."–Russel McLean, *Crime Scene Scotland*

"[*Funeral*] is the novel Samuel Beckett might have written, if he'd been a Galway Arms regular... *A Fifth Of Bruen* is a must for all true Bruen fans."
–Kernan Andrews, *The Galway Advertiser*

Contains Ken Bruen's early novellas & anthologies:
Funeral: Tales of Irish Morbidities / Martyrs / Shades of Grace / Sherry and Other Stories / All the Old Songs and Nothing to Lose / The Time of Serena-May / Upon the Third Cross

A HELL OF A WOMAN:

An Anthology of Female Noir

Edited by 2008 Edgar® Award winner Megan Abbott

Foreword by Val McDermid

Hardback, $26, ISBN: 978-0-9792709-9-4

Paperback, $18, ISBN: 978-0-9767157-3-3

Dark tales of lonely housewives, diner waitresses yearning for more, schoolgirls with dangerous ambitions, hustlers looking for one last score, factory girls with big plans, secretaries with hidden talents, schoolteachers with secrets to burn … and much more.

And each one, *a hell of a woman.*

Featuring original noir stories by Lynne Barrett, Charlotte Carter, Christa Faust, Alison Gaylin, Sara Gran, Libby Fischer Hellmann, Vicki Hendricks, Naomi Hirahara, Annette Meyers, Donna Moore, Vin Packer, Rebecca Pawel, Cornelia Read, Lisa Respers France, S. J. Rozan, Sandra Scoppettone, Zoë Sharp, Sarah Weinman, Ken Bruen, Stona Fitch, Allan Guthrie, Charlie Huston, Eddie Muller, and Daniel Woodrell. *With a bonus 50-page appendix of essays on female noir pioneers.*

Nominated for *Crimespree Magazine*'s Favorite Anthology of the Year!
Cornelia Read's "Hungry Enough"—Winner of the Shamus Award!
Daniel Woodrell's "Uncle"—Nominated for the Edgar & Anthony Awards!
Includes Eddie Muller's "The Grand Inquisitor," which he adapted to the big screen with his short film of the same name.

"*A Hell of a Woman* is not only an exceptionally entertaining anthology, it's an invaluable resource that will be cherished by aficionados of the genre."—*Chicago Tribune*

MIAMI PURITY
by Vicki Hendricks

Now back in print!

The acclaimed first novel by the 2008 Edgar® Award-nominated author of *Cruel Poetry*.
New foreword by Ken Bruen.
New afterword by Megan Abbott.
Trade paperback. $16.
ISBN 978-0-9792709-3-2

"Sex and murder, sunny places and shady people—*Miami Purity* is a modern noir masterpiece."
—Michael Connelly

"*Miami Purity* is the toughest, sexiest, most original debut noir novel ever written, and instantly rockets Hendricks into the list of all-time great noir authors. Gripping, super-sexy, and unforgettably raw."
—Lauren Henderson

"Shocking and supercharged, both reverent and original, this is the novel that amped up a new generation of noir writers."—George Pelecanos

"The authentic heir to James M. Cain, Vicki Hendricks is the high priestess of neo-noir. A fierce and fearless talent."—Dennis Lehane

"*Miami Purity* is as sleek as a well-oiled weasel and tight as the Gordian knot. One of the best of its kind from a very fine writer."—Joe R. Lansdale

"Vicki Hendricks is a true original. She is undoubtedly one of the most important noir writers of the past twenty years, and *Miami Purity* is one of the best crime novels I've ever read, period."—Jason Starr

A. E. Maxwell

Just Another Day in Paradise
Paperback, $13 (978-0-9792709-6-3)
The Frog and the Scorpion
Paperback, $14 (978-1-935415-00-8)

"Maxwell's style is sexy and hard-hitting." —*Publishers Weekly*

"The writing is lean and restrained, and Fiddler, growing from book to book, gives Travis McGee a real run for his money." —*Los Angeles Times*

"Fiddler is to California what Spenser is to Boston and Travis McGee is to Florida. Tough, smart guys who know that sometimes, what looks like paradise, is pure hell." —Paul Levine

David Handler

The Man Who Died Laughing/ The Man Who Lived by Night
Hardback, $26 (0-9767157-8-3)
Paperback, $18 (0-9767157-9-1)

The Man Who Would Be F. Scott Fitzgerald/The Woman Who Fell from Grace
Hardback, $26 (978-0-9792709-2-5)
Paperback, $18 (978-0-9792709-1-8)

"When it comes to digging up the dirt, there's nobody quite like natty ghostwriter Stewart 'Hoagy' Hoag... As bitchily amusing as eavesdropping at Spago." —*People*

Ace Atkins

Crossroad Blues
Paperback, $15 (978-1-935415-03-9) *October 2009*

"An impressive debut by a promising new talent."
—*The Philadelphia Inquirer*

"In Atkins' hands, the characters are as substantial as a down-home breakfast of biscuits and ham with red-eye gravy . . . the riffs on the juke joints of the '30s are sweet."
—*Entertainment Weekly*